O9-AID-961

DREAMED IT

This Large Print Book carries the

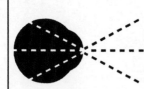

This Large Print Book carries the
Seal of Approval of N.A.V.H.

A DREAMWALKER MYSTERY

Dreamed It

Maggie Toussaint

THORNDIKE PRESS
A part of Gale, a Cengage Company

Copyright © 2019 by Maggie Toussaint.
Thorndike Press, a part of Gale, a Cengage Company.

ALL RIGHTS RESERVED
This is a work of fiction. Names, characters, places, and incidents are either the product of the author's imagination or are used fictitiously.
Thorndike Press® Large Print Clean Reads.
The text of this Large Print edition is unabridged.
Other aspects of the book may vary from the original edition.
Set in 16 pt. Plantin.

LIBRARY OF CONGRESS CIP DATA ON FILE.
CATALOGUING IN PUBLICATION FOR THIS BOOK
IS AVAILABLE FROM THE LIBRARY OF CONGRESS

ISBN-13: 978-1-4328-7576-3 (hardcover alk. paper)

Published in 2020 by arrangement with Camel Press, an imprint of Epicenter Press, Inc.

Printed in Mexico
Print Number: 01   Print Year: 2020

*This book is dedicated to
the First Wednesday Lunch Group.*

ACKNOWLEDGMENTS

Thanks to my husband Craig for continuing to encourage and support me on this writing journey. Thanks also to my critique partner Polly Iyer who helps in so many ways. I also thank Holly McClure for sharing Cherokee courting customs with me. Special thanks to Deborah Holt who won the right to name Dr. Alleen Dabba in this book during a Murder on the Menu auction in Wetumpka, Alabama.

CHAPTER ONE

A sudden jolt propelled me to consciousness. I gazed upon a vast darkness and wheezed air into my lungs. Time passed as I steadied my breathing and slowed my racing heart. Flat on my back, I took stock of my situation. Numb limbs indicated an extended dreamwalk, but I had no memory of any such excursion.

I'd spent a quiet Sunday evening at home with my daughter and Sam Mayes, my Native American boyfriend, who was down from North Georgia for the weekend. I'd gone to sleep in my own bed and awakened here, wherever here was.

Was I alone?

I called upon my flagging energy to do a life signs scan. Using my extra senses, I virtually ranged out from my prone position. Mayes was to my immediate left, and from his low energy levels, as wiped out as I was. He was a dreamwalker, same as me.

And from the cold energy pressing against my leg, my ghost dog watched over us. He'd bark on the spirit plane if someone or something approached, though my scan assured me we were alone.

The void in my memory worried me. My debilitated condition pointed to an extrasensory event, but danged if I remembered contacting a spirit on the Other Side. Strange, because I remembered every other dreamwalk I'd ever made. Why not this one?

So much for me being an expert on the paranormal.

Just when I thought I had the hang of my unusual profession of communicating with the dead, it socked me in the teeth. Crossing over to the spirit realm was something I did often, but the veil between the living and the dead nearly won this time.

This had been no ordinary dreamwalk. Instead of it being a spirit-only event, somehow our bodies had also undergone the shift. That defied the laws of physics, but here we were, body and spirit. Impossible and yet my reality.

Tears misted my eyes, and I blinked to sharpen my vision. A woodsy aroma filled my nose, so we were outdoors. The darkness suggested it was night. My thoughts drifted into a self-healing meditative trance focusing on the breath. Gradually, clarity returned.

As numbness yielded to tingling nerves, sensation seeped into my rigid body. Fatigue rolled in next, and with it, the riptide of bone-deep exhaustion. Despite my weariness, I took heart. This reaction was normal after an extended dreamwalk.

Oliver lapped happily at my face, his whip-thin tail wagging his entire ghostly form. *Good dog, Oliver,* I managed as I joined him on the spirit plane. While here in spirit only, I still maintained awareness of my physical surroundings.

My ghost dog materialized as a misty image of a jet black Great Dane, his body aquiver with happiness. Earlier this summer I rescued Oliver from virtual chains and too-tight collar at a haunted house. No amount of urging had prompted him to the afterlife, and his essence attached to mine. At this bereft moment, I was delighted by his presence.

Oliver showed us the way home through the drift, I realized. It wasn't the first time he'd rescued me, and I owed him so much already.

Despite my dry-as-cotton mouth, I cooed over him while I tried to pinpoint my location. Stars twinkled overhead, framed by

11

tall oaks and pines. Not my treetops, not my yard.

I heard a moan to my left. Felt the urgency as Mayes whispered my name. "Baxley." With a final rub of the ears for Oliver, I integrated fully into the physical plane.

Mayes whispered again, his tone deeper and freighted with authority. "Bax. You okay?"

"Yeah." I managed. "What happened to us?"

"Got no clue."

Sam Mayes had become a fixture in my life, though I'd only known him for three months. I wished I was in his protective arms right this very second.

"I feel like I got run over by a truck," I said. "Last thing I remember is getting ready for bed."

"That's right." His voice roughened. "I shared your toothpaste before we crawled under the covers."

My face heated as memories surfaced. "I remember the before-sleep part fine, but between there and here is a big, fat zero. Except for Oliver. He guided us home through the drift." I tried to sit, but my limbs weren't fully responsive yet. I remained prone.

"I have the same mental gap. I believe we

12

were taken, body and spirit, from your house."

Hearing the words made it real. The impossible had happened. Nothing else explained our physical displacement, the prolonged recovery time, and the shared memory gaps. My teeth ground together as I made another connection. "Unless some other entity kidnapped us, my money's on Rose. Her abilities go beyond the possible. I've never met another spirit entity as powerful."

Allegedly, my otherworld mentor, Rose, worked undercover in the spirit realm, but she claimed to be an angel. Seeing her dark, powerful wings had made a believer out of me. That physical manifestation, her ability to do impossible feats, and her total hold on me proved she was more than a powerful spirit. She'd banished demons, fetched folks from beyond the point of no return, wrestled with selkies, quelled spirit rebellions, and more.

Trouble was, Rose kept changing the rules of our association. By sheer willpower, I managed to draw one hand close enough to study in the starlight. From the faint glow of my watch, it was three a.m. The rose tattoo on my hand was still there. Rose put three tattoos on my body to indicate the

13

hours of my indenture to her. Rats. If she'd gone to the trouble of kidnapping us and erasing our memories, her prominent brand indicated I still owed her the hours of my life I'd willingly exchanged during life-or-death situations of loved ones.

That's right. Rose charged for her supernatural favors, and I'd begged for her help three times. Each time the terms had been the same. A favor in exchange for an hour of my life. I'd agreed due to the dire nature of the situations, but darn-it-all if I wanted Rose to collect. With her rule-bending nature, I could turn into a mass murderer or worse on either side of the veil.

"I keep reminding you, Rose is not your friend," Mayes said.

"I'm aware of that, but I'm stuck with her."

I could wiggle my toes. That was a good sign. "We dozed off around eleven, and my watch says it's three in the morning. It's Monday already," I said, my voice sounding stronger each time I spoke. "I don't know when she took us, but that's four hours of missing Earth time. A lot can happen in four hours. I thought I would die on the way back. Thank goodness for Oliver's help, or we'd still be tumbling through the drift. This transition through the veil of life was the worst ever for me."

"Agreed. It's never been like that for me either, and I'm indebted to your spirit dog for his help." He turned to Oliver on the spiritual plane and said a few words in Cherokee which made Oliver bark with doggy happiness. The spirit dog gave each of us another lick and sat nearby.

"Rose must've burned a mountain of energy moving both bodies," Mayes continued. "She must've assumed we could manage the last part of the journey alone. I wonder what she did with us."

I hated knowing Rose could compel me to do things whether I was awake or sleeping. Times like this I truly felt I'd sold my soul to the devil, and now I'd drawn Mayes into my indenture. "I don't think we want to know. Ignorance is bliss."

"Unless we broke the law."

I swore under my breath. Of course Mayes would consider that angle. He was a lawman with a professional reputation to uphold, while I was merely a police consultant with a landscaping and pet sitting business on the side. My reputation had been established before I was even born. Sinclair County residents had known my family for generations, and in the Deep South eccentricity was expected.

The Nesbitts might be weird, but they always helped others when there was a problem. That counted for a lot around here.

"Sensation is returning," Mayes said. "Where the hell are we?"

"Working on it. Give me a sec." I reviewed the physical evidence at hand. A dim light glowed on a tall pole nearby. Sandy concrete stretched underneath my prone body and radiated warmth. An open expanse yawned to my right, maybe a parking lot. No cars in sight. I glanced at the structure to my left. Plain stucco façade. One story. Double glass doors with one handle slightly askew.

"Wait a minute. I recognize this place. The post office. The satellite office about a half mile from my house, to be exact. We're close enough we can walk home on the paved road."

"Our bodies aren't where we left them," Mayes said. "The only reasonable explanation is Rose or one of her kind abducted us. They used our bodies and abandoned us in the drift."

"Maybe. I'm withholding judgment until I remember what happened." I heard his clothes rustling as he moved. If Mayes was recovering from the side effects of the between-worlds shift, I would be mobile soon.

Suddenly I was blindsided by every parent's worst fear. If we were here, where was my ten year old daughter? "Larissa! Is she home alone? Is she okay?"

CHAPTER TWO

I thrashed like a beached whale until I managed to sit. Mayes was already sitting and actively flexing arms and legs. "Easy," he said. "If we're that close to your place, we can use your extrasensory talent to monitor Larissa's life signal."

He sounded so sensible, so reasonable. Instead of being annoyed by his uncanny ability to divine my thoughts, I felt relieved we were on the same wavelength. My daughter meant the world to me. "I am weak, but I have to know if she's all right."

Mayes crawled to my side. His arms encircled me. "Together we are strong, Walks with Ghosts. Never forget that."

I smiled at his pet Cherokee name for me and drew strength from his embrace until I realized he was sharing his energy with me. He needed that energy to recover so I blocked the physical transfer.

He gently hugged me. "Relax. You need this."

"The experience drained both of us. You need your strength too," I said, ignoring the masculine authority in his voice. "But I like your idea of checking on Larissa with the long distance scan." To my delight, he touched his forehead to mine. Together we formed a mindlink and quested telepathically to my house. One sleeping life form registered. Larissa was at home.

I grinned as our mental probe ended. "Thanks. I feel much better knowing she's resting peacefully. Now we can focus on getting home."

My daughter was fine. Thanks to Mayes sharing some of his energy, I felt strong enough to walk home. My senses were recovering and so was my body. Had I done too much recently?

It had been five days since my last dreamwalk, taken on behalf of a grieving grandmother, and a month since I consulted with the sheriff on a murder case, so I hadn't pushed my extrasensory limits or fried my unusual talents lately.

I ran a few self-checks. *My name is Baxley Powell. I'm a dreamwalker in Sinclair County, Georgia. I own a landscaping and pet care business called Pets and Plants. It's the first*

*week of November. My husband died, and my
daughter Larissa is ten years old. Two plus
two is four. The square root of nine is three.
There are fifty states in the United States of
America.*

So far, so good.

I became aware of dampness in the air, of
dew condensation on my body. Dry clothes
would be the first order of business when I
got home. No. A shower first. I needed to
wash off wherever I'd been, whatever I'd
done. My fingers and toes responded as I
flexed them. The shoes I wore felt stiff and
angled. Definitely not my regular work
boots. In the faint starlight, I glimpsed the
fancy, spiked heels strapped to my feet. The
sequined, clingy top. The hip-hugging mini
skirt.

Mayes noticed my get-up at the same time
and whistled with masculine appreciation.

A fresh horror shivered down my spine.

Not my clothes.

Not my shoes.

Not even close.

Rose.

Mayes was right.

My other-world guide was the only explanation for this bizarre situation. She'd commandeered our bodies and done God knows
what with them. The last time she'd taken

20

over my body, she'd tricked Mayes into making love to me. We weren't a couple then, but her interference had turned out all right. We were a couple now, and I didn't feel alone anymore.

I remembered every aspect of that earlier Rose-takeover, so why couldn't I remember what happened this time? And how odd that Mayes had been included in the abduction.

Rose was giddy when we became a couple, and now I understood why. She planned to use him too. If I had an ounce of energy to spare, I'd vector back through the drift and confront her. The truth dawned rapidly. Rose had to wait because I couldn't leave my body here unprotected. I had to get home and I was already running on fumes.

The easy way Rose moved through time and space, we could've been deployed anywhere on the planet or in any reality, which might account for the terrible transition we experienced. If not for Oliver showing us the way home, we'd still be trapped in that nothingness.

My throat constricted as I noted a dark stain on my fingertips. I sniffed them. Copper scent. Blood. Sad that I knew what blood smelled like, but that knowledge came from being a police consultant on murder cases.

"What's wrong?" Mayes asked as he clambered to his feet.

"I don't know, but I'm scared." I took a deep breath and spilled my bad news. "Mayes, my hands. There's blood."

"Let me see." In the pale starlight, he brought my hand close to his face. He turned it this way and that. Sniffed. "Definitely blood."

I quaked inside. "What did I do?"

"You didn't do anything. Rose did, and don't you forget that. We'll figure this out together, after we've had some sleep."

"What if I killed someone?"

"You didn't. Not enough blood or spiritual blowback for a shooting, no knuckle abrasions from fist-fighting, no obvious signs you stabbed anybody. Most likely cause is one of us had a minor wound."

"You got all that from looking at my hand?" I asked.

"Some of it. Look, let's reassess later, okay. Whatever happened, we're not to blame."

"Maybe, but if someone rides down the road, we have to hide. We're each other's alibi until we figure this out. Unless someone can prove otherwise, our story is that we spent Sunday night at home. You coming?"

"Right behind you."

I scrambled to my feet, knees knocking together as I tried to walk across the unpaved parking lot in the tight skirt and the sparkly pink high heels. We were alone, except for my ghost dog companion, who padded alongside us in a transparent form.

The shoes had to go. Reaching down, I tugged off the heels and strode down the paved road as fast as I could go. With each step, a horrible certainty drummed into my thoughts. We must erase all evidence of our forced outing.

My bare feet smacked the pavement. If anyone saw us, our alibi of being home in bed would fail. An owl hooted in the woods bordering the road, startling me.

I searched for cover possibilities, but the shoulder was shallow, with only a hint of a swale. If a car came along, our choices were to hide on the shoulder or sprint for the pines. We couldn't explain why I had on hootchie-mama clothes.

This wasn't fair. I was getting my life together, just learning how to be myself again. Tears filled my eyes. I blinked furiously, needing to see. Needing to protect Mayes and his reputation. Mercy. How had it come to this?

Oliver materialized in front of us, barking.

Our movement halted as we watched Oliver cock his head. He heard something. I listened harder.

A faint rumble sounded in the distance. A motor. "In the ditch, now," Mayes said.

I scrambled down the grassy shoulder. Not much of a ditch here, but with no ambient light, we should be safe.

"Lay down," Mayes said. "And stay down. Every aspect of your sequined clothing is designed to reflect light."

The ground smelled of grass and damp earth. I shielded my face with my hands. Most people were asleep this time of night. Who could it be? Someone who'd been partying and lost track of time. Someone who was up to no good. Or a routine patrol from law enforcement.

The car rolled closer, the rumble of the engine and the tires on the road getting louder. I thought about raising my head to see who it was, but Mayes must've intuited my intention because he dove on top of me. "Don't move," he said.

While I didn't like feeling trapped, I could breathe and Mayes was a hero many times over. He couldn't help his protective instincts.

The car passed, and the shoulder darkened. Mayes arose and helped me stand.

"Did you see anything?" I asked, reaching for the discarded pink heels.

"Dark sedan traveling down the middle of the road. One tail light busted."

"Doesn't ring a bell." I brushed the sandy dirt from my skin. "But at least they didn't see us."

We continued toward home, Oliver trotting at my side. His loyalty warmed my heart. I ducked low as I passed my next door neighbor's drive. Mayes followed my lead. Mr. Luther's house wasn't near the road, but I couldn't risk him seeing us. Deniability was our best chance at proving we'd stayed home tonight.

"What about these clothes?" I whispered when we were a good ways from my neighbor's place. "They could destroy our alibi."

"We'll deal with the clothes," Mayes said. "I don't trust your associate."

"Smart man." I slowed my pace, looking at the woods flanking the two-lane road. "We could shuck them off right now and fling them in the pines. But then we'd be naked."

"Stay focused. I'm all for getting naked but back at your place," Mayes said.

"Our DNA and God knows what else are on these clothes."

"Point taken. We'll bag everything as we

take them off and stash the bag out of sight until I can burn the items elsewhere. If we use your fireplace, there's a chance something might not burn completely."

"Sneaky, but I like that in a man." That's what we'd do. Bag up our clothing and burn everything later today. No one would ever know about our excursion.

No one.

Not even us.

CHAPTER THREE

Mayes delayed his departure to his home in Stony Creek Lake until noon on Monday, giving us a few extra hours of togetherness. After Larissa climbed aboard her school bus, we gathered the offending clothes, a shovel, and my small gasoline can.

We marched through the woods to a clearing on the back of my property. I'd camped here with my family years ago, and the fire circle was still intact.

Resolutely, I placed the paper sack of clothing in the circle. We gathered twigs and small branches, soaked the lot in gas, and lit a match. With the two of us poking and prodding the fire, everything burned.

After the flames died down, Mayes nodded. "That should do it."

I turned the embers with the shovel and found no trace of the clothing. "I agree. Even if someone finds this ash pile, it wouldn't link us to an event elsewhere.

We're safe now."

"Let's hope that's the case."

Mayes doused the embers with sand and we hiked back to the house. My brain flitted ahead to practical matters. In less than two hours, Mayes would be on the road again, back to his life in north Georgia.

Not what I wanted, but when did the world ask my opinion? I loved the way he made me feel, loved the way he fit in my life, but geography was not our friend.

We stowed the gear in the shed and washed our hands in the kitchen sink. Though we both needed a shower to remove the smoky smell, I didn't want to waste a second of the time we had together.

"We need to talk about the future," Mayes said as we sat on the comfy living room sofa, his fingers entwined with mine. My family pets, three dogs and two cats, settled in beside us. Oliver had returned to the spirit world. "Polls indicate my boss is a shoe-in for governor, I have to make a decision."

"You should run for sheriff in Stony Creek," I urged, wanting the best for him. "That's been your goal all along."

"It was my plan until you walked into my life. My goal changed because of my feelings for you. We are good medicine."

And that was the rub. Our strong feelings

for each other versus reality. His daily life was three hundred and fifty miles away from here. My family and dreamwalker support team lived on the Georgia coast. His Cherokee tribe lived in the north Georgia Mountains. I didn't see how our relationship could work long term, but Mayes seemed less hamstrung by logistics.

Still, someone had to be the voice of reason, but I didn't want to risk losing him. I wanted to believe in his version of our future, only how could I let him miss this career opportunity? I loved him enough to want the best for him.

"I agree we're good together," I began slowly, "but I won't be responsible for wrecking your career plans. You're needed there, I'm needed here."

"I'm reconsidering the Task Force idea."

He'd been asked to head a special squad detailed to difficult crimes, those that had an element of paranormal or were missing person's cold cases. He'd be good at this kind of work, and we already knew we worked well together. Sounded like a good idea except for the catch. Special assignments were dicey and often politically based. If we didn't bow to the right person, our jobs might be at risk.

What were the odds I would meet a Native American man and fall in love with him? They had to be astronomically small. The hallmarks of his Cherokee heritage, his high cheekbones, angular nose, intelligent brown eyes, dark hair clubbed back, and perfect bronze skin were as familiar to me as my own reflection in the mirror. He was the gift I never expected to receive, a kindred spirit who understood the challenges of my life. His height matched mine, and his strength seemed boundless. He was a Cherokee medicine man, a healer, and I suspected, much more, though he was modest about his special talents.

"No comment?" he prompted.

I flushed at being caught staring at him. "I, uh, got distracted."

"Looking at me."

"Yeah. You're thinking big picture and I'm thinking you're leaving again in a few hours. I'm trying not to be sad about another goodbye."

"We can go forward in a new direction, together. The Task Force would be a good compromise. We could base our operations from here."

"But your people . . ."

"I will travel home twice a month to meet with the council to address their concerns, but the rest of the time we would be to-gether."

The incident from last night loomed large in my mind. What if Mayes gave up his cur-rent life, moved here, and whatever hap-pened last night caught up with us? I would be the instrument of his downfall. He could lose his career, reputation, and honor if Rose made us do something illegal.

"Mayes, I can't ask that of you and I can't leave this place permanently. If I'm not the Dreamwalker, the job falls to my daughter. She's too young. I have to stay here."

He covered my hands with his, his dark eyes ablaze with hope. "Don't you see? This plan for our future together is perfect for both of us. You don't have to leave."

I wanted him here fulltime more than anything, but it wasn't as easy as he implied. "I appreciate what you're trying to do, but why should my work take precedence over yours? I don't want you to sacrifice your dreams for me."

"Let me tell you a secret about my career. Being a lawman is a way I can restore order in our crazy world. Working together, you and I can restore much more order. I will still be walking down the right path for me, only I will have you at my side."

His reasoning made sense, so why was my

stomach knotted with doubt? I loved Mayes too much to drag him into the trenches with me. Between my jobs, my family, my dream-walking, and Rose, my life was a three-ring circus. Surely he saw that.

I pulled back, dislodging the Chihuahua and the Shih-poo in my haste to say this right. "You're making assumptions, Mayes. Even if we can swing the Task Force assignment, as a cohabitating couple we face other challenges. We haven't known each other that long. And I can't be on the road all the time. I have a kid who goes to school every day of the week. The Task Force detail isn't the best fit for me."

"I'm certain we're meant to be together. Don't be swayed by the reasons we shouldn't try this. I want a life with you. Can you say the same?"

He sounded so matter of fact, as if I were the next thing on his to-do list. Maybe I wasn't being fair to him, but darn it, my opinion mattered. "My feelings for you are certain but my head isn't convinced about the logistics. I have to be sure before we move down this path in lock-step. Will you give me time to mull this over?"

His eyes went cop-hard for a second, then the gentleness and sweet adoration he always showed me returned. He sang to me in Cherokee, a tender melody that made my eyes glisten even though I didn't understand the words. When he wound down, I nudged his side. "I know what you're doing. You're enchanting me."

He skootched closer, catching my hands in his. "Then we're even, Walks with Ghosts, because you put a spell on me. You are as necessary to me as the air I breathe. I pledge my heart and life to you."

My heart panged at his declaration. His words made me feel cherished and rare. "You don't play fair."

"Not when I want something this bad."

"Even if the career change works out, there's still last night. I will demand a full accounting from Rose, but we could be in big trouble."

His hands tightened around mine. "I thought you planned to let those sleeping dogs lie."

"That was my initial knee-jerk reaction to our kidnapping. After reflection, I need to know. We're considering major life changes, and we don't need big unknowns on our horizon. Something like last night could destroy your career."

He took a moment to reply. "What if Rose won't cooperate? Can you go over her head?"

"I don't have access to whoever has dominion over her, but she has been in trouble with him before."

"Good to know." He drew me close and kissed me in a way that left no doubt of his deep feelings for me. I clung to him, knowing where this was headed and craving that intimacy. Before things went any farther, my cell phone rang. Sulay, my Maine coon cat, padded over to the counter and meowed.

"Don't answer it," Mayes said. "This is our time."

"That's Wayne's ring. I have to answer."

"He has a ring?" A stormy expression crossed his face. "Do I?"

"Yes and yes." I crossed the room to take the call. A few minutes later, I turned to Mayes. "We have a case. Literally. A suitcase. With a body in it. Behind the abandoned dance club."

His eyebrows spiked, his astonishment genuine. "A suitcase murder? Here?"

"Apparently." I wrinkled my nose. "Why? Has this happened before?"

He quickly closed the gap between us. "I'll say. This guy leaves bodies in suitcases near interstate ramps across the country."

I grimaced. "Someone makes a habit of doing this?"

"Serial killer all the way. Law enforcement is always behind the eight ball on this guy. Could be your body is fresher than the ones that've been found to date. I've never worked a suitcase murder, but our extra abilities will prove useful."

"Good grief. We have a serial killer in Sinclair County. That's hard to absorb."

"As I think more about it, I don't believe anyone used psychics to track this killer." Energy radiated from him like crazy. "Don't take this the wrong way, but this case is a career-maker. If we nab the Suitcase Killer, we can have any job we want in the future. This case can be our ticket to tomorrow."

"Whoa!" I thrust a palm in his direction. "Let's not get ahead of ourselves. Right now, the Sinclair County police have a suspicious death. I've been ordered to the scene at the old Club Frisky property. Beyond that, I don't know what will happen. But I do know how my boss thinks. It wouldn't be to Sheriff Wayne Thompson's advantage to toss in a bunch of cold cases, no matter how similar the M.O."

"Time will tell. Meanwhile, I'll contact Sheriff Blair in Stony Creek immediately to request being detailed here. Look on the bright side. With a case to solve, I won't be going home today.

CHAPTER FOUR

After getting a green light from his boss, Mayes and I rode together to where the suitcase was found. On the way, we stopped to feed Peaches and Babyface, the Smith's energetic boxers, and turned them out into their fenced yard for the day. Their owners would be home this evening, and my Pets and Plants business would earn another chunk of cash for pet sitting.

Mayes had his customary Zen thing going on mood-wise, but now that I knew him better, I noticed the telltale signs of his excitement: the tightening of the eyes, the whole body alertness, and the stoic waiting while I tended the dogs.

The detour only delayed us ten minutes. As we neared the site, I gave Mayes some background on the property. "The whole county was in an uproar when Club Frisky opened its doors. According to the business license application, it was supposed to be a hamburger joint. Turned out they served burgers, but the waitresses were topless."

Mayes took his time answering. "Good to know."

"Seriously, they tricked the County Commissioners. Once they got in, legislation was passed to keep similar establishments from setting up shop, but Club Frisky was grandfathered in. The ladies of the county never got over their outrage about topless waitresses and prostitution, and the men joked about being hungry for hamburgers."

"Were you upset?"

"Nah. I was in my vegetarian phase." I made a dismissive gesture with my hand. "What did I want with a hamburger?"

Mayes chuckled, relaxing into his seat. "You're funny."

"The story doesn't end there. A few years back, the manager of our branch of the exotic dance biz made off with a fortune he'd made from those hardworking girls. Upper management closed the club, and the girls were farmed out elsewhere in the franchise. The building's been abandoned ever since, though the cops sometimes chase off long distance haulers who tuck their rigs behind the abandoned building while they catch a few zzzs."

"Thanks for the background. It will come

in handy."

I wondered if he would ogle Club Frisky's gigantic placards of scantily clad women. It still seemed something of a miracle that he wanted me, but I didn't physically measure up to any pin-up queen. I glanced surreptitiously in the rearview mirror. My freakish white hair lurked underneath an Atlanta Braves ball cap, the lack of hair color resulting from a Rose misadventure. I had milk chocolate colored eyes, narrow lips, and tanned skin. I had one of those in-between body types. Not thin and not fat. Manual labor kept the extra weight mostly in the muscular range.

My usual style of dress, jeans, a tie-dyed T-shirt, and work boots shouldn't inspire declarations of undying love. Despite my lack of glitz and glamor, three men had chased me. My late husband, Roland, had been crazy about me. The sheriff kept sniffing my way, and now Mayes wanted to spend the rest of his life with me. He hadn't proposed marriage, but lifelong commitment was in everything he said and did.

The remaining miles rolled by quickly. Bright sunlight spilled onto the road in straight lines through the orderly rows of pines planted alongside the road. Light and shadow seemed to be duking it out for space. Light would win the match for now. This afternoon, the tide would turn.

I veered onto the access road to the interstate. Club Frisky was situated halfway between the state highway and the Interstate, guaranteeing the club traffic from both routes. Most of their clientele hailed from the expressway, but rumors around town suggested the former city council chair and several prominent locals had lifetime passes to the place.

The abandoned building looked sad to me. Those smiling photos on the building's front had been bleached by coastal sunshine until the faces ghosted on the placards. I saw a calculating expression on Mayes' face as we circled the building. Weeds grew knee high in the parking lot cracks and in the gutter along the roof frontage by the road. The energy here felt brooding, tainted with dark pleasure, pain, bitterness, and loneliness. I girded my extrasensory perception. I didn't need an energy reading of the building to know those emotions had been layered in this place through time.

I eased around to the back where three police cruisers idled with flashing lights. My father was there in his role of coroner, along with his assistant, Bubba Paxton. Dad had a good thirty years on Bubba, but both were wiry men of medium height with braided pony tails. Dad's was white while Bubba's was a muddy brown.

Bubba, a former crackhead turned new age preacher and snake charmer, had been part of my dad's dreamwalker team and then partnered with him when he transitioned to coroner this summer. The job posting made sense for both of them since they were accustomed to dealing with the dead.

They'd suited up in white coveralls and had their gurney out and ready to go. Mayes and I walked over to them, the smell of menthol under their noses wafting across the parking lot. "Hey, Dad. Bubba. What's the word?" I asked.

"This is seriously messed up," Bubba said. "Who stuffs a dead person in a suitcase?"

CHAPTER FIVE

I couldn't answer Bubba's question. Worse, I dreaded seeing the woman's earthly remains. Would my boss expect me to examine everything in the parking lot? Though woods flanked us and the old club blocked us from the road, I didn't like the vibe here. The sooner I could leave, the better.

"Is the sheriff here?" I asked Bubba, noting Wayne's Jeep wasn't in the Club Frisky parking lot.

"He caught a ride with Virg and Ronnie," Dad said. "Dottie's car is in the shop getting tuned for the big road trip down to Fort Lauderdale for their anniversary cruise. The kids had sports physicals today, so she commandeered Wayne's vehicle. He's steamed about it, so I wouldn't mention his missing vehicle if I were you."

"Message received." I gazed over to where the sheriff and his deputies stood in a clump by a thick stand of scrub oaks and pines.

Uh-oh. From the look of things, Wayne was already giving out everyone's assignments. "We'll head over and see what our marching orders are."

"Good luck," Dad said.

Bubba Paxton touched my arm. "We're here if you need us, Baxley."

I nodded to show I'd heard, pivoted, and strode away with Mayes padding silently beside me, very conscious of my being the only female on site. Wayne had two female deputies, but they were off duty today. Oh, joy. No telling what the men might say at this risqué site. How many lewd jokes would they tell about the good old days of sneaking into the club?

But maybe the good old boys' network wouldn't be operational today, not with Mayes present. The guys accepted Mayes as a fellow lawman, but he wasn't one of them. I considered that a plus. Not sure how Mayes felt about his conditional welcome.

The sheriff scowled at me. "Glad you finally made it, Ms. Powell. I already ran the briefing for the guys. Here are the highlights for you and Deputy Mayes. No one talks to the media. Not the TV kind. Not the print kind. They'll be here like jackals as soon as this case hits the system. We harvest everything from this crime scene this morning. Once the reporters arrive, anything we miss will be trampled and worthless.

"Virg and Ronnie are on perimeter search. Doug Allister will photograph everything around the suitcase and inside the building. Mayes and Stone will conduct a grid search on the property." He shot a barbed glance at Mayes. "Stone's got point on the search. My consultant and I will vet the club. Any questions?"

No one said a word. I wanted to give Mayes' hand a reassuring squeeze, but he wore his stony lawman's face at the sheriff's blatant move to split us up.

"Get to work." Wayne motioned with his hand and jerked his head toward Club Frisky. "Powell. Let's go. You're with me."

I followed him, with a quick glance at Mayes over my shoulder. My boyfriend seemed fine, so I quit worrying about his potential hurt feelings. "I came as quickly as I could, but I had another commitment," I said. "The Smiths are out of town, and I'm caring for their dogs. They had to be fed and let out."

"You're getting full time pay from my office and I expect you to report promptly when I call."

I gulped. He was right. My pay had been

43

bumped from part time to full time. I was a salaried employee on call around the clock. I hastened to explain "I apologize for being a few minutes late, but I put in my leave papers last week to have this morning off. If I'd known we'd catch a case today, I would've headed out at dawn to tend those dogs. I'm available to work until school gets out, and if you need me for the rest of the day, Mom can meet Larissa's bus. She knows we're working a case."

Wayne stopped marching like he was headed to a fire and swore. "Sorry. You didn't deserve that outburst. It's not you. It's Dottie. She's driving me nuts with this stupid cruise. I told her I didn't want to go on any boat ride cooped up with strangers, but she booked it anyway. The tickets are nonrefundable. If I don't go, I'll have wasted all that money. She trapped me. Again."

"You'll figure it out." We'd all attended high school together. Dottie had a fast woman rep back then, and Wayne had been the football quarterback. She'd caught his eye and more until she got pregnant by him. He'd griped all the way to the altar, but while their marriage had a rocky start, they were still cohabitating ten years later. Sometimes I thought the four boys were the glue that kept Wayne physically tethered to

44

Dottie. She had his kids and his home, but he made it known to every woman he met that he wasn't hers.

Bantam rooster cocky, Wayne carried his two hundred pounds on his five-ten frame with an alpha dog swagger. His thick head of hair and long eyelashes turned heads wherever he went. Rumor was his latest girlfriend worked at the new gift shop.

We stopped near the rear door of the club. It was the only entrance as the side fronting the road was solid wall. There were no windows anywhere in the building. I cleared my throat, very much aware that I'd never been inside this place before.

"You think the suitcase person died in the club?" I asked.

"Never said that. I needed to get you away from the others. What's with your boyfriend glomming onto my case? Sheriff Blair called and insisted she wanted him on this case. He after my job?"

"No. He's got other options in mind for his career path. The state forensic pathologist is pushing Mayes to head a statewide cold case task force."

Wayne swore again. "I hate it when the staties or the feds recruit one of our rank and file. If this is the Suitcase Murderer, we'll have the FBI and national news outlets

45

all up in our business. And if we can't wrap this up before that damned cruise, I'll have to leave one of my guys in charge. Frankly, that scares me more than the cruise. So we better get this case solved or you'll have to tell my wife why I'm not going."

I gulped. No one wanted to cross his wife, least of all me. "What can I do?"

"Solve this case today for starters. Get your boyfriend out of here to finish. We don't need outsiders looking over our shoulders. You and I prefer to avoid scrutiny from the media, so I need you to bring your "A" game to this investigation. Let's git her done."

Pride stiffened my spine. "I always bring my A game. I tutored you in math, remember?"

"Yeah, I remember. You could think rings around me back then. You angling for my job too?"

"No one is angling for your job, not Mayes, and certainly not me. I can't handle another job or responsibility. I'm spread thin as it is."

"Good." He stared around the derelict lot for a moment before pinning me with a needle sharp gaze. "Why didn't you ever go out with me?"

"Because you're a tom cat, that's why."

"I would've mended my ways for you."

I knew better. My head buzzed a little, as if someone wanted to talk to me in mind-speak. Must be Mayes. I blocked the sensation for now. "Dream on."

"Tell me this. If I divorced Dottie today, would you go out with me?"

"No."

"You're a cold-hearted woman, Baxley Powell."

Despite my mental shields, Mayes blasted through on our telepathic link. *Is he bothering you?*

I'm fine. Wayne needed to vent.

That guy wants you bad.

So do you.

Yeah, but I've got you, right?

What was it with the men's egos today? Was Mercury in retrograde? I didn't keep up with astrology but something was causing this cluster of masculine insecurity. *Yes. Why the doubt?*

Your sheriff wishes I'd go away.

He has wife problems. He's calmer after venting.

Good. Ping me if you need backup.

Thanks.

Something shook my shoulder. "Huh?"

"Baxley," the sheriff said. "Where'd you go? Is it the case? Are you getting a vision

47

out here?"

I glanced at the sheriff, momentarily blindsided by the genuine concern in his lady-killer eyes. "Umm. No. Sorry. I was thinking about something else. I'm ready to go inside if you are."

"You were talking to him, weren't you?"

"Sheriff, I'm ready to do my job."

"Some guys have all the luck." He clomped up the metal steps, his heavy feet making more noise than necessary. "I'll show you around inside."

I drew my arms across my chest to keep from touching the handrail. No sense connecting with all the lusty emotion laid down on the rusted rail. "You're familiar with this place?"

"Sugar, me and my dad kept this place in business."

I steeled myself against the thick miasma of lust leaking through the doorframe. "I should've known," I muttered under my breath.

"What's that?"

"Nothing."

He opened the dented aluminum door. "This place was unlocked this morning. Unusual, but there are still some keys in the community."

"You have a key?"

"I do."

Was he doing the gift shop lady here? Gross.

Wayne glided through the narrow opening and switched on his flashlight. The shadow drenched room held two dingy loveseats, three café tables and chairs, and a fireman's pole at the end of the room. Visions flooded my consciousness, without me initiating a dreamwalk or touching anything. Just stepping over the threshold was all it took for the tide of lusty emotion to overwhelm me.

I tried to mentally shut down, but the lust-fueled activities overrode my failsafe. Faces of men in the throes of release surged into my head, one after another in kaleidoscope fashion. I couldn't get a good look at the people because the image sequence zipped by like a movie reel on fast forward.

Under the mental assault, I staggered, lost my center of gravity, and dropped when my knees buckled. Wayne caught my head before I hit the floor, and still the visions raced through my mind. It was too much. The pressure in my head shot from tolerable to excruciating. The last image I saw before I blacked out was Wayne's glowing face in the throes of lust.

CHAPTER SIX

"Hey you," Mayes said.

I blinked and blinked some more. Mayes' austere face was framed by a bold blue sky. I was outside of the club, laid out in the parking lot from the looks of my surroundings. Unlike the bizarre dreamwalk Rose forced on us Sunday night, I remembered what happened before I conked out in the dance club. "Too many faces," I muttered.

Mayes leaned down and rubbed his cheek against mine. "It's okay. Just a few more minutes."

I felt better immediately. That's when I realized he was transferring energy through his hands, which were intertwined with mine. "You can't keep doing this," I said. "You need your strength."

"We need you at full speed to work the crime scene. It's important," Mayes said before his lips touched mine. Energy sparked in the three places we intersected.

The resulting current charged my entire body with a satisfying hum.

"I'm not paying y'all to make out," Wayne said, annoyance coated his voice, sunlight glinted off his dark glasses. "Bax. You coherent enough to tell me what happened?"

Mayes touched his forehead to mine before going upright. "Back-off. You took her into a blackout zone."

To me privately on our telepathic link, Mayes said, *Your boss is a jerk.*

He didn't know I'd pass out.

Sorry you went through that.

I never want to go in there again.

Maybe you won't need to.

"Baxley?" Wayne said. "Answer me. What the hell happened?"

"Enough." I untangled myself from Mayes and managed to sit under my own power. I wasn't at a hundred percent, but I didn't need to be. Eighty percent would do. "What happened was that you took me to a place with layers upon layers of emotion and sexual activity. The experiences in that building ran through my mind like a movie reel on warp speed. I couldn't process the rapid-fire input, so I passed out."

"See anybody you know?" Wayne asked.

Though I didn't care for the leer on his face, I valued my job. I drew in a bracing

51

breath. "No one stood over a dead body or carried a suitcase full of bones, if that's what you mean. There was not one suitcase in the entire sex parade. What I saw appeared to be unrelated to the case."

"Pity." He stared down at me in a calculating manner. "While Mayes sat with you, I scouted inside, and nothing seems out of the ordinary. I'd rather you have a go at the suitcase now. We need your input on the luggage."

Not liking being at a height disadvantage for this conversation, I scrambled to my feet, ignoring the helping hand from Mayes. "How'd the person in the suitcase die? Surely you must have opened it."

"We won't know how this victim died until the Medical Examiner takes a look," Wayne said. "There's a compressed mess in the suitcase right now. It appears there are no clothes, no accessories like glasses or watches, and no bullets. Save yourself from a nasty visual. I'm thinking you could get all you need from the suitcase exterior. We will, of course, exclude your prints and DNA from the samples collected."

I tried not to think about the dead person stuffed in a suitcase and thrown out like garbage. I was acutely conscious of Mayes standing close behind me and grateful to have him at my back. "I'll examine the suitcase now, if that's okay with you."

"All right. We can walk over there, if you're strong enough."

Time I made my demands known. "I want Mayes to accompany me."

Wayne studied the two of us. His thinking expression of pinched brows and scowling mouth came and went. "He fixes you when things go wrong?"

I met his level gaze. "Yes. He does. The physical contact recharges me quickly. The more contact points, the better."

"Okay. I'll change the pair ups. The two of you collaborate at the suitcase, and I'll process the club's interior surfaces. I'll keep Stone on the grid search."

Never let it be said that Sheriff Wayne Thompson couldn't think on his feet, especially when he'd seen me pass out on the job and be rescued by another man. Wayne and I needed to talk about Mayes soon. He needed to understand that Mayes wasn't going anywhere.

As Wayne hurried to retrieve his evidence kit, Mayes and I strolled toward the crime site. His hand reached for mine. "I'm sorry," he said. "I should've protested the assignment and gone with you."

"Forget it. Stuff happens in this job."

He glanced back at the sheriff for a moment. "You told Wayne you didn't see anything helpful, but did you see anyone you recognize?"

I pinched the bridge of my nose, not wanting to lie but feeling loyalty to my boss. "Sorry if I sounded snippy before. This is a difficult case and I didn't sleep much last night. Tell me about the victimology."

"There is a chance this is a copycat killer, but this M.O. is nearly identical to a suitcase murder a year ago. We might have a leg up on solving the case, which may in turn tie into other Georgia Suitcase Murders."

"How so?"

"There were a few persons of interest the lead agent suspected."

That made sense. A bit more of my unease melted away. I began walking again. "You have access to that data?"

"I surely do. And I'll be checking to see if any of those men passed through here recently."

"How?"

"Phone records, cell towers, credit card receipts, surveillance cameras."

"Don't you need a warrant for all that?"

"Not a problem. My buddy in the Georgia Bureau of Investigation will get the warrants we need."

I groaned aloud at the thought of the intrusion. I felt the same way about outside agencies as my boss. "Not the GBI again. We don't want Burnell Escoe around here impeding our investigation."

"Escoe won't get this cherry assignment, especially if my guy wants to close his case."

"Does Wayne know about this GBI guy?"

"I'll read him in if he doesn't know Lavene."

"Whoa." I halted again. The sun seemed overbright and harsh. The humid air cloaked me like a wet blanket. The environment hadn't changed so quickly, but my perception of it had. Mayes was operating under a different set of ground rules.

"Wayne doesn't work that way," I said. "Get him on board before you call your friend."

Mayes had the grace to look sheepish. "I phoned him as soon as Virg updated me on the suitcase findings."

"I'm telling you, if you work for Wayne you do things his way. You should tell him now."

"No rush. We'll read the suitcase first."

My gut clenched. "You may be number two deputy in your county, but you're not even a number here. He expects to make the decisions. This is his case."

"We do things differently in north Georgia, and the world still turns. I'll tell him. Soon as we finish with the dreamwalk."

I squeezed my eyes shut. Why couldn't things be straightforward? Was I loyal to the sheriff or looking out for my own hide?

I met his gaze. "I love you but Wayne should be informed of the lead. That's the protocol here."

"Understood. I'll tell him, but I'm watching out for you by delaying the conversation until after we read the suitcase."

"This won't end well if you wait. I've got dreamwalker help with Bubba Paxton and my father here, so if Wayne reacts poorly, I won't be alone."

"All right." Mayes raised his hands in surrender, his voice sharp. "I'll ask Lavene to delay sending information until I have the sheriff's approval. I'll tell the sheriff now, if you go with me."

"Now who's chicken?"

CHAPTER SEVEN

Mayes shrugged and urged me toward the former club. My work boots felt ten pounds heavier. Wayne would blow a gasket when he heard the GBI news.

I didn't want Mayes to be on Wayne's bad side, but I needed to stay on my boss's good side however this played out. I nodded toward the crime scene behind us. "Did you try a dreamwalk with the suitcase already?"

"Nope. That's your jurisdiction."

"But you could. Dreamwalk with the dead on your own."

He gazed at the sheriff watching our approach before he leaned down to whisper in my ear. "One of these days we'll talk about how talented you are. My process is hit or miss. The dreamwalks you make are straightforward; mostly I'm an infant whereas you're an elder when it comes to spirit crossings and encounters."

"You've done solo dreamwalks before. I

57

don't understand."

"Out of all the dreamwalkers I've met, you're the only one who does what you do. The rest of us lob trial balloons in the same general direction. You're a rock star in our world."

I strangled out a bitter laugh. "Not in this lifetime."

"Deny it all you want, but it's the truth."

"Hey," Wayne called. "Y'all gonna get to work or keep strolling around my crime scene?"

"In a minute," I said as we stopped in front of the sheriff. "Mayes has something to tell you."

"This case," Mayes said. "It's very similar to a case that happened near my jurisdiction."

The sheriff set his evidence kit on the ground and planted his hands on his hips. "And you're just now telling me?"

Mayes seemed tongue-tied. I jumped in to fill the gap. "Tell him."

My boyfriend shot me an exasperated look. "I called the investigator who ran the other case. A GBI guy who's a friend of mine."

Wayne let out a blue streak of cuss words. "You sicced the GBI on us?"

"This guy is different," Mayes insisted.

"Getting Roger Lavene engaged right away will net us expedited new warrants on his suspects. We can close this case faster and minimize the media frenzy that's soon to follow."

The sheriff shook his head and glared. Negative energy radiated from him in thick waves. "I'm not asking you to think outside the box, Mayes. You're on loan from your department. I'm supposed to have an extra body to help work this case, and extra set of hands that have no downside. All I want from you is to do the job as I see fit. Understood?"

"Yes, sir."

Mayes worked with a looser rein for his sheriff. He believed he'd done the right thing to move the investigation forward, while Wayne was certain Mayes had screwed him beyond measure.

Their unhappiness and anger permeated the air, battering me in a way that made me nauseous. A little voice told me I'd caused this upset, which brought a wave of shame and regret.

"We're changing assignments again," Wayne said after an uncomfortable silence. He leveled his gloved index finger at Mayes like it was a gun. "You're on the evidence collection inside the club. I'm handling the consultant."

"I want him with me," I said.

"It doesn't work both ways, Bax. If he doesn't follow orders, I can't trust him with my most valuable asset."

"Give Baxley your phone," the sheriff said. "That way you can't get into more trouble."

Stark emotion etched his dark gaze. "I made a mistake. It won't happen again."

"Damn straight it won't. Oh, and one more thing," Wayne said. "Who did you say you called?"

"Roger Lavene."

"Don't know him," Wayne said.

"Rog's number is last on my called list. Phone him yourself. He knows this suitcase killer inside and out."

Wayne stalked toward the suitcase. I pivoted and followed my boss across the lot for the second time that day. Good grief. Could this day get any worse?

Once we were out of earshot, I tried to soothe Wayne's ego. "He tried to help."

"He should've come to me first," Wayne muttered. "I tolerate a lot in my shop, but I have no doubt about any of my people's loyalty."

"Will you phone Roger Lavene?"

"Maybe. After you visit our dead person. We need fresh leads."

I handed him Mayes' phone, but an eerie feeling haunted me. Would Wayne do more than banish Mayes from his team? Surely not.

Wayne stopped. "Hold up."

"What?" I stumbled to a halt.

"They're moving the body now."

I glanced up and saw my father and Bubba Paxton wheeling a suitcase-shaped body bag toward their vehicle. Their grim faces suggested they'd seen the decomposed body inside the case. A telling aroma emanated from the sealed body bag. I wished I had some of the coroner's menthol under my nose to combat the odor.

My heart went out to whoever was in there. They'd been disposed of without a care, tossed into the woods as if their life meant nothing. *Whoever you are, I will get justice for you.*

"New plan. You can read the suitcase inside the air conditioned coroner's van. Someone will sit nearby to monitor your status."

It would be too much for my dad to handle and Mayes was currently persona non grata. "I want Bubba to be my wingman."

"Figured as much." He glanced over his shoulder. "Boy toy won't like you dreamwalking with another guy."

I ignored the ugly jibe. Mayes wouldn't like the situation no matter what, but Bubba wouldn't join me. He'd sound the alarm if something went wrong though. Not that it would go wrong. I could handle a dream-walk on my own. "Mayes is a professional. He'll handle whatever you throw at him."

"I'll hang here for a bit, but if this runs long, report to me at the office when you awaken."

How aggravating. The sheriff wanted me on his team, but if my special abilities took too long for his convenience, I was to find him. I pasted on my coldest professional smile. "No problem."

CHAPTER EIGHT

After dipping into dad's menthol supply to keep the pungent aroma of death at bay, I scrambled in the van beside the collapsed gurney and the suitcased body. Just an odor, I told myself when my instincts urged my flight from this pungent, confined space. Natural processes at work I told myself, processes that were not the victim's fault.

I tried not to imagine the body's decay, and I hoped like anything the dreamwalk wouldn't include the decomp process. I tried to hold onto my outrage over the victim's means of disposal, but the truth was I wanted this over with as soon as possible so I could escape this stench.

Heart pounding in my ears, I unzipped the heavy duty bag. The rotten odor intensified and my breakfast turned to stone in my belly.

I stared at the black canvas suitcase for a moment, unable to bring myself to touch it.

I braced myself for a spontaneous dream-walk, but nothing happened when my fingers hovered in the air above the case. No flicker of a photographic slide show. No sense of passing through the veil.

Rats.

My only option was to touch the suitcase. I didn't wear gloves because that thin barrier made it harder for me to dial in the dreamwalk. Anything I got on me could be washed off, and I could take a shower to get the unwholesome stench out of my hair. I lowered my hand to the canvas surface, braced for the freefall of a transition and the bending of reality. Nothing.

Was I broken?

That wasn't good.

Wait. I wasn't doing this smart. Fear had made me stupid. I needed to touch the suitcase handle or the zipper pull. The killer may not have touched this side panel of the luggage. Steeling my nerves again, I reached for the handle.

Right away, I felt the tug and tumble as my spirit detached and traveled through the drift, the other-worldly veil between life and death. You weren't supposed to have physical sensations in this turbulent channel, but I always felt cold and alone as I pitched, whirled, and plummeted through the darkness.

As usual, my stomach wanted to revolt, and I longed for the orientation of gravity. Just when I thought I couldn't take another second of freefalling through nothingness, everything changed. The midnight intensity of my surroundings lightened to a dull murk. Sound returned, though everything I heard was distant and garbled.

I waited for the framework of the Other Side to appear. Usually an empty hallway spanned before me with closed doors that I could open one at a time. Or a direct touch like this one would vector me directly into a past scene from the victim's life.

My nerves skittered at the delay. Why wasn't the dreamwalk beginning? I called for Rose, my mentor and guide, but she didn't respond. Usually, she arrived in less than a second, eager to help me out, but today she was a no-show.

Rose wasn't my only lifeline over here. Oliver, my Great Dane ghost dog, was an earthbound spirit who could cross the veil. I summoned him, and he loped out of the melancholy fog to be with me. He barked happily and wagged his tail. I gave him ear rubs, which he lapped up like the affection starved spirit he'd become, and then I drew the big dog spirit into my virtual arms for a big hug before I stood and focused on the dead woman again.

Woman? Did I know she was a woman before now? I couldn't remember. But I felt cramped. As if I was in a tight spot. My chest burned as if I couldn't take a full breath, only there was no breathing on the Other Side.

So, this confinement and darkness was a memory the dead woman was sharing with me. She'd spent time in a small space. Locked up? Hiding? I didn't know the answer.

"Show me what else you want me to know," I said, even though that wasn't the way dreamwalks worked. Typically, spirits shared bits and pieces of their lives. There was nothing linear about this process. Usually the first scene I saw, unless it was an I-can't-believe-I'm-dead moment, was something that had a visceral impact on the victim. The timeline could be anywhere in his or her history.

Like this oppressive sense of confinement I was feeling. This woman had been caged somehow during her life. It may or may not be relevant to her death. As a child, I liked to hide in tight places, but this didn't feel adventurous. This felt like she couldn't leave

66

the area.

Being stuck in a small place would certainly be something one wouldn't forget.

Oliver whined at my feet. Like him, I was impatient for more information. I tried to reason with the spirit. "I know you can hear me. I get that you spent time in a confined space, but unless you show me something else, I can't help you. Who did this to you?"

The pervading sense of feeling trapped wavered. A slice of sunlight glimmered through a crack in the tiny prison. Beyond the narrow opening was green everything. Green yard. Green trees.

"So you could see outside," I said. "Were you in a shed or a vehicle? Could you smell fresh air? Were there any landmarks?"

The verdant image remained steady and the lack of noise implied that this woman could see the world but not hear it. "I want to help you, ma'am. I want to bring your killer to justice. Can you show me what he or she looked like?"

The thin sliver of foliage might as well be a snapshot since it remained static. "Is the reason you aren't hearing anything because you were mute in life?"

Nothing from the woman.

I shouldn't have asked so many questions. Wayne only asked one question at a time in an interview. I needed to start doing that. "Ma'am? I need your help. Please show me something to help us figure out what happened to you."

Like a desert mirage, the verdant green shimmered and faded to black. I heard the incessant whine of insects. A rumble of a diesel motor. And another sound. Something high pitched like a pump. Or an industrial machine.

The sounds reminded me of a pastoral setting. "Are you on a farm?"

A wispy spirit materialized near me. She wore a loose, shapeless shift that was easily two sizes too big for her. I quickly scanned her body for anything remarkable. She wore no jewelry. Her longish hair curtained over her face. Her arms and legs resembled toothpicks perched atop tiny bare feet.

I repeated my question and she nodded the smallest little bit. Just that slight effort seemed to take forever and cause her infinite pain.

"Did he hurt you?" I asked.

The shade stared at me as if I were the biggest mystery of all time. Figuring I wasn't going to get much more from her, I gave her The Talk. "I'm a dreamwalker, and my name is Baxley. I'm here to help you. We found your remains in coastal Georgia.

Someone left your body in a suitcase in the woods near the highway."

She seemed interested in what I was saying. She nodded again as I got to the word highway. The woman repeated it. "Highway."

The black thinned to the pervasive murk of the Other Side, with the shade fading into the murk. I wasn't ready for the vision to end. "Wait!" I shouted. "What's your name?"

The reply was so faint I nearly missed it. "I am nobody."

"Nobody," I muttered. "I am nobody."

"Don't sell yourself short," a man said. "You are very much Somebody."

I smiled inwardly at that familiar voice. Mayes. I swam up the rest of the way from my dreamwalk savoring his warm, strong hands on my shoulders. The first thing I saw was the formal café curtains, so I knew I was still in the back bay of the coroner's van. I'd been working a suspicious death about a woman in a suitcase.

From the steady stream of energy coursing through my body, Mayes was sharing his life force with me again. "Shouldn't be here," I said, meaning Mayes.

"My place is with you, Baxley," Mayes

69

said, moving his hands from my shoulders to my forearms. Warmth and wholeness flowed from his gentle touch. "Don't you ever forget it."

"Where's Bubba?"

"Once you started coming around, he and your dad made a lunch run with Deputy Stone at the behest of the sheriff."

"That's nice."

"Where's the body?"

"The out-to-lunch gang took the victim to the morgue on their way to eat. The case was small enough to fit in Stone's trunk."

My world populated in layers. The familiar pull of gravity, the miasma of death in this vehicle, the faint undertones of ripening fall forest, and blessed silence. As my vision crisped, I recognized the familiar shapes of officers moving about the Club Frisky parking lot.

Reality. Boy, how I loved reality.

My parched throat limited me to speaking in short phrases. One day I'd figure out why I always came back so thirsty from these dreamwalks. Pin and needle sensations tingled through my numbed arms and legs. A few more minutes of recovery and I'd climb out of this deathmobile under my own power.

I glanced out the open tailgate, and the

sun was near the center of the sky. If it was early afternoon, I needed to make arrangements for my mom to meet my daughter's school bus. "What time is it?"

"You weren't dreamwalking long, two hours max. It's just before noon," Mayes said. "What do you remember?"

"Nobody. She said she was nobody."

"The suitcase person is definitely a woman?" he prompted.

"Yeah."

"Anything else?" he asked.

"Not much that made sense. She was confined in a tiny space for some time."

Mayes went all steely-eyed. The brackets of his mouth tugged down into a frown.

"That poor woman. She'd been prisoner for so long, her captor brainwashed her. She didn't even know her own name. We need to catch this guy."

"You're our best shot at nailing this killer."

A yawn sneaked out. "Maybe so, but I need a nap."

"No naps for crime fighters. I've got a soda and a candy bar waiting outside to recharge you. Eat and we'll add you to our search team. It's a sure bet the feds and the media will catch wind of this by afternoon. Bottom line, we'll lose this scene today."

Reluctantly, I pushed up to a seated position, wiggling my fingers and toes to get my circulation going. "The sheriff?"

"Got called away as soon as you did your thing."

No wonder Mayes felt free to climb in the coroner van with me. "Another case?"

"Same case. Roger Lavene's info came through on his email, and Wayne tore out of here. If the sheriff has half the sense I think he has, he'll invite Lavene here as soon as possible. Otherwise, he's inventing the wheel all over again."

"Gotcha." Wayne wouldn't like playing second fiddle to the GBI, but he'd love catching a bigtime serial killer. He didn't aspire to a higher political office, but he darn sure thought he was king around here. Solving this case would boost his reputation and his ego.

My fingers and toes moved freely. Everything seemed to be on track with my body's dreamwalk recovery. I wished I'd learned more, but first time encounters with a client, and yes, I thought of murder victims as clients, were often tricky. The dead didn't always recognize their altered status. My sudden appearance in the land of the dead often spooked them.

After scooting to the edge of the vehicle, I stood. Mayes remained within reach. I knew he acted out of care and concern, but he was hovering. Someday we'd have to talk about that. I wasn't spun glass that would break at the first hint of strong winds.

"Feeling better?" he asked.

"I'm fine," I said automatically. Out of reflex, I touched the moldavite pendant at my neck. The gem was a gift from my late husband, and it centered me. Right now it was drained from the dreamwalk. Thanks to Mom, I had a replacement in the truck, along with a supply of charged crystals.

Mayes followed me to the truck, a little wary, but who wouldn't be crabby after an energy draining experience? Briskly, I ate the chocolate bar and soda. Then I replaced my necklace and pocket of crystals with the fresh ones. My mood elevated several notches.

"What have you found in your grid search so far?" I asked.

Mayes blushed, the crimson stain on his cheeks looking out of place on his bronzed face. "Uh, we found multiple items, but whether they have any bearing on the case is questionable."

"What kind of items?"

"Sex toys."

CHAPTER NINE

At his unusual admission, I hurried from the truck to the array of paper sacks. At first glance, it appeared we were creating a luminary display in the parking lot. For holiday celebrations, many coastal communities lined their streets and sidewalks with lunch sack sized bags, though luminary bags held sand and votive candles, not items from an adult entertainment store.

"Holy cow. All of these are sex toys?" I asked, my voice cracking a little. "There must be forty evidence bags here. Wayne will go bankrupt processing all this stuff. No one will believe this."

Mayes had the grace to look sheepish. "The majority are sex toys. We found a few undergarments and in that larger bag over there, a deflated blowup doll in the mix. Given the quantity of artifacts we've already collected, I'd say the items had more to do with the former nature of this location than the body dumping site."

I peered in a few bags and felt my cheeks sizzle. "I don't know what half these things are."

"Fine with me," Mayes said.

"Do you recognize them?"

"I've seen similar items on other cases."

I backed away from the bags like they had the mange. "What should I do?"

"Help us search the remaining grid sectors. Tape your pants to your boots and spray with insect repellant."

I glanced at the dense undergrowth of palmetto and vines, thankful for my thick canvas pants and work boots. "Yeah, tick-proofing is the only way to go."

Once I was ready, I joined the men, stomping our feet as we moved through the wooded area near the body dumpsite. Presumably any self-respecting rattlesnake would hear us coming and retreat from all the noise we were making. The latex gloves I wore came in handy when I picked up discarded items. Nothing even remotely related to a suitcase or a missing woman was discovered. My shielded senses didn't ping, and no spontaneous visions occurred. Bummer. Like Wayne, I wanted this case to be over, but it was just beginning.

We convened in the parking lot afterward.

"Do your thing, Baxley," Mayes said, gesturing to the open bags.

The thought of touching all those objects turned my stomach. "Probably not a good idea. Sensory overload will short circuit me again. Why don't you do it?"

"My talent doesn't work that way. Besides, it won't be as bad for you this time. You already know her energy signature," Mayes said. "Enter into a light trance and run your ungloved palm over the top of the open bags."

I let out a sigh of relief. I didn't have to touch them. Thank goodness. "That might work."

"It will work, u ge-yu-di."

The tone of his voice was kind, but years of people treating me as an outsider and calling me names made me curious. I arched an eyebrow at him. "What's that mean?"

"It's my new name for you in Cherokee."

"You're not calling me a goose, are you?"

He shot me an enigmatic gaze. "Let's finish up here and get home in time for your daughter's school bus."

"And the nickname?"

"Very complimentary, *lovely.*"

Lovely. I wasn't lovely, but he made me feel that way. And I really liked how he'd called my place home. I smiled. "It's a plan."

Since I'd already encountered the victim once, I did a slow sensory scan over all the evidence bags searching for her distinct energy signature. It wasn't there. One bag with a torn thong smacked of another familiar energy. Wayne's. He'd told me he'd visited the club. He must've also *visited* the woods as well.

"There's nothing here with her energy on it. I believe this junk is of little value to our case," I stated, stepping back from the area.

"Good. Means our work here is done." He motioned to Virg and Ronnie. "These are ready to be sealed and turned over to the sheriff."

The two deputies jostled each other as they swaggered over to our location. "You want us to tape them bags?" Ronnie asked.

"They sure do," Virg said, with a not-so-gentle smack to the back of Ronnie's head. "Don't act dumb as that mayor in Tampa."

Tampa. That Florida city name rang a bell but for the life of me I couldn't figure out why. "What's this about Tampa?" I asked.

Virg preened, his grin infectious. "I love it when the mighty become the fallen. The goody-two-shoes mayor got caught in his boxers. Claimed two wild eyed gunmen stole his clothes and forced him to his office in the middle of the night. His secretary found him tied to his desk chair this morning, with drawn-on lipstick kiss marks all over his torso. The media is going bonkers with the story, and that's not all."

God help me, I shouldn't encourage Virg, but I couldn't help myself. "Oh?"

"His wife is madder than a sack of wet cats. She refused an interview with the press when the story broke this morning. Now helicopters are circling her house, and reporters are camped out on her lawn."

Poor woman. Her husband violated her trust and now she was being stalked by the press. "Where's the Tampa mayor now?"

"Cop shop. Word through the grapevine is the mayor's been up to no good with city funds."

"That won't end well," I predicted.

"Heck no. He'll be lucky if he ever sees daylight again. They're saying now that all the surveillance cameras in City Hall were wiped clean over the weekend. It smacks of an inside job."

"Be that as it may, the Tampa mayor has nothing to do with our case," I said. "I'll call Wayne and let him know we've cleared the scene. Mayes and I are heading home for a late lunch."

Ronnie shoved Virg. "Lunch. Right. I wish I was going for *lunch.*"

Surrounded by so much evidence of sexual activity, I flushed. "It's not like that."

But less than twenty minutes later, it was exactly that.

"I have a gift for you," Mayes said once we were dressed again and I was making us peanut butter sandwiches in my kitchen.

Sulay, my Maine Coon cat, watched from atop the fridge. The dogs and little Ziggy vied for space around our feet. I froze as still as the large cat.

Oblivious to my distress, he finished setting the table with forks for our fruit salad and water glasses. "I was saving it until I left, so that you'd something to remember me by. But my leaving has been postponed and I wish to present it to you now."

It was hard for me to take a breath but I forced one inside. Surprises weren't my thing. Years ago, I'd gotten trapped in a dreamwalk merely by sitting in my uncle's chair. My brain knew Mayes' surprise wouldn't be a paranormal event, even so, I tensed.

Fighting down the sudden rush of adrenaline, I covered my distress by speaking softly. "You should've warned me. I didn't know we were exchanging gifts. I don't have anything for you."

79

"You're all the gift I need." Mayes kissed me on the forehead. "I'll be right back."

I finished making the sandwiches and carried the rest of our lunch to the table. My late husband used to complain about my deadpan reaction to gifts. He was never sure if I liked his gifts or not. I wasn't keen on surprises, and I wished I had something to offer Mayes to keep the situation balanced. No matter what he gave me, I'd make sure Mayes knew I liked it.

He returned from his vehicle and handed me a small pouch. The energy coming from the package felt right. "I like it already," I said as I stroked the soft leather and carefully withdrew the carved comb. I loved the weight and feel of it in my hand. The smile on my face was genuine. "It's beautiful."

"It is traditional among my people for men to give this gift to their women." His brow furrowed, and he shoved his hands in his pockets. "Do you accept my gift?"

He seemed anxious about my reaction. Good grief. I must be making a weird face or something. I really looked at him. Was that sweat on his brow? The poor guy. I had to fix this.

My hands closed possessively over the comb and pouch. "Of course, I'll keep it. Why wouldn't I?"

His exhalation was noticeably deep. "Then I am also pleased."

I gave him a hug before returning to gaze at the exquisite comb. "I've never had anything like this before." I fingered the delicate flowers carved into the solid material. The comb was too ornate to use every day. "I'll treasure it. Thank you."

He lifted the comb from my palm and gazed longingly at my hair. "May I?"

If he wanted to comb my boring white hair, who was I to argue? Seconds later, he was easing the pretty comb through my shoulder-length hair, and I was savoring his gentle touch. I sighed with contentment. How long had it been since someone other than me combed my hair?

"Keep that up and I'll make sure we catch a ton of cases so you'll stay," I warned.

His chuckle warmed my heart. "So long as you aren't doing the crimes."

Back at the office, Wayne directed us into the conference room. He slid a sheaf of pages to me and another to Mayes. Another set rested in front of the sheriff. "Familiarize yourself with these three homicides and suspects."

Mayes and I exchanged glances as we accepted our assignments. From the official

Georgia Bureau of Investigation logos and letterheads, it appeared that the sheriff was on good speaking terms with Mayes' GBI friend. Each stapled section began with a photo of a female victim and her name. The last section contained three male suspects.

"The same guy killed all these women?" I asked.

Wayne nodded tersely. "That's Roger Lavene's theory, though there are other suitcase murders all across the country. The GBI believes these three homicides in Georgia were committed by the same person."

"Lavene's cohort are all Georgia murders," Mayes added. "He's frustrated he couldn't close these cases. He wants to examine our evidence for linking factors he may have overlooked. We have the afternoon to come up to speed on the cold cases. He will be here tomorrow to meet with us. We need to evaluate how our case conforms or diverges from the previous cases."

I glanced at Wayne to see if he reacted to what Mayes said. He didn't seem any tenser, but he was already tightly wound. I gestured to the paperwork. "Are we adding these cold cases to our investigation?"

"Undetermined at this time, but we must be thorough. If our suspect killed four women, we want rock solid evidence for his prosecution."

Ah, yes, the prosecution. After a few months as a criminal consultant, I was learning more about the second half of the justice equation. Catching the bad guy was one thing, but making the charges stick was another matter. Dreamwalking wasn't solid evidence; therefore, I had to leverage my extrasensory findings into tangible evidence. So far, my insights had proven helpful to solving cases. I hoped that trend continued.

"What about the women?" I asked. "Did they know each other? Where'd they go to church, school, or work? Did they shop at the same stores or have the same hairdresser?"

"I'll get Lavene to share more of their personal histories after the briefing. Meanwhile, here's what he told me over the phone. Deb Teal of Atlanta clerked at an eastside grocery store on the swing shift. Chaundra Mallory worked six days a week at a South Fulton County Library. The Savannah woman, Hannah Blake, worked as a marina receptionist on Tybee Island."

I spread out their photos on the table as he spoke. Deb, Chaundra, and Hannah all had a friendly vibe in their pictures. "Each victim had a meet-and-greet job. Every day they met and interacted with strangers."

"And?" Wayne asked.

"And they might not have been careful around a predatory stranger. If their natural intuition alerted them to the danger of the man who killed them, I believe they would've ignored it because that's what they were trained to do. They were blindly hospitable, and I don't see how our painfully shy victim fits that mold."

"We don't have all the pieces of the puzzle yet," Wayne asserted. "If our Jane Doe was a serial killer's victim, we'll uncover evidence to prove it."

Hmm. He had so much faith in our investigation. Serial killers. They had patterns and set ways of doing things. Rituals, even, that required practice. An idea popped into my head. "This may sound dumb, but did any of the previous victims survive?"

"The cases I handed you are homicides," Wayne said in a curt tone reserved for dumb questions. "Two victims were found after substantial decomposition. Only one Atlanta woman, Chaundra, was discovered within a few days of death."

"Let me rephrase my question. Was there anyone found in a suitcase and alive?"

An edgy, considering silence blanketed the room. Wayne's face looked blank, and he started rooting through his stack of papers.

Beside me, Mayes went from reptilian stillness to grinning. "Excellent question," Mayes said, leaning forward in his chair, his eyes bright. "We should add those keywords to the database searches. Killers often demonstrate a learning curve. It's possible a victim from his early days got away."

"Point taken," Wayne said. "I'll add those keywords to the searches I'm already running. While y'all are catching up, I'll be in my office working on my press release statement for this afternoon."

"I noticed we had a media-free parking lot," I said as he rose. "How'd you swing that?"

"Everyone here is under a gag order until we've met with Lavene in person. Assuming we're of like mind, he and I will hold a joint press conference after our staff meeting tomorrow mid-morning."

"When will we hear from the Medical Examiner about our Jane Doe?" I asked.

Wayne's chest puffed up like a rooster's. "I already spoke with Dr. Alleen Dabba. Due to the body's advanced state of decomp, it won't take Dr. Dabba long to clean the bones. So far, she says Jane is definitely female of small stature and thin-boned. She took dental X-rays for comparison and observed, based on dental development, that Jane Doe was an adult. She collected hair, a molar, and femur bone marrow samples for DNA analysis."

"What are the victim's vitals?" Mayes asked.

"Five feet tall — that's a definite. Dr. Dabba estimated her weight between ninety to a hundred and ten pounds. Hair color was brown. Her age? Based on the bone ossification centers, anywhere from eighteen to thirty."

"Should I input the data into Missing Persons?" Mayes asked.

"Ahead of you. As soon as I had the data, I added Jane to the Georgia system, then I expanded to neighboring states. Those searches are running. If I strike out in the southeast, I'll query the national system."

Despite our sparse information, the investigation was perking along in good order. This morning's dreamwalk showed our Jane Doe had been terrified. We had to do better for her, but we needed better leads. "Is that all the ME learned from the body?"

"She's still examining the remains. She's determined to identify this woman."

"I'm not sure how helpful I'll be in determining her identity," I said. "The suitcase dreamwalk yielded little information. We have no clothing, jewelry, or even a murder scene. With the disposal site so close to a major highway, she could've been killed anywhere and transported here."

"Which is why we're also reviewing these cold cases and talking with the guy who's worn these shoes before. We're combining solid experience with fresh eyes and a novel investigative approach." He glanced my way. "They haven't used a psychic before."

"Whoopee." I wasn't keen on being labeled a psychic. As a dreamwalker, I technically qualified to be a super psychic because of my multiple talents. Basically, my senses, normal and extra, were strong investigative tools. But extrasensory perception scared many people. If calling me a psychic made people feel better about my contribution, I'd keep my mouth shut about my extra gears.

Wayne lost his cheesy smile. "We have more than the suitcase, and if it comes to that, I'll have you try another dreamwalk with a bone. Meanwhile, you and Mayes familiarize yourselves with the related cases so that everyone has the same information when we meet with Roger Lavene tomorrow."

After the sheriff left, we dove into the case files. Keeping in mind what meager facts we knew about our case, I looked for similarities. At first, the cases were just words on a page, and I thought this would be a wasted effort. I much preferred field work to reading cold case files.

But details from the prior cases intrigued me. One victim had been found fully dressed. Another had been discarded with a newspaper. And another had bunny fur in her hand. "If you focus on the differences," I thought aloud after we'd been at it for nearly an hour, "you can't get anywhere, but each of these women seems to be on the slight side and in the general age range as our victim."

"The hair colors don't match," Mayes said. "Overall, the victimology shows limited overlap."

I'd noticed the same trend. "I was hoping for a signature talisman inside each suitcase."

"The suitcases are from different manufacturers," he continued in the next breath. "The colors vary too. One of the cases is plaid. Who buys a plaid suitcase?"

"Somebody, apparently," I said. "It seems like the killer went out of his way to make the evidence different."

Mayes got a faraway look in his eyes before he nodded. "Brilliant deduction.

These cases are alike because they are each so different. This man isn't a spree killer. He's methodical, and he thinks like we do."

"Hold it right there." Aghast, I pushed back from the conference table. "I do not think like a person that murdered four women."

Mayes studied the chair across from him. The corners of his lips quirked. "Pardon me. I misspoke. You don't think like the killer. The killer thinks like a cop. Or a lawyer. He knows how the law and order system works. He's playing us."

"Someone in law enforcement did this? A cop? Or an attorney?"

He shrugged. "Bad guys exist in all professions. The ones on our side are better at hiding it, for a time."

He was right. I studied the gridded ceiling tiles to gather my scattered wits. Men and women killed for love, power, greed, revenge, and the like. I'd seen family members murder each other to protect their secrets. Some killers had accomplices, from this world or the next. Others worked alone. That left an infinite suspect pool.

I glanced through the suspect packet again. The three men who stared back at me had real jobs and real lives. The trucker, drug rep, and doting grandfather weren't slackers, had no priors, and spent most of their time driving. Their information wouldn't settle in my thoughts. It spun round and round in a dizzying whirl.

I'm sure Wayne secretly hoped I'd get a hit from studying the case files. That wasn't happening. All I was getting was a headache from trying to make connections when there were none. In disgust, I pushed the stack of paper aside and stared at Mayes until he noticed. "Tell me straight. Who did this?" I asked "The butcher, the baker, or the candlestick maker?"

"No one stands out in my mind," Mayes said. "But if we're going the nursery rhyme route, I always thought Little Jack Horner was a braggart and a discipline problem. Think about it. Why else would he be sitting in the corner?"

Grateful for the distraction, I ran the singsong rhyme through my head. "How did he pull a plum out of a pie using only a thumb? Did he even wash his grimy hands first?"

"Good one." We both laughed, and then he said, "Nursery rhymes have special dispensation for germs. But whoever made the pie might've been upset by the plum removal and the kid's attitude. Plus, there's the whole punishment issue. Was it even his pie? And if he wasn't being disciplined in the corner, was he hiding there?"

Hiding. My thoughts sobered. In my dreamwalk with the suitcase, the woman had been in a tight space. I'd assumed she was being held against her will but what if she'd been hiding to spy on someone? Would that someone have been upset enough to kill her? "Do these cases involve punishment for the victims or their families? Who benefitted from these victim's deaths? Who lost?"

Mayes took a moment to flip through the cases. "Don't see assets listed in the file. Not much in the way of family mentioned for Deb, Chaundra, or Hannah."

I rubbed my throbbing temples. "Makes me wonder what else is missing."

"Good thing Lavene is coming here tomorrow."

"He has some 'splaining to do."

CHAPTER TEN

Roger Lavene didn't look sporty or athletic. For some reason, I'd pictured him as long and lanky, like a baseball or tennis star. Instead, he resembled a height-challenged linebacker as he sat next to Wayne. Further, from the guilty way the pair startled apart when we entered the conference room on Tuesday morning, it seemed they had become closely acquainted already.

Lavene shook hands with Mayes and then nodded in my direction. No handshake was offered, but that was par for the course for how most people treated me. I could count daisy petals to list the people brave enough to shake my hand. Everyone else shied away from touching me. They didn't want to be read any more than I wanted to read them.

Perhaps my stark white hair was off-putting to the GBI man. I wasn't in uniform, so Lavene didn't have to show professional deference to a fellow lawman. In fact, his leery reaction was typical of most cops to psychics. They expected us to be scent dogs and lead them to evidence on command. Other than that, they gave us a wide berth.

Virg, Ronnie, Tamika from dispatch, and several admin staffers filed into the conference room and joined us for the briefing. We sat across the table from the sheriff and Roger Lavene. Glancing at the others, I noticed no one else brought files or notepads to the meeting. Were their memories that good? Another mystery I couldn't solve.

After Wayne's introduction, Lavene rose. "I'm delighted to talk with the Sinclair County sheriff's department about my cold cases. How can I help?"

"Everyone in this room knows we found a body in a suitcase yesterday." The sheriff rose and loomed over the shorter man. "The evidence we recovered is minimal. So far, we have a suitcase and a victim. Nothing else. I'm hoping we can pool resources and catch this guy."

"You already know it's a guy?" Lavene asked.

"We do." Wayne jerked a thumb my way. "My consultant is sure of that much."

Lavene's shrewd gaze settled on my face. "We surmised as much from the FBI profile we received on our suitcase murders and the suspects we developed." He gestured toward me. "Do you have proof?"

"Nothing that will stand up in court," I admitted, hating the sound of that admission.

"Can't use it then," Lavene said, dismissing me with a wave of the hand and turning back to Wayne. "How are you hunting the killer?"

"The M.E. is scouring the remains, so database searches are our primary focus right now."

"The database is only as good as the people entering keywords in each case," Lavene scoffed. "Though, I applaud you for checking to see if any women found in suitcases were alive, even though that search was a bust. That's an avenue I never explored." He fell silent for a moment. "Y'all have questions for me?"

"Why narrow your search to the suitcase victims found in Georgia?" Mayes asked. "Is our killer a Georgia resident?"

"Economics, unfortunately, limited the scope of my investigation." Lavene grimaced, his face creasing in deep ruts. "Our travel allowance took a big hit two budget cycles ago. And, yes, I realize that suitcase murders are not confined to Georgia, but my boss decided that narrowing our focus was our best shot at finding the killer. We coordinated with the FBI agent assigned to the national investigation, but our profiles were slightly different from the other cases. It is the FBI's belief that we have a copycat killer down here."

The FBI belief and GBI/FBI coordination on past cases was news to me. "That wasn't in the files you sent," I added. "What's different?"

"Most of the national cases had an element in common. That linking factor was never released to the media, and only your sheriff has the clearance to know specifics about the signature item."

Another sour expression crossed Lavene's face. "Politics. You think it wouldn't be a factor in police work, but it is. My boss is into political correctness so your files were scrubbed. But I'm here for you to pick my brain and to assist in your investigation. Anything I know, except for that national signature, is yours for the asking."

Sounded reasonable. Mayes said this guy was solid, so I should move on to my other questions. "What about victim ID? Was there any one thing that speeded that process along in your cases?"

"Solid investigative work," Lavene added,

puffing up like a toadfish. "We tracked down every lead."

"And the Missing Persons database. How helpful was that?"

"Not as much as you might think," Lavene said. "Two of the cases, including the one in my jurisdiction I worked the most aggressively, were in the Metro Atlanta area, while the other was in Savannah. I got a sketch artist to make a rendering of what my victim must've looked like, and I floated it past the metro Atlanta cops. A beat cop recognized the woman's photo. Once I had that ID, and I saw another suitcased body had been found in the same district, I thought I had my killer's home territory. I even found three men that connected the two Atlanta victims. I thought sure I would wrap up the case in a few hours once I had solid suspects, but I didn't have enough to arrest any of those guys."

"And the Savannah case?" I continued. "One of your victims lived in Atlanta before moving to Savannah. Her suitcase was found near the port."

"What was the connection?" Wayne asked. "You must've had solid ties."

"I did. Jared Springfield is an independent trucker who makes intrastate runs. He answers to no one, and he hauls all over the state."

I flipped to the info about Springfield in my folder. During the estimated window of death for the Savannah victim, he traveled to Savannah five times. They'd searched his home and his rig and found nothing untoward. He didn't even own a suitcase, using a duffel bag for his travel gear. He answered questions frankly, becoming upset when he wasn't released from police custody right away.

"Of your three suspects," I said, "who is your most likely candidate?"

"Can't say because each of them could've come in contact with more than one of the victims. Otis Clement is a pharmaceutical rep with a lucrative territory in Atlanta. He drives a large SUV with tinted windows. He vacationed in Savannah during the window of death for the Savannah victim. My other suspect, Darius Bronson of Macon, has grandkids in Atlanta and Savannah. He keeps the road humming going to his grandsons' sporting events. His luxury sedan has a big trunk. With their travel schedules, their large vehicles, and their ability to crisscross the state at the drop of a hat, all of my suspects appear to have had the opportunity to encounter the victims. I couldn't zero in on a single suspect."

"Have any of these men passed this way recently?" Mayes asked.

"Checking on that now. You can learn a lot about a person's whereabouts from the cell tower information. I got warrants issued for their mobile phone usage before I headed down to Marion."

Sounded like this collaboration wouldn't go very far. Something had to give. "Any possibility these men know each other?" I asked.

"Each of them took lie detector tests. Clement failed every question so I can't say for sure about him. Springfield and Bronson passed the test without any red flags. They are either innocent or very accomplished liars."

"All things being equal, who does your gut say is most likely the killer?" I pressed.

"Doesn't matter," Lavene said. "Can't take my gut to court."

"But it might give us a tighter focus for our investigation."

"That's where you're wrong. We narrowed the scope before and failed. You need to develop fresh leads. If they connect to my suspects, fine. If we head a different direction, fine. We must stop this killer."

Good plan, only we had no new leads.

Something niggled at the back of my mind, but I couldn't shine a light on it.

"You got anything else, Powell?" the sheriff asked.

"I do." I glanced down at the victim photos as I gathered my thoughts. "I saw only one or two family members mentioned for Deb, Chaundra, or Hannah. Each victim had someone who eventually notified police of their disappearance. Did their family benefit from their deaths?"

The packed room grew quieter with each second that ticked by. Given Lavene's now florid complexion, I wondered if I was supposed to keep questioning our case expert. Did Wayne do this to pit the team against one another?

"These victims had little of value in their personal estates," Lavene said in a soft voice. "Family was investigated in each case and rejected as suspects. We worked through their connections, but these women weren't heavily networked. They had no best friends or boyfriends who noticed they were missing. In each case, the suspect had days with the victims before an investigation was mounted."

"That seems relevant," I observed, lobbing the conversational ball back in his court.

Lavene gave a terse nod. "From what we observed, the Georgia Suitcase Murderer selects victims who are small in stature and weight, introverted, and isolated."

Our Jane Doe fit the criteria. Still, how did one guy pull this off? "Did the killer abduct the women or did he somehow gain their trust to insure voluntary cooperation?"

"I believe he took them," Lavene said, "though I can't prove it, given the lack of witnesses or evidence. Why do you ask?"

"In my dreamwalk, our victim watched the world through narrow slits. She was in darkness and the world beyond was in full color. I wasn't sure if she was hiding and watching the killer or if she was imprisoned. Were any cages or old sheds or trunks found near your murder locations?"

"We only found the dump sites. Nothing like that was near where the suitcases were found."

Great. We were looking for a man who probably lived a double life. An invisible needle hidden somewhere in the haystack of Georgia.

Wayne shot me a questioning glance. I shook my head, not knowing what else to ask. "Anyone else?" he asked.

No one said a word.

"All right then," Wayne said. "Here's our

play. We'll track down Lavene's suspects, find out where they've been for the past few weeks. Every patrol shift will have their ID and vehicle information. We'll also keep an eye out for suspicious behavior during our patrols. Powell, you and Mayes head to the morgue. Lavene and I will review the press release I've drafted and hold a press conference on the lawn within the hour. The press should be gathering outside by now. No one but me or Lavene speaks to the press. I want results, people. Everyone is to be on the lookout for suspicious persons and suspicious activity throughout the county. Dismissed."

I rose, tucked my paperwork under my arm, and silently trailed deputies Virg and Ronnie from the conference room.

Once we were out of earshot of the sheriff, Virg elbowed Ronnie. "That's some warped dude doing this stuff," Virg said. "If I see any of those suspects, you betta believe I'll light 'em up with my Taser."

"Make sure he's resisting arrest first," I cautioned. I'd been on the wrong end of Virg's Taser once, and I hoped to never repeat the experience. "You don't want to make a mistake on a case like this."

Virg snorted.

"I'll tell ya who's lit up," Ronnie said,

coming out of his quiet funk and sounding like a bona fide redneck. "That mayor down Tampa way. Caught in his skivvies with his hand in the till. Boy, is he dumb or what? Heard tell his wife already threw all his clothes out the winda and he had to move in with his mom once she posted his bail."

I felt a twinge at the mention of the Tampa news again. Something about that situation in Florida didn't feel right to me.

Don't say anything.

I stumbled at the unexpected voice in my head. *Mayes? What's going on?*

He steadied me and continued our conversation in the telepathic mode. *I didn't mention this before. I found something in my pocket from the other night. A cocktail napkin from a Tampa bar.*

The other night. Our lost night? Was he kidding? I turned and caught his eye. He stepped up to walk beside me. *That was us? No way.*

His expression tightened. *The real question is why would your spirit guide need us to make an example of this man? Embezzlers don't strike me as major threats to those in the afterlife. What made Rose target this man?*

Tampa. I know something about Tampa. Come to think of it, what I know about Tampa had to do with Rose. In one of our early encounters she had me relay a message to a woman down there.

Mayes opened the door to the employee lot, and we stepped out into blazing sunshine and high humidity. In tandem, we lowered our dark glasses to protect our eyes from the glare. He held out his hand for the keys, and I willingly relinquished them.

"Name?" he asked when we were alone in my truck. Vents blew cool air on our warm faces.

"Rose claimed the woman was her sister. Raymondia LaFleur. It took me a while to find her, but the message Rose sent was 'the proof's in the pudding'. The message had something to do with a bank robbery. The woman in Tampa had me take this message to Rose — that she sat on her sister's glasses in second grade. Nothing about that messaging made any sense to me. In retrospect, I believe the exchange was a test, to see if I would do Rose's bidding in this world and the next. And I wouldn't mention it now except for the Tampa connection and the fact that banks or money may be involved."

"Do you still have this woman's phone number?"

I twisted to place my notes and folders behind the seat, then I reached for my seat belt. "No. Wayne got it for me because it wasn't listed in the phone book. If I ask him for it again, he'll make the connection with the current news from Tampa. I'd rather not remind him of that possible connection until we figure out what the heck went on down there."

"I know how to get unlisted numbers."

"Great. Problem solved."

"Except the act of getting the number will leave a record. If you remember the date of the incident, we may have an easier time searching the calls from Wayne's office on that day."

Sneaky. I beamed my approval. "I can narrow down the timeframe. It was a few days before we arrested a man for murdering his brother."

"The Gilroy case."

He said it casually, but the case hadn't received attention in the state-wide media. I studied him openly. "You know about it?"

"I have an interest in you. I've read your case files."

He was telling the truth. He'd been checking up on me. "Wow. Should I be flattered or creeped out?"

"Flattered. You came into your power suddenly and managed like a pro. Not many dreamwalkers could have done so well."

"I've made my share of mistakes."

"We all have."

"You?" I scoffed as he drove us out of the employee parking lot. "No way. You are so self-assured and in total control of your abilities."

"It wasn't always so. One day I'll share a few of my mistakes. Not today. We've got other priorities." He glanced toward the chaos of the main parking lot, where vans, cameras, and people hunched and squawked like a flock of grackles. "Like avoiding the press, for one."

Like handling a dead woman's bones for the other.

CHAPTER ELEVEN

"Your morgue is in the next county?" Mayes asked as we motored across the last of five bridges to reach the county line.

I savored the view from the top of this tall bridge, enjoying the sight of the bustling marina and the gleaming vessels docked there. Beyond the moorage, endless stands of ripe marsh grass framed the sediment-heavy freshwater of the Altamaha River. If only human matters were as steadfast as rivers flowing to the sea.

I turned my thoughts to our pending morgue visit and to reading Jane Doe's bare bones. "It is now. Our former coroner and M.E., Dr. Sugar, conducted autopsies in his medical office. My father came on board as coroner after Dr. Sugar got fired and lost his medical license. Since my dad isn't a doctor, the county outsourced the service. For a while, we paid another county's Medical Examiner to come over and use the doc's facility, but Wayne hated waiting for the part-time employee to clear his schedule. It's only twenty minutes door to door to Flynn County's morgue. Best of all, our people get equal priority this way."

"Makes sense." I noticed brake lights flaring ahead. Should I say something to Mayes? Probably not. My hand crept over to grip the armrest. "Your population and your crime rate need to rise exponentially before you can afford a fulltime M.E."

"Funny. We always thought of Dr. Sugar as a lecherous old goat. Who knew he was doing our county such a service?"

Mayes braked as he approached a fully loaded log truck. "Who replaced him as your community doctor?"

"No one. We got a satellite clinic from the hospital. It's staffed by P.A.'s mostly. The days of the old-school country doctor are behind us."

He nodded. "With a fulltime M.E., you're more likely to have a thorough autopsy."

To my immense relief, the log truck veered onto the interstate spur road. I preferred having the open road before us instead of a logger. Once years ago, I'd witnessed a crash involving a big truck like this, with the tree trunks spilled all over the road. One trunk speared the roof of a car. Not something I ever wanted to happen to me. I was glad Mayes wasn't riding this guy's bumper because I might have to reveal another strange thing about me to him.

"What can medical examiners tell from Jane Doe's bones, other than height and gender?" I asked, glad to talk shop instead of obsessing about log trucks. I let go of my armrest and tried to relax in my seat.

"The condition of the skeleton can be evaluated."

"I don't understand. They're bones."

"Some may be broken. If so, the M.E. can determine if the break occurred before or after death. That may indicate a violent death."

"Oh." Should I have known this? I'd held bare bones before for dreamwalks, but never thought of them as forensic tools. "You've studied this?"

"I've attended a number of autopsies as part of my job," Mayes said.

He spoke so matter-of-factly. On some level it bothered me that anyone could see death as routine. "Does it get you down, dealing with death all the time?"

"We don't get many murders up at Stony Creek Lake, maybe one every quarter or six months. We have more natural deaths, which may require autopsies, depending on the circumstance. The difference is I've been doing this for years. My experience is cumulative."

Whereas the sum total of my experience was a crash course over the last six months. I sighed. "I seem to find dead bodies everywhere I go."

"Lucky you."

The medical examiner, Dr. Alleen Dabba, introduced herself in the reception area of the Flynn County Hospital. She filled out an oversized set of mossy green surgical scrubs. Intelligent blue eyes stared back at me from behind black circular eyeglass frames. Owlish eyes, I thought.

In silence, she escorted us directly to the morgue. I'd never been here before. One wall held a bank of stainless steel vaults with tags on them. Two person-sized exam tables were present, one empty, one populated with skeletal remains. Drains accented the buff-colored tile floor. Every counter was shipshape and gleaming. A faint chemical aroma of bleach tainted the air.

"No sense wasting time in my office. Let's get your analysis underway. I've got another autopsy in two hours, an old timer who died alone. No indication of foul play, but I have to check." Dr. Dabba shot us a puzzled look. "Which one of you is the psychic?"

I cleared my throat. "I'm a dreamwalker, Dr. Dabba, not a psychic."

"What does that mean?" She scrunched her nose, making her eyeglasses waggle. She reminded me of a shifty-eyed comic when she did that. Why couldn't I think serious thoughts about this woman?

I cleared my wayward thoughts and tried to sound professional. "I see certain scenes from the deceased's life. We use that information to generate leads for the investigation."

She turned to Mayes and studied him. "You're her bodyguard?"

"We're associates," Mayes said.

Neither Mayes nor I elaborated on our personal or professional relationships. Far as I was concerned, Dr. Dabba was on a need-to-know basis about me. I still clung to the fantasy that I could solve crimes with dreamwalking and publicly maintain a low profile.

"I see." Dr. Dabba ushered us toward the skeleton. "Your Jane Doe is on the far table."

"Any broken bones?" Mayes asked as we flanked the table. The odor of bleach was much stronger.

"Good question. She had a prior injury on her left tibia. The bone is knit together, so this injury happened years ago."

"What about means of death?" I asked.

"Nothing stands out. We found no bullets, no severe head trauma. Unless something comes back positive in her tox screen, I will be putting 'unknown' as the cause of death."

The sight of the skeleton laid out on the exam table was grim. Earlier, this Jane Doe had called herself Nobody, but she was somebody's daughter, somebody's loved one. It was my job to figure out where she belonged and to seek justice for her.

"What do you need from me?" Dr. Dabba asked.

I saw a wheeled stool nearby. That would work nicely for my field trip into the Beyond. "Dreamwalks are solo efforts. We're good. Thanks."

"Have at it, but don't take all day. I've got a stack of reports to proof and sign." With that Dr. Dabba strode briskly out of the room.

"Where do you want to start?" Mayes asked once we were alone.

"I was thinking her head, but I've never done this before with so many bones to choose from. Is there a chance that each bone will generate a different reading?"

"Always a chance, but I think it's unlikely. Why the head?"

"The skull is one of the larger bones."

"Got it. Am I to follow you in or do damage control on this side of the veil?"

"I've never dreamwalked here, so I'd appreciate it if you'd keep watch. I thought I'd sit on the stool beside the table. That way I wouldn't disturb the bone placement."

"Your call. This is new to me too."

"I've done a bone dreamwalk before. Not much different than any other." I wheeled the chair around to my satisfaction. With a final glance at Mayes standing nearby, I lowered my hand to the cleaned skull.

I braced for the disorientation of crossing over, but everything felt spectacularly ordinary. No sense of transition, no jolt of wispy vision. I raised my eyes to meet my boyfriend's. "I got nothing."

Mayes took his time answering. "If it was the same scenario as the suitcase, you would've seen a replay of that scene, right?"

"Yes. But there's nothing here."

"Try another bone."

Nodding, I reached for the hand bone. Again, I steeled myself for the crossing of the Veil of Life but I didn't receive so much as a flicker for my efforts. I opened my eyes again. "Nada."

"Hmm. The sheriff told me Dr. Dabba

112

bleached the bones. Were the last bones you read bleached?"

I thought back and couldn't remember. "I don't know."

"From what I know about chemistry and bleach, the bleach may have quenched the residual energy. If only a trace remains, you may need to amplify the detecting capability."

"Makes sense to me. Grab a chair, and we'll both cover this hand bone." We got situated and touched the bone together. A glimmer of something flashed in the distance. I jolted out of the meditative state and met Mayes' level gaze. "You see that?"

"Yeah. Something remains, but we can't get at it this way. The only way to boost our amplitude is full body contact, with the bone between us."

I'd been getting a lot of full contact with Mayes these days, not for work purposes either. The prospect held appeal, but we'd both be vulnerable to prying eyes or intruders. "Uh, we don't have anyone to stand watch over the door."

Mayes grinned and rose. "That's what locks are for. Dr. Dabba already knows we need privacy. She should respect our wish not to be disturbed."

We found a clean sheet in a drawer and

laid it out on the floor of the locked room, around the corner from the stainless steel exam table. I tried not to think about where the sheet might have been prior to this. Mayes lay down on the sheet, facing up. He placed Jane Doe's hand bone on the sheet beside him.

I straddled him and collected the bone in my left hand. "Ready?"

"Ready."

With that, I eased down on top of him, our energy already humming in the chilly room, interlacing our fingers together. I pressed my forehead to his and then my lips to his lips. Heat and energy and light flowed between us until our auras merged. I focused on the bone in our joined hands. *Where are you, Jane?*

Reality wavered. We skipped the plunging chaos of the drift and vectored to a tiny cubicle. A dark-haired woman typed at a lone computer. The office lights were turned down low, creating an intimacy in the small illuminated space.

"Jane?" I asked.

The woman ignored me, but her wan face lit up when her computer chimed. I maneuvered behind her. *It looks like a message board,* I said to Mayes in mindspeak. *She's conversing with someone online.*

Lean closer and read the exchange aloud, Mayes said. So I did.

Good Buddy: When can I meet you?

Nobody's business but my own: Why ruin a good thing? This is better than an in-person relationship. Nothing will interfere with our friendship. No longing, no lust.

Good Buddy: Speak for yourself. I long to meet you. To hold your hand. To look into those brilliant eyes of yours.

Nobody's business: Then you'd be disappointed. No one sees me. No one hears me. I might as well be a ghost in this call center.

Good Buddy: You're not invisible to me. I hear the purity of your spirit, the growing angst with your daily life. Life is short. We mustn't waste time. We should meet.

Nobody's business: I'm scared.

Good Buddy: No need to be scared. I'm a regular guy with similar feelings of isolation. Tell you what, I'll be in your area on Friday. I'll use the Wi-Fi at the truck stop to reach out to you around lunchtime. If you want to meet up, join me. If not, I'm moving on. I need you in my life, so I hope you'll be there.

Nobody's business: Why can't we leave things as they are?

■ ■ ■ ■

The cursor blinked on the screen, but no more responses followed. Nobody's business lay her head down on the desk and sobbed.

"Hello," I said, gently tapping her shoulder after a decent interval of weeping passed. "Won't you please tell me your name?"

Instead of glancing my way, the woman faded from sight. Mayes and I stared at each other in the murk, shrugged, and vectored back to the Flynn County Morgue. As with my other Mayes-assisted dreamwalks, I awakened fairly quickly in his arms and felt minimum energy drain.

"Ahem," a woman stated in a peeved tone. "I don't know what kind of whack-job people you are, but trying to get some on the floor of the morgue is morally reprehensible and disrespectful to all the medical professionals who work here, along with the dead. I'm notifying your boss of your behavior and that you are hereby banned from our facility."

CHAPTER TWELVE

Sneering faces ringed us on the morgue floor. I scrambled to my feet, Jane Doe's bone nestled deep in my curved palm. "I can explain."

"No explanation needed," Dr. Dabba said, hands planted on her hips, her face pyracantha berry red. "I know what's going on in here. I'm not blind."

"Please, this is a misunderstanding. Because the bones were bleached before I read them, I couldn't connect with our Jane Doe. Mayes and I were amplifying our signal reception." I searched her eyes, hoping for a flicker of understanding. All I got from her were waves of fury. I gestured with my arms to add emphasis to my plea. "We meant no disrespect, and the procedure worked. It worked. We have new information for the sheriff."

"I'll bet she does," another woman behind

Dr. Dabba said. "She's probably doing him too."

"Shh." Dr. Dabba made a dismissive gesture at the crowd behind her. "Move along, everyone. The show's over."

No one questioned her authority. They left amidst some muttering and dirty looks. I sensed Mayes on his feet behind me. Like him, I felt off-balance from the abrupt end of the dreamwalk and the loss of telepathic whole body communication from our entwined position.

"You have one minute to explain, Ms. Powell," Dr. Dabba growled. "If I don't buy it, you're permanently banned from this morgue."

Yikes. I swallowed around the lump in my throat. "I did explain. I'm able to read some objects. Not every time though. We needed to learn more about this victim, and I couldn't get a read alone. Multiple contact points between me and a helper amplify the signal. I was doing my job. I offer justice for the dead and solace for the living."

Dr. Dabba didn't move, didn't bat an eyelash, didn't even breathe. I hung in that void of uncertainty, hoping like anything my explanation meant something to him.

Why didn't Mayes jump on the re-assurance train? It felt like I hanging out in the wind alone. I didn't much like the feeling.

"The door was locked," Dr. Dabba said, "as if something nefarious was going on in here."

I glanced at Mayes again. He seemed as if he'd been struck mute. Good grief. I really was on my own.

"We locked the door for this very reason. People misinterpret the process," I began slowly, feeling my way and hoping my words eased the doctor's concerns. "I tried a solo dreamwalk and it didn't work. Mayes and I have had success on dreamwalks where we joined forces like this. We locked the morgue door to prevent misunderstandings from passersby. We weren't up to anything hinky in here. Merging our energy is best accompanied by full body contact. Consider filling a glass from the sink. Do you get a full glass quicker with a trickle or the valve opened all the way? That's what we were doing. Opening the energy valve between us all the way to quickly and expediently do our job."

Dr. Dabba gave Mayes a calculating glance. "He's also a psychic?"

Mayes was somewhere between a Cherokee holy man and a medicine man, and a man of considerable paranormal power.

There were depths to him I hadn't begun to understand. Saying he was psychic was like saying there was only one kind of marsh grass. "He is."

She scowled at both of us. "You two are also a couple."

I nodded. "We are, but that has no bearing on our work. We speak for the dead when they can't."

"Give me that," Dr. Dabba said, pointing to my hand.

Heat rushed to my cheeks as I realized I still held the bone. I handed her Jane Doe's bone. "Sorry. I intended to return it when I awakened. I'm apologize for the misunderstanding. We didn't mean to disrupt anything at the hospital. Nontraditional investigative techniques such as ours are often misconstrued."

"Your *fraternization* hit every one of my trigger points," Dr. Dabba said after an awkward silence. "This is my corner of the world, and I have zero tolerance for unprofessional conduct. I don't believe your explanation, but I believe your sincerity. I'll verify your story with the sheriff and let him know my decision about your future access here. Meanwhile, stay out of my morgue and out of my sight."

"Yes, ma'am." I nodded to Mayes, and we

exited the building silently. My cheeks stung as I walked past the admin area, and folks glared at us.

With each step I took, my emotions churned. How Mayes managed to maintain his silence when we were accused of lewd conduct was a mystery to me. No. It was more than that. It was a lack of support.

In the parking lot, we paused to don our sunglasses against the brightness. Mayes extended his hand for my truck keys, and I hesitated a minute, not sure if I wanted him to drive me anywhere, but knowing I was too upset to focus on safe driving.

I smacked the key set in his palm. "What an unfortunate scene. Why didn't you back me up in there?"

"No need. You provided the explanation. More talking would not have helped our cause. Dr. Dabba wasn't ready to hear the truth."

"How do you know that?"

He fell silent for a bit. "How do you know the sun rises in the east or a seedling becomes a tree?"

No fair. He was retreating into generalisms. I stalked to the passenger side, allowed him to open my door, then I stewed until he joined me in the cab.

My thoughts wouldn't settle. He'd called

me out. I had to respond. "Until we walked into that morgue, neither one of us ever met this coroner. How do you know what she thinks or does?"

He cranked the truck and adjusted the air conditioning to maximum flow, but he made no move to shift the vehicle into gear. "In the same way I know you need to be mad right now. Your feelings were hurt because our perceptions of that confrontation were different."

"You think my pride is hurt?" I fired right back at him.

He reached for my hand and caressed it. "We share many talents, family values, ethics, and philosophies, so that's why your pride is hurt by this specific cultural difference. From birth, I had to get along in a world that values perception over truth. Whereas, it's my observation, your worldview expects perception and truth to be identical. Until you consider the truth from other viewpoints, you will only see the world one way."

A quick retort threatened to erupt from my throat. Words pulsed with angry urgency, needing to defend my thoughts. But this was Mayes. He wasn't saying this to put me down. He was stating his opinions. They were as valid as mine. Maybe even more so because he'd presented them calmly and rationally, knowing I wasn't of the same mindset.

I drew in a few deep breaths, allowing the first flush of emotion to fade, allowing myself to hear the words he'd spoken. Perception versus truth. I knew what it was like to be misunderstood. I knew people who'd changed life paths, like my father's friend Bubba Paxton, and yet some in our community didn't trust him not to become a drug addict again, much less to lead a worship service.

Was I blinded to my own preconceptions?

Mayes shifted the truck into gear and headed to Sinclair County. The coastal highway ribboned before us, and neighborhoods and trailer parks passed in the wink of an eye. As I gathered myself, I realized I owed him an apology.

"I'm sorry," I said. "I shouldn't have lashed out at someone I care for, when I wanted to light into those small-minded folks at the morgue. They were off-base saying we were fooling around in there. We were entirely professional."

I only saw the softening of his jaw because I was studying his profile intently, and that minor expression change told me he'd been more on edge than his calm demeanor suggested. I hurried to better explain what I meant. "I mean, we were doing our job, for Pete's sake. I was raised better than to think I could do anything I wanted whenever I wanted. It wasn't like I was jumping your bones or anything."

A slow smile filled his face, though he kept his eyes on the road. "For the record, you can jump my bones anytime, anywhere you want. I'm happy to oblige."

My head reared back into the neck rest. "What? Are you serious? You'd make love to me in the morgue? Have you done that before?"

"Never," he admitted. "But with you, I want to grab every minute and every intimacy. I savor every opportunity to touch you, to kiss you, to make love to you."

Nothing came out of my mouth. I tried to speak again. Couldn't. I shook my head and strangled out a cough. "At the morgue?"

"You are the sunrise I never expected to see, the beautiful eagle winging amongst the clouds. Every part of me wants to soar with you and see the world through your eyes." He uttered a phrase in Cherokee, taking his eyes off the road on a dangerous curve, to snag my gaze.

"Eyes on the road," I said. "What's that mean? The stuff you said to me in your

124

language."

"When I feel things strongly, I express them best in my native tongue."

"But I don't know what you mean."

"You will when you are ready to hear that truth."

Darn him for being cryptic. Did he expect me to suddenly understand Cherokee?

"You've asked me many questions, my lovely," he said. "I have one for you."

The emotion in the truck ramped in intensity. My body heated in response to the sensual challenge in the air. Mayes had both hands on the wheel and his focus on the highway, but it felt like he was stargazing in my soul.

"And?" I asked.

"One minute." He put on his turn signal and turned off the highway into a deserted boat ramp parking lot on Butler Island. He faced me, his hand caging mine. He brought my fingers to his lips, a hint of mischief in his eyes. "About the morgue . . . Was it good for you?"

CHAPTER THIRTEEN

"It was certainly memorable," I said in a wry tone. "Speaking of which, I've been so busy venting that I forgot about damage control. We need to tell the sheriff what happened. Jane Doe's message board exchange may have bearing on the investigation."

"There will always be cases," Mayes said. "Look around. For the first time today, we're alone. Nobody is here to interrupt or misconstrue or criticize. We're all by our lonesomes."

Ignoring the cheesy way he waggled his eyebrows, I leaned in for a quick kiss. "We're alone right this second, but how long until someone pulls off to offer assistance? My truck is well known in the community, and people will think I'm stranded. We can't do anything here."

"Just checking," he said, drawing me close. "A man likes to know he's appreciated."

"Oh. Well. I, uh, very much appreciate you in that regard, just not here or now."

His turn for a quick kiss before he released me and shifted the truck into gear. "You're all right, Powell."

We rolled down the highway and over the remaining bridges toward Marion. "I've been thinking more about that full body dreamwalk we took to Tampa or whatever a whole-body teleportation is called. I tried reaching Rose about it once already and got no response. It's weird she's incommunicado. Weirder still that we have matching memory voids. Doesn't sound like anyone was killed in Tampa, which is a blessing from our perspective."

"We need to be careful with conducting our inquiries," Mayes said. "If the Tampa investigation leads to our door, we have more deniability if there are no searches for Tampa incidents on our phones or personal computers. Use one of the communal computers at work if you feel compelled to check into the situation."

"Gracious. I hadn't even considered that phone or computer angle. I wish I knew what Tampa was all about. Not knowing makes me anxious. I hate that Rose dragged you into this mess."

Mayes shrugged. "What's done is done.

We can't undo it. Best we can do is remember the events of the night at your house. Larissa will verify we were home Sunday night."

Not even the populated fishing pier framed against the bright blue sky cheered me up. "There are video cameras everywhere. What if there are pictures of us in Tampa?"

"What if-ing leads to more worry. We destroyed the clothing in a fire. Nothing material links us to Tampa. No one will believe we could travel there and back via Rose, and there wasn't enough time to drive roundtrip, much less interact with anyone from Tampa. Even our cell phones will register your home cell tower because they remained at your place. As long as we didn't leave fingerprints down there, we can't be persons of interest for tying up a dirty mayor."

"Thanks a lot. I felt better until you mentioned fingerprints."

"As law enforcement personnel, our prints are in the system. That's why I mentioned it," Mayes said. "However, Rose and her accomplice had access to our thoughts. My mind would've insisted on eliminating all traces of our presence."

"This isn't fair. Every time you reassure

me, you add another cause of concern. Rose had an accomplice?"

"It's unclear how she bent the laws of physics to take us there, but logically, it would be difficult for her to inhabit us simultaneously. I believe another spirit used my body while she took over yours."

I hadn't considered the biomechanical aspects. Mayes was right. Two otherworld entities would be needed to operate two bodies. What had I gotten us into? What had been in our bodies, angels or demons?

"The first time I saw Rose, she was with a pack of bad boy spirits. Ever since then, she's been alone. I have no idea who she consorts with. And if body snatching wasn't enough to ruin your life, details of our dreamwalk posture are spreading all over the hospital. Seems like all I do is apologize to you."

"We all come with baggage, lovely," Mayes said. "Yours just happens to be supernatural."

Soon as we walked into Wayne's office, he stood, a vein pulsing on the side of his flushed face. "About time. I need you at the Ballenger house. Stat. We've got a missing person's report."

"The Ballengers? Who's missing?" I asked.

"Kitty. No one's seen her since Friday."

Kitty Ballenger. I knew her as a shy young woman who rarely made eye contact with anyone. I couldn't imagine her wandering off. "What happened?"

Wayne herded me toward the door. "That's what I need you for. Mayes, help Virg contact other jurisdictions about our missing person. He can bring you up to speed on what information to pass along."

I opened my mouth to protest but caught the glint of warning in Mayes' eyes.

He needs to talk to you privately about what happened at the morgue, Mayes said in mindspeak. *This is better for us anyway. I can get that phone number for you and check the Tampa information while y'all are out.*

I dislike being split up, but I understand, I answered back. *I always feel better with you at my side, though.*

Goes both ways, Bax. Stay safe and try to figure out where the missing woman went.

I turned to the sheriff. "All right. I'm ready."

Ten paces down the hall, the sheriff said to me, "Y'all were doing it again, weren't you?"

"I can explain the situation at the morgue," I said.

"I got an earful from Dr. Goody Two

130

Shoes. Best if you two avoid the morgue for a while," Wayne said, ushering me toward his Jeep. "Y'all were doing that silent communication again in my office. I hate that."

"Not all conversations are about you, boss man."

"I don't trust Mayes."

"He says you're jealous of him."

"Maybe. You're distracted when he's around. I want you focused on your work."

I shook my head. "Fuss all you like, but Mayes is going to be in my life."

"It's that serious?"

"It is. We can't quite wrangle the geography yet, but he wants to marry me."

"Whew. He sure moved fast." He gave me a sideways glance loaded with calculation. "You moved fast."

I didn't care to discuss my private life with the sheriff, but the air needed to be cleared before Wayne would accept this new reality. "We have a lot in common."

Wayne halted. "You moving to north Georgia with him?"

"No."

He nodded and resumed walking. "That's a relief."

"Mayes and I are a work in progress, but we're together. If you can't wrap your head around that, we have a problem."

Wayne raised his hands in surrender. "No problem. I'm happy to have you stay on my team."

"Good. Now that that's settled, tell me more about our missing person's case."

"In a sec." The sheriff ushered me outside and into his Jeep. "Kitty Ballenger's abandoned car was found at the truck stop. She wasn't there. No one saw her enter or leave the parking lot."

I visualized the scene as I strapped in and we hit the road. Single girl. Alone in a high traffic area. Surrounded by strangers. Anything could happen.

By Wayne's quick, economical driving motions, he was worried too. "The truck stop?" I repeated.

"Yeah. That mean something to you?"

I shuddered at what could be happening to Kitty if she was alive. "The cases we're working may be connected. One of our suitcase murder suspects drives a semi. Wayne, the suitcase guy may have Kitty."

CHAPTER FOURTEEN

The sheriff's lips pressed together in a scowl as he drove at high speeds to the Ballenger place. We passed few houses and vast acres of forested land. The curving road and the towering pines enhanced my senses that we were alone.

I quickly reviewed what I knew about the missing woman. Kitty lived with her older brother. Her parents divorced years ago and both drifted away to the streets of Miami. Both died of heroin overdoses. Merry Moore, Kitty's maternal grandmother raised both kids until she passed away right after I moved back home a few years ago.

"How old is Kitty?" I asked.

"Nineteen," Wayne said. "Didn't go to college. Started working at the convenience store right away to help pay bills, but that didn't last long. Her acquaintances from high school lost touch after graduation. No boyfriend that I know of."

"Why didn't her brother notice she was missing for four days?"

"Shawn travels for his job and then he spent the weekend with friends in Atlanta. He returned home late last night. When Kitty didn't answer her cell phone yesterday afternoon, he made calls to their extended family as he drove home. His neighbor, Bo Measly, came over and they rode around the county all night until they found her car at the truck stop an hour ago. Neither her phone nor purse are in the unlocked car. It's eerie how there's no trace of her."

"That's awful." I thought for a moment, gazing at the thin clouds overhead and then turning to Wayne. "Does she have a computer? If she was conversing online with a guy, there'd be a record of it."

"I don't know if there's a computer. Tell me why you think the suitcase guy has her. Just because her car was at the truck stop doesn't mean she went there to meet anyone. Lotsa folks go out there for the cheese grits and fluffy pancakes."

"Forget the food angle. I can connect these dots for you," I said. "Mayes and I got a new lead at the morgue. Using our amplified signal, we connected with the suitcase Jane Doe. You remember I told you after the first dreamwalk that Jane called herself

Nobody?" He nodded. "We saw her at a call center having an online conversation with a guy. Her screen name was 'Nobody's business but her own'. The man she chatted with had the screen name of 'Good Buddy'. He asked her to meet him at the truck stop on a Thursday night."

"I can add that information to the search for Jane Doe's identity. If Kitty is into online dating, we'll tag her file likewise," Wayne said. "Anything else from the vision?"

"There's a little more. Jane and Good Buddy were using an online chat room. She wanted to keep their relationship platonic, but he demanded to meet her. Afraid of losing his friendship, she agreed. She should've trusted her instincts because now she's dead."

"And you see a parallel between our Jane Doe and Kitty?"

"I do." I ticked off the similarities on the fingers of one hand. "Same lonely hearts personality, same slight build, and same intention to keep people in real life at a distance. If so, we have a new prospect for our Suitcase Killer. We need to know how he targets his prey."

"Maybe, but let's not be hasty. We go to Kitty's residence with an open mind, listen to what the brother has to say. If Shawn's

135

lying, tell me. He got into trouble with the law once upon a time, so he isn't Mr. Clean Cut, even if he looks the part."

It was a sad state of affairs when family members were suspects, but I'd already seen that family members would kill each other without a qualm. "All right. I'll listen carefully. You want me to try to touch him too?"

"Yeah. I hope you're wearing your bird dog shoes. I want you to track this missing girl."

"I can't do that. Maybe my ghost dog can, but I can't. And Oliver can only track her until she gets into a vehicle. You haven't moved her car yet, have you?"

The sheriff swore, then called a number on speed dial. "Cancel the tow truck. I'm sending a tracker out there in half an hour. Stay with the vehicle for now and only the K-9 unit is to search that car. Once I give the okay later today, you can move the car to the impound lot."

There was a squawk from the other end of the line. "Don't worry about the call rotation to the tow companies," the sheriff said. "You still have this towing job."

Wayne ended the call. "Got that turned off. I'm counting on you, Bax. Kitty is one of our own. Homegrown and homespun.

Her life depends on the choices we make today."

"I'll need to walk in her shoes and sit behind the wheel of her car. The emotional energy in her bedroom and car will be strong. The rest, including using Oliver to track her, is iffy, as you well know."

He slowed to turn right. "I'll take whatever you can give us."

I pointed out the obvious. "Mayes is a better tracker than I'll ever be."

"No." The sheriff's tone left no doubt as to his state of mind. "Mayes sits out the field work on this case. He's detailed to us for the Suitcase Murder case. Roger Lavene is bringing in one of his former suspects this evening. Mayes will assist on that interview. If we finish up in time, we can watch from the observation room."

My gut instinct was to argue my point for having Mayes assist me, but I was learning a thing or two about guys. Men like Wayne and Mayes needed to be in charge. They also needed to be the sole authors of a solution.

I liked being in charge too, only I was smart enough to let men think they were running the show.

"I don't know where Kitty is." Shawn Ballenger had the build of a doughy athlete who'd forgotten how to shave or groom his thinning hair. He paced the tiny blue–hued dining room in the boxy house. The house had the distinct smell of a rank gym locker. The room we'd walked through to get in here was littered with clothing on every surface. "We need to stop wasting time. You should be searching for my sister."

Wayne shot a glance my way. *He's lying,* I mouthed, perching on the edge of my seat.

"No one is buying that, Shawn," Wayne said. "We know you're lying."

"I don't care what you think," Shawn said. "Kitty's in trouble. I know it."

"How do you know?" Wayne asked in the next breath. His voice held a dangerous edge, one that caused most criminals to eat their words.

Shawn's index finger jabbed at the table-top repeatedly. "She never leaves home, that's how. She's a nervous wreck if I make her go to the grocery store with me. She won't leave home for anything now, not un-less I force her to accompany me. For her to be out of touch for days is wrong. Dead wrong."

"I have every cop in Georgia looking for her right now. We'll continue searching, but I need to know where you were for the weekend."

"Staying with friends in Atlanta."

Wayne shot me a questioning look. I shook my head to indicate no. "Try again," Wayne said. "This time tell the truth."

"This is the truth." He pounded a fist into his open palm. "My sister is missing. She rarely leaves home, much less vanishes for an entire weekend."

"We need to rule you out as a suspect in her disappearance. I need the name and the address of where you stayed."

Shawn swore up one side of the dining room and down the other. He stabbed his fingers through his stringy hair. "I can't. My buddy . . . he'll kill me."

"Should of thought of that before you left your fragile little sister home alone all weekend."

I reached across the table in an expression of sympathy and patted his arm. Steamy scenes flashed in front of my eyes. People kissing and doing a whole lot more. The man in the image was clearly Shawn. I didn't recognize the acrobatic brunette.

Shawn tugged away from me. "Keep your witchy hands to yourself, lady. I know who you are."

"Then you should know I'm here to help your sister," I said. "We can't move forward with the investigation until you are honest with us."

He groaned and stomped toward the window. The matchstick blinds were bent out of shape, as if someone had careened into them. "Why is this happening to me?"

"Nothing is happening to you," Wayne said. "But if your sister was abducted, her chances of survival are slimmer with each moment that ticks by."

Shawn sagged into the doorframe, his shoulders bent nearly to the breaking point. "You think she's dead?"

"There's a possibility her case might be linked to another one we're investigating, one that involves a serial killer."

His head bobbed up, and his jaw dropped. "Serial killer? After Kitty? You're joshing me."

"This is a serious matter, Shawn," Wayne continued. "If you refuse to talk with us, we'll invite you to spend the night in our guest facility."

"Huh?"

"Cooperate or go to jail," I translated for the distraught guy.

Shawn waggled his hands in the air. "I can't go to jail. I'll lose my job."

"And what is your job these days?"

"I transport shipments for indies."

"What's that mean?" I asked, looking to Wayne for a translation. I mouthed "lying." Wayne's eyes widened in acknowledgement.

"Sounds like he's moving drugs." Wayne whipped out his cuffs. "Hands behind your back, Shawn."

"No. I can't be out of pocket that long. I've got too much riding on this. I'll tell you what you want to know."

Wayne gave him a stern look, must've thought it over, and put away the handcuffs. "Go on."

Shawn shuddered and held his peace for a long moment. "My buddy was out of town. He asked me to look in on his wife. She's always had a thing for me and I was feeling lonely, so we hooked up. All weekend."

"Name and address."

Shawn swore some more and spit out the information in staccato bursts. Wayne stepped outside to make a call to verify the man's alibi.

"Will you show me Kitty's room?" I asked.

"You gonna do your voodoo in there?" Shawn asked, drilling an accusing gaze into me. He didn't move from the doorway.

I didn't appreciate his tone or his insinuation. Really, some people thought they knew everything. They were too uninformed to know what they *didn't* know. "I don't do

141

voodoo. I tap into residual energy. That's all."

"But you saw me with Robin."

The brunette? "I did, but only because you were thinking about her when I touched you. She made quite an impression on you, I take it."

He looked away for a moment. When he gazed at me again, his neck and face were a vibrant pink. "Yeah, but so what if we had fun in the sack? I should've come straight home. Then I'd know where Kitty is. Gramma Merry was counting on me. Kitty's my responsibility."

His last sentence caught me off guard. "At nineteen, she's an adult in the eyes of the law."

"That don't mean nothing. Kitty ain't tough. She can't hold down a job, and schoolwork gave her headaches."

Kitty sounded like a wounded spirit. Perhaps she had medical or social issues that interfered with reasoning. I'd ask Wayne to check into that. "But she uses a computer?"

Shawn pounded on the wall, the thuds echoing through the house. "Do we look like a computer family? I'm lucky to pay the utilities on this house most months. Kitty has a smart phone, one of those government

142

freebies, cuz of us being so poor."

"Does she have friends?" I asked, my heart going out to the lonely girl with a violent and negligent brother.

"Not that I know of."

"Was anyone hassling her?"

"I. Don't. Know." He seemed to be having trouble opening his mouth. "She never talked about anything unless I asked her specific questions. She liked being swept away in shows and movies. That's all I know about my little sister's life. I'm a lousy brother, all right?"

He was telling the truth now, and I sympathized with his distress. "You called your neighbor as soon as you knew something was wrong. That's what a good brother does. We will do everything we can to locate Kitty."

"I want her to come home and to be all right."

"Then help us by cooperating. The more information we have, the greater the chances we have the right leads."

While Shawn absorbed that in silence, I tried to assemble the facts in my head. Kitty lived an isolated life in poverty. With her being a young-for-her age nineteen, she would yearn for something else in her life. "I'd still like to see her room."

"Me too," Wayne said, striding back into the cottage. He seemed deceptively at ease and yet I knew he was entirely focused on this case. "Your alibi in Atlanta checked out."

Shawn stood tall, hope dawning on his face. "My buddy doesn't know?"

"He knows and he's livid, gauging from the swearing I heard on the phone. I requested a Dekalb County unit visit there for a possible domestic disturbance."

Shawn rammed a fist into the paneling. I started at the sickening sound, automatically retreating from the angry man. He withdrew his hand, and a fist-sized hole appeared in the wall. Shawn cradled his scraped knuckles. "So much for that job."

"What were you hauling for the man?" Wayne asked.

Shawn looked down. "Various items."

"You mean drugs?"

"No drugs. Just imported stuff he brings in at the Jacksonville port. I go down there, fill up my truck and haul the merchandise to Atlanta for him. That's it, I swear."

Wayne shot me a questioning look. "He's telling the truth," I said.

The sheriff glanced at his watch again. "Show us Kitty's room."

Shawn walked quickly to the nearest

144

bedroom. Unlike the disarray in the rest of the cottage, this room was neat as a pin. Clothes were lined up in drawers or on hangars in the closet. Shoes were soldier straight on the floor. Someone fastidious lived in this room. At first glance, it didn't appear that there were any gaps in the clothing, but I had to ask.

"Are any suitcases missing?" I asked.

"We don't have any suitcases."

"What about her toothbrush and shampoo? Are her personal hygiene items here?"

"Yeah. Her bathroom stuff is here. So what?"

"It's unlikely she left of her own accord because she would've taken personal items."

"You getting anything?" the sheriff asked me.

"I haven't looked yet. May I have some privacy?"

"Sure," Wayne said. "I'll question Shawn in the other room. We'll need something of hers for the scent dogs."

Shawn shrank into himself, banging his head as he backed into the hallway wall. "Wait. Is she dead? Did I get my sister killed?"

"Let's not jump to conclusions," Wayne said. "Right now, she's missing. I'm using every tool at my disposal to find her."

Including me.

146

CHAPTER FIFTEEN

While I resented being called a tool, my job of reaching out to the dead and reading energy on inanimate objects very much made me a person detector. The overall feel of Kitty's room was tidy but impersonal. No posters or photos hung on the walls, not a single mirror was present anywhere. The colors of her clothing ranged from black to gray. Every teenager I'd ever known had yearned for true love or travel or adventure or riches, but this room, this girl, seemed to be a blank slate.

What are your dreams, Kitty?

I opened my senses, expecting to be bombarded with snips of her life, but I got something different. A low level hum of satisfaction. Kitty loved hanging out in this room. She enjoyed keeping it tidy. No, she needed it to be tidy. Mess and chaos made her uneasy. This was her sanctuary.

No way would she abandon this room or

this life. What I saw as unembellished, Kitty saw as quiet contentment. I brushed my fingers over her boxy dresser, her clothing, even the few pieces of jewelry I found. There was no trace of strong energy, no trace of emotional distress.

The only surface where I noticed any sign of conflict was on her white pillowcase. An image flashed in my head of her sobbing. She'd cried soundlessly in the bed, letting her tears fall unchecked. I focused on the pillow, touching it with both hands, losing myself in the moment.

Layers of emotion came through my fingers. Loss, grudging acceptance, hope, and trepidation. Kitty had been awash in this odd emotional mix and conflicted about her future.

My image of her expanded to see her curled into a fetal position in the bed, her hand wrapped around her phone. Such a mishmash of feelings — was I fooling myself by hoping she was alive? I wanted to find her on this side of the Veil of Life, but I needed to know if she was already gone.

With her personality so firmly imprinted on this pillow, I could easily reach her released spirit through a dreamwalk, if she was dead. I sat on the bed and dream-walked, hoping against hope that I wouldn't find her spirit on the Other Side. I vectored through the drift, keeping Kitty's spiritual signature firmly fixed as my destination through the soundless falling and arrival in a realm where time had no meaning. The air thickened around me, misty, murky, and empty.

I called her name.

No answer, not even the usual teasing and catcalls from roaming spirits. This whole place seemed deserted. Not possible.

No change in the inky mists as I tried again. "Kitty Ballenger! Are you here?"

No Kitty.

She wasn't in the realm of the dead, but I had one more resource I could try.

I called for Rose, my Other World mentor and guide. No answer from her either, which was starting to bug me. What kind of partnership was this if she didn't hold up her end of the deal?

Though I could keep looking for my mentor, that effort seemed counterproductive. I'd have to figure out what happened to Rose later. Kitty's disposition was my immediate concern. I drew back inside my body and awakened in Kitty's bedroom.

My spirits flagged, and it took a minute to gather myself. *She's still alive,* I told myself. *You still have a chance to find her. Get up and keep looking.*

I tried her bathroom items next. Her toothbrush had a similar mixed vibe as her pillowcase. Something was different about Friday, the day she'd last used this toothbrush. I went deeper into a meditative trance to seek a lead to her current whereabouts. Nothing popped into my head, though as I roused, it seemed a man's shadow hovered in the mirror behind me. I stared at it for another moment, but the only thing looking back at me was my own reflection, a hollow-eyed woman with a white ponytail under her ball cap. I whirled and confirmed I was alone in the bathroom.

When I returned to the living room, Wayne held a large paper sack in front of him. "What's in there?" I asked.

"Shawn loaned me Kitty's favorite sweater. For the hounds."

I nodded and shared my findings. Wayne then asked Shawn for the pillowcase on her bed, which he bagged separately.

"She's not dead?" Shawn asked, ogling me as if I had two heads. "You can really tell that?"

"In my humble opinion," I stopped to clear my throat, ignoring Wayne rolling his eyes, "your sister is alive right now. That's good. We need to find her so she stays that way."

"To be clear," Wayne said. "We have your permission to search your sister's vehicle now and her cell phone once we locate it?"

"Sure. Whatever it takes," Shawn said. "Find her before she gets dead."

Moments later, we headed out with Kitty's sweater and pillowcase, each stashed in a separate paper bag. Wayne carefully stowed the evidence and drove to the truck stop. "You shouldn't have promised anything to him," Wayne said. "If we find her dead, that boy will never forgive you for that false hope."

His criticism rankled. I'd been trying to keep Shawn from giving in to despair. "He deserved the truth. He blames himself for her being missing."

"He had no business getting involved with a buddy's wife."

Given Wayne's history as a roving tom cat, his barbed remark made me snort out loud. "Aren't you being all judgy today."

A cheesy grin filled his face. "I may be a cheater, but I have rules."

He had some nerve. I couldn't let that slide. "You slept with married women before."

"Yeah, but they weren't hitched to my

151

buddies. Shawn crossed a line."

The more he explained, the more irritated I became. "So his sister deserves his bad karma?"

"No. He does."

I released my pent-up breath. Getting upset with Wayne wouldn't solve anything. I needed to direct this conversation back to the case. "I only know Kitty by sight. The way Shawn was talking about her, she sounds like a Special Ed student."

"She does things in her own time, and she is entirely too trusting. I remember hearing about a few incidents in middle and high school where other kids took advantage of her, but she doesn't have special needs. Her granny was a former teacher and could've homeschooled her, but she mainstreamed both kids for socialization. She expected them to go to college."

Granny's stance seemed harsh to me. If my child couldn't cope in public school, I'd do something about it. Everyone thought this woman was wonderful for taking in her grandkids, but it sounded like she provided room and board and nothing else. No wonder Shawn and Kitty had adjustment issues.

"I don't understand why folks think college is a golden ticket," I said. "Kids graduate college with a general degree, loaded with debt, and can't find a job. Why start off in the hole?"

He opened his palm and gestured broadly. "Maybe they should all grow up to have superpowers like you."

"Ha ha. I am a Nesbitt. With my heritage, I had no choice in the matter."

"From where I'm sitting, you got a better slice of the genetic lottery than I did."

My expression sobered. Wayne's father had been a notorious womanizer. He'd inherited that fraternal tendency, while I'd gotten the extrasensory jackpot. Suddenly, visits with dead people sounded pretty darn good. "Guess it's all a matter of perspective."

"Get me a solid lead," Wayne told me when he parked beside a forlorn looking sedan at the truck stop. "I want to know what she was doing out here."

As he spoke to me, a deputy with a K-9, Clark Ryan, exited Kitty's car. "Is the dog finished?" I asked.

"Not yet. Sit tight while I take the sweater to Clark."

The police K-9 sniffed Kitty's sweater and the perimeter of her car. Then he trotted to a parking place between the car and the truck stop. He lay down on the spot. Kitty must've walked to a nearby vehicle and been driven away.

The dog got a treat and Clark loaded him back in the squad car beside the idling tow truck. Wayne waved me over. "Your turn. I'll ask if he found anything while you're reaching out to Kitty. Do your job. I expect answers."

Man. His caustic tone smarted, but his frustration came from not knowing what happened to Kitty. "Aye, aye."

He gave me a sharp look. "We have to find this girl. Her car should be a gold mine of information for a dreamwalker. Get me something useful, Powell, and do it fast."

I had my marching orders. If I didn't get a lead from the car, we were done. We had nothing else to go on. Talk about pressure. A woman's life hung in the balance. With a quick touch of my necklace, I girded myself for the task at hand.

Kitty drove an old Camry that had seen better days. On the driver's side, the front door and the back door were different colors from the washed out gold of the hood and trunk. The driver's bucket seat had been duct-taped together, but the tape had worn away to dirty threads.

Gently, I eased onto the tattered seat. Like

her bedroom, Kitty's car was tidy. No empty cups or candy wrappers lying around. No spare change or umbrellas or purse. No nothing.

The lack of clutter worried at me. It seemed like Kitty was determined to leave a minimal footprint in the sands of her life. While I applauded her orderly habits, I felt sad for her. I wanted her to know joy, love, and acceptance. I wanted her to experience all of life.

Everything of hers held an underlying sense of pathos. Did she embrace it or despise it? Had loneliness and isolation taken its toll on her? Was sensory deprivation what ultimately caused her to make poor decisions?

The answers had to be inside this car. The sedan's interior was a neutral shade between tan and fingerprint gray, while the steering wheel was a faded black. The gear shifter dominated the center console. Cautiously, I opened my senses to my surroundings. Something brushed at the back of my mind but I couldn't make it out.

I eyed the steering wheel with trepidation. If I grabbed that, I'd risk plunging into the same rabbit hole that swallowed her. *Get over it, you're here to do your job,* I told myself. To center myself, I drew in three deep breaths, then I gripped the wheel with both hands.

Light fractured and bent. In my vision, I felt the steady hum of the car engine beneath me, saw the white-knuckled grip Kitty had on the wheel. From the wild beating of my heart and the butterfly gymnastics in my belly, Kitty's fear felt raw and elemental.

She'd pulled up exactly where the car was now parked, but she made no motion to leave the car. My vision blurred. She was crying, and since I was looking through her eyes, my vision blurred too.

Why are you doing this, Kitty? I asked.

Of course Kitty didn't answer. I was viewing a past scene from her life, a rerun of something she experienced while in the grip of terrifying fear.

I dashed the tears with the back of my hand and immersed myself in the flow of the scene.

Kitty lowered her head to the wheel and sobbed. A tap on her window startled her into crying out. Her entire body trembled.

"You okay in there, miss?" a deep voice said.

Kitty nodded, her gaze on her black jeans. Her sobs intensified. She gasped for breath because her nose was clogged.

"No need for all that, missy. He ain't

worth it, whoever he is," the stranger continued.

The man's voice sounded kind, compas-
sionate even. Kitty choked back her sobs,
wiped the tears away again, and glanced at
him. A man with a shaded face met her
gaze. He wore a ball cap and eyeglasses,
along with a button collar Oxford shirt,
open at the neck. A black star necklace
centered above the vee of his shirt.

"There you are," he said through the
closed window. "How about some water? I
have a bottle right here."

"No," Kitty said.

"That's okay," the man said. "I wouldn't
take anything from a stranger either. But
look." He raised a small water bottle up to
window level. "The seal isn't broken. I know
your throat's parched after all that crying."

"Go away. Please. I planned to meet a
friend, but I can't do it. I need to go home."

"Good idea, but I'd feel better if I helped
you. Just crack your window enough for the
bottle. I want to help."

She froze momentarily. "Will you leave
me alone if I take the bottle?"

"If that's what you want."

"All right." Kitty lowered the window
about five inches. The end of the bottle
came toward her. She took it and rolled up

the window afterward.

"Have a nice life," the man said.

Kitty watched him walk toward a cluster of cars near the restaurant. She sat there, blurry-eyed and sniffing, until she remembered the tissue pack in her purse. She found it, blew her nose, and blotted her face dry.

"This is stupid," she said softly. "I knew better than to come all the way out here. I knew a stranger couldn't really be interested in me. The pretty girls have everything. Wallflowers stand on the sidelines."

Her breathing slowed until it was a normal rate. She could go home right now and Shawn would never know she'd been so foolish. She'd make a bowl of soup and take a nap. But first she'd get a big glass of water.

Wait, she had water right here. She glanced around the parking lot, fearful that her Good Samaritan might be spying on her. There were cars parked near the store area of the truck stop and big semis out back. No one strolled around the parking lot. No one was there to witness her humiliation.

So much for meeting her new friend. He'd lost his nerve too. Now she'd drive home, back to her ordinary life, back to being invisible like a fly on the wall. The only person who ever noticed what she did was her brother, and he barely came home anymore.

Kitty took another look at the bottle. Might as well drink some of the water. Then she'd head home.

The bottle's seal cracked upon opening. She drank a shallow sip and then another. The moisture felt heavenly on her dry throat. She drank heavily. The weight of liquid in her belly made her feel better. No more butterflies cavorting around in there. No pressure about anything now that she didn't have to meet with anyone.

Her breathing slowed and still she sat there. *I should go home,* she thought, but she made no effort to put the car in gear.

I want to go home, she thought, willing herself to follow through. But she couldn't move. She tried and tried but nothing worked. *No! This wasn't right. What was wrong with her?* There was a sudden noise to her left. The sky whirled, and she felt herself being lifted.

"Good girl," a man whispered.

CHAPTER SIXTEEN

I awakened from my Kitty dreamwalk exhausted and weeping. Three dreamwalks in one day was surely a record. The rumble of my stomach reminded me I'd skipped lunch. But what was one meal when a young woman had been missing for four days?

Quickly, I swiped the moisture from my face, glad to be me, to be seeing the world through my own eyes again. More tears rolled down my cheeks. This couldn't be happening. I rarely had meltdowns on the job. I had to be tough around these cops so they'd accept me. I had to prove I could cut it through thick and thin.

Sheriff Wayne Thompson leaned in the driver's side window, an impatient scowl on his face. "Cut the waterworks, Powell, and tell me what you saw. I don't have all day."

Knowing dawned as quickly as a rainbow, my spirits lifted, and my pluck surfaced. "They're not mine."

160

"They sure as hell aren't mine." He hesitated. "You telling me the missing gal was crying?"

"Yep." I could feel my heart racing from the moment Kitty realized her fate. My pulse still thudded in my ears. Kitty had been duped. Worse, she'd been incapacitated and paralyzed. "He did this to her," I said.

"Who did what? You're not making any sense, and the clock is ticking."

"The water. He gave Kitty a bottle of water. He seemed friendly and kind. He seemed concerned about her. She'd been crying and he offered her a bottle of water. She accepted because the seal was intact. Except, it wasn't just water. That's how he got to her."

Wayne squatted beside me. "Tell me everything and don't leave a word out."

"She came here to meet someone, but she lost her nerve. Never even got out of the car because she was too afraid. Instead, she cried her heart out." Sitting in her car made the recitation of events feel like it was happening all over again. "A stranger approached, consoled her through the car window, and offered her a bottle of water. Only it was a trick. He drugged her. The stranger must've been the man she was meeting."

161

"What'd he look like?"

"He looked tall. He seemed innocuous. He wore a ball cap, blue jeans, and a nice shirt."

"What race was he?"

I reran the scene through my mind, shocked to find no crisp image there. "I didn't notice his skin color. How is that possible? Nothing about him was remarkable. He blended in, like a chameleon. His facial features are blurred in my memory too."

"That's not helping me find her. I need specific details. Was he wearing any jewelry? Did he have tattoos on his arms?"

I summoned the fading scene again. "No tattoos. No rings, though his fingernails were nicely rounded. His hands looked soft too, like someone who didn't do manual labor."

"You're killing me, Powell. What about glasses or an earring?"

I couldn't remember those details. "His face was shadowed from the ball cap, and I didn't see his ears." Something jogged in my memory. "He wore a short necklace. It was black and star-shaped."

Wayne rocked back on his heels. "That's precise. Why the hell can't you tell me what he looked like?"

"I can't control what they show me. I only

report the dream sequences. For some reason, she focused on his necklace. But this vision wasn't a waste of time. We learned something. He drugged her and then moved her to another vehicle."

"There are no cameras in this parking lot. I checked. Other than credit card charges made at the cash register inside, don't know who was here last Friday night. The clerk inside said he worked that evening. He's an older, mustached Hispanic man, so it wasn't him pretending to be her friend."

I raised a hand in protest. "Wait. It wasn't night time. Kitty and the stranger met in the daytime. I saw sunshine behind him and blue skies overhead. He abducted her in broad daylight."

"Huh." Wayne glanced around the busy lot." That timeline doesn't make finding her any easier. People come and go here twenty-four/seven."

"Someone might have seen her. A man carrying a woman is not a typical sight."

"No one saw him move her, or we would've heard by now."

His critical tone annoyed me. I was doing the best I could. I pushed back. "You don't have to be so grumpy about my visions and interpretations. I'm the messenger here."

"A chameleon met a young woman in this

lot, drugged her, and kidnapped her on Friday afternoon. It's been four days now. Our odds of finding her get slimmer every minute."

We couldn't give up. Kitty needed our help. "Nothing about this case is straightforward. Judging by the difficulty I had in reaching her, she's still alive."

"Where's the proof? I want to find this girl and get her safely home, but I need solid leads. I need to know where to look."

His words rang with truth, softening my irritation. "We all want that."

"You're not trying hard enough." Wayne rose from his squat beside Kitty's car and swore.

I exited the small sedan and trailed after him. "I'm doing my best. It's hard to find someone among the living. We can't quit. Kitty's counting on us to find her. What about her phone? You said something about it earlier, but I can't remember what you said."

He shook his head and gazed around the lot, as if he was willing the abductor to rise from the pavement. "It wasn't here. We've pinged the phone, but it's not registering. This guy is slick. We're the bumbling amateurs nosing down a cold trail."

I understood his frustration because I felt

equally helpless. "You're a good cop, Wayne. You follow the evidence. That's how you close cases."

He gave me a sidelong glance cloaked in a scowl. "This your version of a pep talk?"

"Depends." I arched a brow at him. "Is it working?"

He barked out a harsh laugh. "Maybe. Keep talking."

"Request her phone records from the carrier and find out who she contacted. You've already sent her photo to the Missing Persons registry. Cops all over Georgia are searching for her."

"Is Shawn's boss behind this?"

"It's possible but unlikely. In the vision, Kitty didn't recognize her attacker. He was a stranger."

"Which leaves out most of the locals."

"That's good, right? We don't want to believe one of our friends and neighbors would drug and abduct an innocent young woman."

"Without a local focus, everyone else in the world is a suspect." He paused to stare at a pair of wood storks winging across the sky. "I'll have you get us an ID of the necklace. That's a start."

There were plenty of jewelry vendors online. Surely, I could find a similar pendant and the right weight of chain. "Can do."

A wave of exhaustion overcame me. I touched my pendant and nothing happened. It was spent, and so was I. My knees wobbled. "I need to sit down."

"Wait for me in the Jeep while I check in with my wife. She won't be happy if I don't take her call."

"Thanks." Wayne cranked the motor and blessed air conditioning blew on my overheated face. I leaned back in my seat and pulled my ball cap down over my eyes. Should've brought a snack, I thought, and extra crystals. Outside the vehicle, Wayne's voice rose as it often did when he skirmished with Dottie. I tuned out the familiar white noise and tried to focus on the case.

Kitty could be all the way across the country in four days. Heck, if she was placed on a ship, she might be halfway around the world by now. What a mess.

I ached for Kitty and her brother, for their bad breaks and poor choices. This sucked. I renewed my determination to find her. I would be her advocate.

My fingers curled in frustration. Like Wayne, I wanted to bring Kitty home alive. Focusing on the universe of what we didn't know led nowhere. We built cases on solid information, one lead at a time.

Kitty was alive. We knew more about her abductor. He'd make a mistake, and we'd catch him. We would find her.

Wayne opened my door and bent down to my level. "The K-9 search was a bust. What about your ghost dog?"

My flagging energy surged. "I'll summon Oliver right now."

Chapter Seventeen

From the comfort of Wayne's air-conditioned Jeep, I transitioned into a dreamwalk, going partway into the drift and focusing on Oliver and the living at the same time. The dual mindset veered me into lucid dream territory and the disorientation I usually felt after the transition to spirit form faded as I virtually stood outside the sheriff's Jeep.

As an earthbound spirit, my ghost dog could cross the veil of life permanently, but he'd elected to remain near me. I whistled and called his name. Oliver bounded up to me, wagging his ghostly body at my presence on his plane. This Great Dane's spirit honored me with his loyalty, and I hoped the affection I returned made up for all the things I asked of him.

I don't speak dog and Oliver doesn't speak human, but time after time he seemed to understand what I wanted. He eagerly sniffed Kitty Ballenger's car and her sweater. His first reaction was to bound over to where the K-9 had lain. He gazed at me expectantly.

"Find Kitty," I said, pointing toward the parking lot exit.

Oliver took off down the access road toward the interstate. I shadowed him at a virtual dead run. He kept his nose to the ground as he followed the scent. A speck of hope blossomed in my body. This was working!

The ghost dog loped down the interstate ramp toward the northbound route, as if he had all day to find her. He hadn't hesitated on the access road, so I believed he was still trailing her. He might have all day to find her, but I did not. I'd started this with low energy and spent crystals.

Suddenly he veered off to the shoulder and circled. I hustled over to him. "You find something? What is it, boy?"

The dog barked excitedly, then barreled straight into the woods. I followed the path he made through the underbrush, grateful that thorns and briars couldn't harm my spirit self. Oliver barked by a palm-sized object on the ground. I peered through the pine straw covering it and crowed. "Good dog, Oliver! You found her phone."

Since I couldn't physically grab the object, I made note of the location. The pines here weren't evenly spaced. A twinset of pines stood to my right and another cluster of two pines to my left. The pine closest to the phone had a spindly branch with four pine cones on it directly over my head.

I pieced together what must've happened. Kitty's kidnapper must have stopped on the shoulder and tossed her phone out the car. He'd known enough to turn it off, but now that we knew where it was, we had a better chance of figuring out who he was. Maybe we'd get lucky and collect his fingerprints.

"You're a good dog, yes, you are." I gave that sweet spot between Oliver's ears special attention. He moaned in delight.

"Thank you for helping us," I said to him. "I appreciate your friendship."

Oliver faded into nothingness, and I vectored back to reality. Coming to, I felt the harsh pull of gravity reassert itself. My arms and legs felt like they weighed twice their normal amount. It took every bit of energy I possessed to sit upright and breathe. It felt like an elephant stood on my chest.

"Report, Powell," Wayne said from the driver's seat. "Where'd he take her?"

That was the sheriff for you. No question

about my status. He cut to the bottom line immediately. So would I. "The kidnapper drove out the access road and onto the northbound ramp of the interstate."

"You sure?" Wayne asked.

"Absolutely certain." I yawned, unable to cover my mouth in time for politeness sake. Man, I was beat, and I could use some food.

"This job boring you?"

"The job is fine, but the dreamwalks take a toll. I got nothing left."

"You're in luck," Wayne said. "Mayes is on his way out here now to get you recharged. While you did your thing, I thought about what you said about my resource allocation. The Jane Doe case in important, but the missing teen is our top priority. We'll keep working both, but I'm diverting our effort to locating Kitty Ballenger."

Though I was surprised by his about-face on Mayes, the sheriff wasn't one to squander resources. He'd needed time to process my suggestion until it became his idea. "The cases might be related," I said.

"If so, we'll have a better chance of following the fresh leads. You weren't out long this time. Fifteen minutes max. How come you're so zonked?"

"Because it was my third dreamwalk today and because Oliver and I ran all the way to the northbound interstate ramp. That's why."

He stared at me for a moment. A slow grin dawned on his face. "That's a decent time for such a distance. We'll make a top notch police officer out of you yet."

"Not happening. I'm fine with being a consultant."

"I'm fine with that as long as you work for me."

"Park your ego at the door. I want to find this girl too."

"Ego has nothing to do with it. I'm talking common sense here. View me as an ally. I'll keep the press at bay. Think of me as your personal buffer."

He'd love to be more than that, but I wasn't interested in being his anything. "We need to make this triangle work, you and me and Mayes."

"I already said I'd respect your wishes. You want him in the picture, I'm on board."

"I do. Want him on board. I'm glad he's coming here now. I haven't done a completely unassisted dreamwalk in a while. Mayes fixes me by taking away the power drain as I awaken."

"I didn't separate you guys to punish you, I did it because I'm a jerk. I can't promise I won't be a jerk in the future, but I can

172

promise you that I'm on your team. You and I are going to solve a lot of cases together."

He was telling the truth. My eyelids drifted shut. But before I fell asleep, I roused to mention one more thing. "Oliver found her phone."

"What? Where? Tell me."

"Long as I don't have to move." I directed him to where the ramp merged onto the interstate. Wayne parked in the spot I indicated. "The guy pulled off the paved shoulder onto the grass. He chucked Kitty's phone under that pine tree with the crooked branch and four cones. There's a bit of pine straw on top of it, so it's been there for a few days, which fits with our abduction timeline."

"Sit tight," Wayne said, reaching for gloves. "I'll retrieve it, but I have to photograph it in place first."

"I'm not moving until I get sugar, caffeine, and energy." I dozed while he darted through the thicket. The phone was there, I'd seen it. Seems like I'd barely closed my eyes, and my door opened. I sensed movement around me. "I'm still here," I said, without opening my eyes.

A warm touch to my shoulder and a perfect kiss on the cheek did what Wayne couldn't do. It made me smile. "Took you long enough to find me," I murmured drowsily.

"The sheriff had all kinds of errands for me on the way here." Mayes placed a drink carrier on my lap. It held a large, icy cola and a supersized candy bar. "I called your mom and said we were working late. She'll meet Larissa's bus. I also stopped by the house and got Elvis and fresh crystals."

I already felt the positives of his minimal energy transfer. My little Chihuahua rode in the crook of Mayes' other arm. I reached for Elvis and crooned happily as he tucked into my chest. This was living. Mayes and doggie comfort plus a sugary caffeine rush. Nothing could be finer.

"I'd come in there with you," Mayes said, "but there's not room with the extra gear and gizmos Wayne has in the front seat."

"It's okay." With Elvis plastered on my chest like an infinity scarf and Mayes giving me a modest energy transfer, I helped myself to the soda and chocolate bar. One bite and I was humming with delight. The rest of the snack went down easy.

Wayne returned with a sly-fox smile and a smart phone in a sealed evidence bag. "It was right where you said it would be. Thank your ghost dog for his help. This could break this case wide open. Mayes, where's Roger

Lavene right now?"

"Dublin, sir. He has Otis Clement and will be here in two hours and some change."

"Great. The suitcase murder investigation is finally going somewhere. And Kitty's case just landed new leads." I gave Mayes a quick rundown of my findings.

"You dust for prints?" Mayes asked, turning to the sheriff.

"Not yet. Tell you what. Let's head to the station. We'll dust the phone, pull a copy of the data off of it, then you and Baxley can do another dreamwalk with the phone. Let's see if we can get Kitty home tonight."

I mentally groaned as I polished off the last of the chocolate bar. The fall from superstar to worker bee in a matter of seconds felt meteoric, but truthfully it was another day at the office. I was the sheriff's new app. Instead of point and click, I'd become point and sniff.

CHAPTER EIGHTEEN

Mayes and I stopped for a late lunch on the way to the sheriff's office. It felt good to do simple things with him. I allowed myself to daydream that every day could be like this. We could put Larissa on the bus for school, and both head to the cop shop for work. I'd get to hang out with Mayes at home and at work. That would be so lovely.

I sighed over the last mouthful of hamburger. With my personal finances having been tight for years, it was still a treat of the highest order to eat out.

Mayes eyed my empty food wrapper. "I can get you another burger if you're still hungry."

"No thanks. I'm good. Between the candy bar, soda, and now a burger, I've consumed half of my daily calories."

"You look fine." Mayes tossed the wrappers in the trash. He held out his hand and I took it. We strolled outside like any other couple stopping for lunch.

A family of four clamored by, the two youngest jostling to be first to the door, the parents looking like they needed caffeine. What did people see when they saw us together? Did they see a couple in love?

The "L" word. It hit me like a gale force wind. I loved him, and it was about time I admitted the truth to myself. Okay. We were a couple in love. Further, I wanted Mayes in my life permanently. Wow. Such clarity from a hamburger. Now I needed the right moment to tell him.

We climbed into the truck, Mayes behind the wheel. Elvis barked excitedly to see us, licking both of us before curling up in my lap. I stroked his soft fur and chickened out on sharing my realization with Mayes. I wasn't being a coward. I wanted more time with Mayes when I told him, and privacy mattered.

What to talk about instead? Kitty's abduction? The Suitcase Murders? The situation in Florida? The last one. I turned to Mayes. "I nearly forgot. What did you learn about Tampa?"

Mayes waited for a break in the traffic before he turned left toward the sheriff's office. "I found the phone number you need. Now you can call Rose's Tampa contact and question her. I looked into the mayor's troubles. He's on the board of a bank being investigated for fraudulent practices. That plus his troubles at City Hall with the missing municipal funds and his affair will keep him occupied for a long time. The bank charges are serious. He will go to prison if he's guilty."

"I wonder what made him take all that money."

"Greed is my guess, but they aren't saying he took the money. Only that it's missing and he had access to both funds. That's all I could find out right now."

I touched the rose tattoo on my wrist. That extra zing it used to have was gone. Did Rose use us to steal money? Or was her motive to expose the mayor's misuse of office? "Did they mention how much money is missing?"

"About ten million at the bank and another eight hundred thou from the city."

I whistled softly as I petted Elvis. "That's a lot of money! Where is it?"

"Most likely the funds were transferred to offshore accounts."

"Can Tampa get the money back?"

He shrugged. "They have to find it first."

"Does Raymondia's name come up in the mayoral investigation?"

"I couldn't access the investigator or his files without tipping people off to our interest in the case. We don't want them coming after us."

A sudden flash of internal heat had me adjusting my AC vents so they blew straight in my face. "You're sure the queries you made can't be traced back to either of us?"

"No worries. I only looked up a few things at the office. No one will ever know you and I went to Tampa."

"Speaking of Tampa, I tried searching for Rose during my last dreamwalk. She's not there. I don't even feel her energy through my rose tattoos. There's a void in my extra senses where she should be. I miss her, strange as that sounds, but she was my backup."

"What happened to her?"

"Not sure, but once before she got sanctioned by her boss. That time though, I sensed she was connected to me, but she couldn't help me with anything on the Other Side. Maybe she crossed a line or two by kidnapping us."

"Ya think?"

His wry tone surprised me. Mayes didn't usually indulge in sarcasm. Guess he was fed up with Rose interfering in our lives. "And maybe she got a different punishment this time."

"I hope that's true. She shouldn't be messing with your head or your life."

"You've never liked her."

"I've never liked that she had her hooks in you. She has a hidden agenda where you're concerned, and I don't trust anyone or any*thing* with an agenda."

"Don't worry. I won't put her on our Christmas card list." The remark slipped out before I knew it. Would Mayes and I be sending out mutual Christmas cards in another month? How would I broach the subject of my feelings when the time came?

Mayes did his customary man of silence thing, making me sweat bullets as I waited. The urge to explain rose in my throat, but I tamped it down.

"Good to know," he said, and I breathed easier. "Will she be invited to the wedding?"

My turn to be caught off-guard. Did I really want to have this conversation right here, right now? "Rose does as she likes, but, no, I wouldn't invite her to any family event."

"You skirted the question," Mayes observed after a long moment.

I could say something now. I needed to tell him. "In a world where I had no responsibilities, I would have stayed in the mountains with you. If you don't know that, we're not as in sync as you think we are."

He reached across the console for my hand.

I welcomed his tender caress. "Though I'm pulled in different directions by life, every day, I believe we're right for each other. I don't want you to go home to north Georgia."

He nodded tersely, his eyes on the road ahead as a trio of cars passed going in the opposite direction. Moments later we were decelerating on a grassy shoulder. He brought the pickup to a halt and switched off the motor.

Draping one arm over the wheel, he faced me. "You have my full attention, and I'm overjoyed to hear your words. We can work out the details." His eyes searched mine, his right hand holding securely onto my left. "Are you saying yes? Will you marry me?"

Emotion made it hard to speak. My vision blurred, and I reached deep for my voice. "Yes. I'll marry you."

He whooped and reached for me, hugging me close, murmuring soft, delicious words in Cherokee. Elvis scuttled out of the way, barking his agreement. I luxuriated in the embrace before I pulled back. "One thing though."

Mayes stilled. "What's that?"

I gathered the Chihuahua in my arms. "I tell Larissa first. Not a word to anyone until then."

He beamed again. "Deal, my lovely."

Safely inside the sheriff's office, it seemed as if I could still hear the clamoring reporters outside our locked doors. The din wouldn't leave my head, especially since several reporters had called out my name asking for comments about the suitcase murder victim. I'd ignored them as per protocol and hurried inside.

"Use my office for the phone dreamwalk." Wayne said, rising from his desk chair. "You two wait here while I retrieve Kitty Ballenger's cell from the evidence locker."

Mayes and I settled into the guest chairs at Wayne's spare table. He'd cleared the perennial stacks of folders so we had plenty of room. I hoped like anything that our actions today would lead to finding Kitty because each hour she was in captivity increased the chance she wouldn't see the next sunrise.

I fingered the moldavite pendant on my necklace, but it felt cold and lifeless. The gem needed a recharge. The crystals in my pocket still had some zing though. Four dreamwalks already today, and now the sheriff expected another miracle from me. I would push myself beyond all bounds to attempt five dreamwalks in a day.

Except I wasn't alone, and Mayes had recharged me twice by transferring his energy. He'd be here for me again when I concluded this phone dreamwalk. That wasn't all. Elvis the Chihuahua would help me recover after the dreamwalk. We'd left him with the dispatcher when we arrived a few moments ago.

"Nervous?" Mayes asked, reaching for my hand.

My cold fingers curled around his warm ones. "A little. Plus, it's been a long day."

"I got you."

I nodded, knowing he meant it on so many levels.

Wayne bustled in. "Okay, we're running the prints on this now, and our computer guru is running through all of her call history and apps on the SIM card." He tossed the clear evidence bag on the small table. It clunked as it hit the wood surface. "Do your thing, Bax."

"Don't expect too much," I said. "Even though this is a different object and will possibly yield a different vision, the steering wheel of her car is likely the last thing she touched. This probe may be a repeat of the same details."

"I need information, and I need it fast. We need to find Kitty Ballenger." Wayne took a few steps toward the door, then pivoted to face us. "I'll check on you in about fifteen minutes. Gotta do another press conference first."

Disengaging from Mayes, I reached for the plastic bag and withdrew the phone. I opened my senses to the emotion on the phone's outer surface and received a jumble of feminine anxiety. Though I probed and mentally circled the emotional well, I could go no farther in figuring this out alone. I set down the phone and gazed at Mayes. "The energy is too generalized. Kitty's afraid of something, maybe everything, but I can't refine the search with just me right now. My crystals are low on energy, and I don't have enough juice."

"I'll go in with you, if you like," Mayes added.

"I like." We interlaced our fingers. Our auras blended and resonated so that I felt supercharged. I opened my senses to the emotions on the phone in my other hand. The zap of fear through the link was so intense I dropped the phone.

"What was that?" Mayes asked as individual consciousness returned.

"Kitty's deathly afraid of something. Whatever it is, it scared me too."

"She's been kidnapped, so her fear is reasonable. Try again. She might have seen his face, vehicle, or tag number. Every minute we delay she's someone's prisoner."

I drew in a shaky breath. Though I'd released the phone, Kitty's fear still infused my body. The only way to examine it was to open myself to her possibilities. My quickened pulse rushed her fear everywhere until I was as paralyzed as she'd been. Mayes bent to retrieve the phone. I could see him moving, but I couldn't mirror his motions. I couldn't do anything. He offered it to me, but my hand wouldn't respond to the prompt my brain sent it to move. I wasn't sure if I could talk anymore either. Tears welled in my eyes as Kitty's reality became mine.

Her thoughts resonated in my head. Why was I so stupid?

Why wasn't I going home right now?

The world didn't dish up happily-ever-afters for the likes of me.

Hopes and dreams hurt. Reaching for them would only lead to more misery. I tugged at the crewneck collar of my gray T-shirt. The only path for me in this world was to eke out an existence out of the public eye. No one noticed or needed me, so hiding for the rest of my miserable life was the best thing I could do.

It was safe.

My fingers coiled into fists with the thumbs poking through between pointer finger and tall man. The nails of my thumbs poked into each other as I tapped them together. I am fine. I am safe. I am all right. The litany repeated over and over in my head.

Light fractured as if someone exploded a bolt of lightning inside my head. Someone shouted near my ears. Too loud, I thought, cringing. The light. The noise. The world swirled into a dizzying kaleidoscope and faded to black.

"Baxley! Wake up. Open your eyes and speak to me."

The voice faded and I entered the drift. When the tumbling stopped, I squinted through my eyelids at a bright, outdoor scene. This wasn't Wayne's office, not by a long shot. I saw trees and grass and white ground. What was that white stuff? Sand? Did grass grow at the beach?

I liked puzzles, so I opened my eyes some more. From the recesses of my head, I heard the frantic man shouting for Baxley again, but I ignored the stranger's voice. With legs like a newborn foal, I wobbled to an upright position. The space seemed quite small, confined and yet open. I gripped the steel bars before me, peering out. A breeze lifted my hair and the world shifted gently. I swayed with it, as if I were on a swing. I tried to focus on my immediate surroundings, but this place wasn't familiar at all. It was a cage. Quickly, I glanced around the enclosure. No exit. With hands that weren't my own, I shook the bars and screamed my frustration.

"Sing, birdie," a voice said.

Fearfully, I gazed around. No one was in sight. "You're not real," I said. "I am not crazy."

A diabolical laugh erupted from the adjacent tree. I scanned the tree branches until I saw a little box. No one was really here. Only some techie gadget meant to scare me.

I paced the boundary of my new world, five steps in every direction. *Look around you,* a foreign voice in my head urged. *What do you see?*

I saw trees, grass, and white stuff, same as before. There were no houses, no cars, no people. Just me, stuck in a cage in a tree. I dashed the tears away. The white stuff.

There was something I needed to remember about the white stuff. It looked like someone had taken a big bite out of it. Like it had been mined or something. I gazed at my hands on the bars. A dusty film covered everything.

No. Not dust. Chalk. Or to be more precise, kaolin. Kaolin was what they called the chalk mines in Georgia.

My cage hung in an abandoned kaolin quarry, and my worst fears had become reality. No one that mattered knew where I was. I was completely invisible now.

188

CHAPTER NINETEEN

My skin didn't fit. My arms and legs felt numb and tingly at the same time. I braced against the swinging motion I'd become accustomed to, only nothing was moving. Not even me. Cautiously, I cracked an eye open.

"There you are," a man said.

It shocked me to see anyone so close. How'd he get here? I was alone. And invisible. "What do you want?"

"Where've you been, lovely?"

"Out," I said, not sure of how to answer this curious stranger. I shrunk into my chair. "Can you give me some space?"

His eyebrow arched. "Baxley?"

He stood between me and the door. If I felt better, I'd dart around him and leave this strange place, whatever it was. Nothing seemed familiar. Not the desk or the chairs or the stacks of file folders. It freaked me out. "I don't know any Baxleys. I wanna go home."

"Nobody's going anywhere until I know what happened to Baxley." The man sounded angry, upset even. "Who are you?"

I squirmed under his intent gaze, aware that I couldn't stand or run. I was trapped. Again, only this time the cage wasn't visible. I sighed. "Kitty."

He let out a string of swear words. "That explains a lot. Kitty, where did the man take you?"

My vision flickered, and I nearly puked. I'd hold my belly if I could move my hands. "What man? Who are you? You can't keep me here. I'll call the police."

"I'm Deputy Sam Mayes, and I *can* hold you here at the Sinclair County law enforcement center. My friend Baxley left to find you and now you're here but Baxley isn't. Did she stay behind?"

I stared resolutely at my lifeless hands, willing them to move. Disappointment crushed my hopes when they didn't even twitch. "I don't know any Baxleys."

"What's the last thing you remember before waking up here?"

I recoiled inwardly as the room spun slowly. "No. You can't make me. I don't want to think about that scary place."

"Kitty, please focus. Then we'll get you and Baxley back home."

Focus. How could I focus when everything freaked me out? Why wouldn't he leave me alone? "I don't belong in a tree." I ground my teeth together, wishing I hadn't revealed my shame. Now he knew I was caged like an animal. Now he'd send me back to that awful place.

"It's okay, Kitty. We know a man took you from the truck stop parking lot. We can rescue you if we know where you are. Do you recognize the place?"

He was stroking my hand, and his touch felt oddly reassuring. He wanted to help me. I relaxed and blurted out my woes. "I shiver at night and sweat in the day. I'm thirsty and hungry. Sometimes I wake up and find an apple, but those apples make me sleepy. I stopped eating them."

"Good girl. He's probably drugging your food. How long did the drive last from the truck stop to the place with the tree?"

A wave of nausea washed over me, and the room spun a little faster. My insecurities flared again. He was a stranger. I didn't talk to strangers, but he wanted to help. He was a police officer. I could trust him. "The dash clock said seven when he stopped, and it was dark. Maybe three hours, but I don't know. I was out of it."

"How did he contact you?"

191

"My phone, but it's a secret." Oops. I wasn't supposed to tell anyone. He'd punish me for sure. My body started trembling. I hated being so afraid.

He looked puzzled. "You gave him your number?"

"No. I didn't know him before. We met online. That's how he contacts me."

"Where?"

"He told me how to hide the app. My brother doesn't know about it." My vision faded to black. I flashed hot and cold and the whirling increased. I tried to focus but nothing worked. I screamed. "What's happening? Make it stop."

"Hang in there, Kitty. We're searching for you."

"Baxley? You in there?"

A familiar voice. Mayes. Finally something I recognized on this bizarre dreamwalk. I fought through deep layers of darkness and exhaustion to get to him. My stomach roiled and writhed as if I were trapped in the drift. I wasn't in limbo, but I'd been some place very odd. A place where I couldn't move, where I felt vulnerable and alone. The feeling intensified, giving me the shivers.

"Baxley, it's time to wake up," Mayes said. "Open your eyes right now."

My eyes wouldn't open, no matter how I tried. A strange sound filled my ears. Gurgling. It sounded so near. What on earth was it? Should I be afraid? I tried to speak, and I heard the odd sound again. Great. It was me making the noise. Something was wrong. I was here in the room with Mayes, but I wasn't.

"I'm right here, Bax. You're safe now. You're in Wayne's office, and nothing bad is going to happen now. But you have to wake up."

I heard him just fine, but I couldn't see, and I couldn't speak. I tried to move my hands to reassure him I was there, but they wouldn't work. Everything felt hot and the intense fever spiked into a killer headache on an out-of-control roller coaster. Something awful was happening to me. My gut cramped and heaved. I heard an awful sound, the sound of someone being sick to their stomach. The cramping and heaving went on and on until I collapsed, a sodden mess.

"That was interesting," Mayes said.

His voice sounded clinical, as if he were observing a science experiment. I tried again to speak. More gurgling.

"Easy, now. I want you to stay present with me, but I'm calling for reinforcements.

We need your mom and dad here to help you reintegrate properly. Be calm, but don't slip away."

Funny. All I wanted to do was sleep. Returning to the drift would be easier than staying here where nothing worked. I heard voices murmur in the background, then Mayes began singing his Cherokee lullabies to me. I clung to the soothing music. As long as I could hear him, I was safe.

After a while, more hands touched me with compassion. Energy flared on the spiritual plane, a steady glow enveloped me in love and light. In that welcoming cloud of vitality, I felt and recognized my parents and their friends Running Bear and Gentle Dove, even Dad's assistant Bubba Paxton was there. And my medium friend, Stinger, and Elvis our therapy Chihuahua. They were all here for me. To help me be me again.

The group's energy seeped into my empty spaces. I felt their joys and pains and especially their concern for me. I loved every one of these people. A contented sigh, a very loud aah came from my lips as I felt myself becoming retuned. My life force brightened and flowed through all my meridians instead of circling in place. It felt like I was breathing without my nose or mouth. Like a baby in the womb, I realized.

Energy flowed in four directions, warming and invigorating me. My fingers twitched, and I heard my Mom say "It's working."

With each breath, I seemed calmer and stronger. Sensation and thought melded, and I grew more uncomfortable with who I was. I'd been so scared, so terrified of what I'd seen, that I'd forgotten everything else. The strong fearful emotion was dissipating with each silent breath. I was more than a single paralyzing emotion. I was a beloved daughter, and I treasured my own daughter. I was in love with Mayes. Letting go of the fear allowed me to feel other things.

Something was licking my neck. Elvis. Even the dog wanted me back to normal. Each hand on my body flowed with love and affection. Such an outpouring of caring from my family and friends. I felt so connected to them on every level.

I could feel my bones now. No longer porous, they felt strong and whole, ready to support and sustain my body. Life was so precious. A kernel of joy welled within my heart, blossoming and filling me. Warmth radiated from my body. And light. I could see the steady glow beyond my eyelids.

"Come home, Baxley," Mom said. "It's time."

My eyes opened, and I sensed the spent tears on my cheeks. I'd fought a hard battle to return, but I couldn't have managed without everyone in this room. "Thank you," I somehow managed. "Thank you from the bottom of my heart."

"Welcome back, dear." Mom kissed my cheek. "Larissa is fine. Your neighbor is taking care of her."

"Thanks," I said.

"Love you, daughter," Dad said.

"You are our family," Gentle Dove said as she and Running Bear beamed over me.

"Glad to see you," Bubba Paxton said with a lopsided grin.

Stinger's face appeared, his skin aglow. "I am so happy you're back." Elvis launched himself into Stinger's arms, and I laughed as they made a big to-do over each other.

Mayes leaned over me and kissed me full on the lips in front of everyone. His eyes held so much caring I nearly wept. "Thank you for fighting for me," I said. "I was truly stuck and couldn't pull it together."

"Always," Mayes said.

The door opened, and Wayne stuck his head in. "Good. She's awake. Can I have my office back, people?"

I glanced down, surprised to see I wore a different shirt than I put on this morning.

Mayes had a different shirt on too. The smell of an antiseptic cleaner filled my nose. I flashed back to what I'd gone through and realized someone had cleaned up after I'd vomited.

"Give us a sec," I said, pushing up to a sitting position. I braced for vertigo but I was so full of energy and love that I felt strong enough to leap mountains.

Wayne edged in the room. "I'm more interested in a full report. What'd you run into that laid you low for hours?"

"I'm not sure what happened. One moment I was holding the phone and getting ready to look for Kitty, and the next, I was stuck in Kitty's body. It was not a pleasant experience. She was so afraid, had been so afraid, that all I could do in her immobilized body was look around."

"Just so you know," Mayes said, his fingers interlacing through mine, "your body went rigid too. I don't know why I wasn't affected, since we were questing together, but it was not a good experience from my perspective either."

"How is that possible?" I asked. "Some kind of astral projection? How do I stop it from happening again?"

Everyone looked at my dad. He glanced at Running Bear. "All things are possible,"

Running Bear said. "I can only surmise that young Kitty is under extreme duress. When you reached out to her, she found a means to escape her situation temporarily."

I shuddered, and Mayes drew closer. "I'm okay now," I managed. "Being trapped in her body was terrifying. I couldn't wake up, plus I felt so disjointed and broken. Then, my rescue party healed me on the spiritual plane. I owe you all so much. Thanks doesn't seem like a big enough word for what you've done."

"You are courageous," Running Bear added. "It could have gone badly even with our help."

"But we had a great outcome," Dad said, his hand on my shoulder. "I'm proud of you, daughter."

"Okay. I get it," Wayne said with a dismissive flip of his wrist. "Everyone is grateful to everyone, but what did you see over there, Baxley?"

"Should I tell everyone?" I asked.

"No. You're right. We need the room to talk about the case, so all of you clear out."

"She needs rest," Gentle Dove said, standing nose to nose with the sheriff. "She goes home with us."

"That's right," my mom said, moving between Gentle Dove and me, blocking

198

Wayne from my sight. "Your police work nearly killed her today. I'm not leaving here without Baxley."

Wayne sighed and edged around the human barriers. "Report, Baxley, and then go home."

I nodded, but it took me courage to turn my thoughts back to that scary episode. "She's in a metal cage, suspended in the air about six feet. The cage is held by a chain on a pulley on a tree branch. It looked like she was in a kaolin mine, lots of white surfaces everywhere, and the ground was shaped like a bowl. Water puddled in the distance and it looked to be the turquoise color of the Caribbean."

"Did you see any vehicles or people?"

"No, but if you put me with a sketch artist, I can recreate the scene for you."

"I will do that today." As my family and friends stepped forward as one, Wayne made a show of surrender with his raised hands. "But tomorrow is soon enough."

My mom wrangled me away from Mayes to walk down the hall and outside into the evening. The grass glistened with newly fallen dew. As she installed me in the passenger side of my truck, she whispered, "I know you've got a secret. When will you tell everyone the good news?"

My jaw dropped, and that was quite something after the day I'd had. How'd she know about my brand new engagement to Mayes? Was everything I knew or experienced exposed during an energy share?

"Uh, Mom, it is a secret. I'm not making any kind of announcement until I talk to Larissa first."

My mother gave me a hug. "I'm so excited for you."

I whispered in her ear. "Does everyone know?"

Mom's mouth came close to my ear. "I don't think so. But, being your mother, I recognized the signs. Don't worry, your secret's safe with me."

CHAPTER TWENTY

With my engagement so close to being public knowledge, I needed to broach the topic of marriage with Larissa as soon as possible. It was nine by the time we pulled into the driveway beside Mr. Luther's car. A phone rang, but not my ring.

Mayes pulled out his phone and checked the display. "I need to take this," he said. "Tribal business."

"Take your time," I said as I hurried inside to relieve my neighbor. Mr. Luther rose from the sofa when I opened the door. He seemed spry for a man in his late fifties.

"There you are," Mr. Luther said.

"Here I am," I replied. "Thank you for pitching in with childcare tonight. I am so grateful for your help."

"Not a problem, dear. Are you all right now, Madam Dreamwalker?"

Self-consciously, I touched my cheek. "Can you tell something happened to me?"

"You look fine, but I know it was serious if you needed your folks to help you back from the Other Side."

I'd known Mr. Luther all my life, first as my grandmother's friendly neighbor and now as mine. He wasn't in our circle of sensitives, but he always seemed to know things. Still, I didn't want to confide that I'd been possessed by the kidnapped woman's spirit. That kind of thing could be bad for Dreamwalker business.

"It was a different kind of dreamwalk, that's for sure, but I'm good now." A yawn slipped out. "And ready to go to bed."

Mr. Luther nodded toward the back porch where Mayes was speaking with his tribesmen by phone. "Your new fella. He gonna stick around?"

A genuine smile filled my face. "Yes. He's staying." I couldn't say more without blabbing my news, and Larissa came first. She would hear the news from me first.

"Good to know." He patted his pockets and withdrew his keys. "I'll get out of here so you can get some rest."

"Thanks again. Soon as we knock out this case, I'll have you over to dinner," I said.

He waved a hand as he departed. "Thanks, I'd like that."

Alone at last, I darted upstairs to check

on Larissa.

She stirred as soon as I stepped into the bedroom. "Mom?"

All three dogs looked at me without raising their heads, but the cats gave me the stink eye for waking them. "Yeah, sorry I'm so late, kiddo. I did five dreamwalks for the case today and the last one was a doozy."

Larissa sat up, eyes wide with alarm. "You're okay, right?"

"Yes. All is well, thanks to Mayes and my parents." I hesitated. "I have something to tell you, but it can wait until morning."

Reaching over, Larissa clicked on her light. "Tell me now. Please."

Silence yawned between us. "This is harder than I expected," I began, sitting beside her on the mattress. The cats jumped off the bed, annoyed by my presence. "I barely know where to begin, and your opinion means the world to me."

Concern darkened her features. "What's wrong? You're all glowing and everything this evening. I don't understand. Is this about work or Mayes?"

"Mayes." I chewed on my thoughts a while longer, then I blurted out, "I love him."

"Everyone knows that." Larissa giggled. "It's written all over your face."

My hand went to my cheek. "They do? It is?"

"Yeah, it's kinda cute. He's got the same goofy look about you."

"Well, as to that . . ." my voice trailed off as I steeled myself for anything and everything. "Nothing will replace your father in your life, and I'm not asking you to set aside your love for him." I blew a breath up my forehead. Why was this so danged hard? "I hope you have room in your heart for more love because Mayes asked me to marry him."

"Depends."

That single word and her solemn expression iced my heart. "On what?"

"On what you said. Are you going to marry him?"

My lungs felt like they were caught in a vise. "I want to. What do you think?"

"I think I'm the luckiest girl in the world, that's what I think." Larissa threw her arms around me and shrieked happily. The dogs barked happily. "I get to be in the wedding, right?"

I hugged her back and the chill inside melted away. I drew a deep, full breath. "Of course. He only asked me a few hours ago, so I hadn't thought about more than getting your approval. I had a big wedding with

204

your dad, and I'm not sure that's appropriate second time around. I'd rather have something small with immediate family and friends, but Mayes has a say in this as well."

"Did someone say my name?" Mayes asked, lounging in the doorway, backlit by the hall light. His normally composed face seemed drawn. Did he hear bad news from his tribe?

"Someone did," I said, beckoning him to join us. "I told Larissa about our engagement. She's happy for us."

Mayes embraced us both, with the dogs milling around, barking and licking our hands and faces. I couldn't remember being so happy.

"I will take good care of you and your mom," Mayes promised Larissa.

"I know you will, silly," Larissa said. "It's what I've been wanting for a long time."

Her remark struck a strange chord within me. "How long?" I asked, wondering if I'd botched the job as a single parent.

"Ever since this summer when the Colonel and Elizabeth tried to force me to stay with them. I've been wishing and hoping we could be a family again. We finally know what happened to Daddy, and we said our goodbyes. I miss him, but I'm glad we met Mayes. He doesn't think we're weird, and he has a kind heart. I want him to live here with us. I want us to be a family, the sooner the better."

"Oh, honey," I said, drawing her in tight to my chest. "I'm sorry your grandparents hurt you. They can't take you again. I won't let them. The sheriff won't let them. And now, Mayes won't let them either."

"Good because that's what I want. More than anything."

Mayes and I got ready for bed. I wanted to sleep for six years, maybe more.

"You happy?" he asked.

"I am. Larissa's seal of approval means a lot to me."

"She has become family to me."

"Thank you for that."

"About the wedding date."

"Cut me some slack." I groaned. "I just got the engagement cleared with my daughter, and there's still everyone else to tell. Except my Mom. She confided this evening that she already knew our good news, so our engagement won't be a surprise to my parents."

"I still have to formally ask your mother for your hand in marriage," he said. "But given that she's happy about me being here, the negotiation won't take long."

I stifled another yawn and slipped under

the covers. "My mom, not my dad?"

"Cherokee custom is to ask the mother's permission. Your Dad may also be present, out of respect for your culture, but you become a member of my tribe when you marry me."

"I have a lot to learn."

"You'll be fine. Cherokee women are held in high esteem, and you are a woman of great power. My people already hold you in high regard for what you did for White Feather."

White Feather was a young maiden who fell under the spell of a psychic vampire. I couldn't stop her death, but her killer paid for his crime and her spirit accepted the victory. Now White Feather and her boyfriend, Haney, were greeters on the Other Side.

"I didn't do anything for her that I wouldn't do for anyone else."

"Exactly, which is why you're amazing. Now, back to my question. It's the first week of November now. What date works for you? This week? Next week? Thanksgiving week?"

Each date sounded soon. "I guess a long engagement is out of the question."

"Yes. With the governor's election coming next week, I need to decline the possible opening in the sheriff position so that someone else can be vetted. I hope Duncan gets the job."

"You shouldn't give up your career because of me. Can we maintain residences in both places?"

"Residences, yes. Careers, no. My place is by your side. I will remain available for tribal matters." He kissed my nose. "Truthfully, I don't want to dissect the details tonight. I want to lock in a wedding date."

Aack. He had a one-track mind. "You're relentless."

"You have no idea." He grinned. "I'll stop by probate court and get the paperwork for the marriage license tomorrow."

I sat up, appalled. "Tomorrow? You want to get married tomorrow?"

He took my hand, a sheepish look on his face. "I didn't say that. I said I'd take the burden of filling out the paperwork off your hands. Let me handle the pesky details."

"Oh. That's okay, then." A wave of relief washed away the coiled tension I'd been feeling. "This has been such a chaotic day. I'm ready for it to be over, but I want to thank you again. For saving me."

"You're my heart." His voice softened. "I'd move heaven and earth to save you."

"Nice." A yawn snuck out. "I mean,

thanks. I mean, I need to go to sleep. With you."

"Good answer."

thanks, I mean, I need to go to sleep. With you."

"Good answer."

Chapter Twenty-One

Wednesday dawned with such radiance it took my breath away. Even the hawk that nested by the state highway basked in the brilliance. Songbirds chirped happily, echoing my great mood. Under the thick canopy of live oaks and pines, we navigated the double "S" curves, passing by beautiful, stately Victorian-style homes. Back when timber was king here, this settlement was where the townies came to escape the summer heat.

Like them, I knew a good thing when I saw it.

I was in love and engaged.

Finding someone who valued and understood my differences was a miracle. Dreamwalking might never become routine but my life partner would be a helpmate and source of comfort. Without Mayes, I could never have survived five dreamwalks in one day. He was such a blessing for me and for the souls I served. I savored the glow for several more miles before thoughts of the case intruded.

Did Kitty Ballenger survive the night? I hoped so. That poor woman. Imprisoned. Thirsty. Hungry. Alone. She didn't have many tomorrows. Urgency thrummed through my veins, until the must-rescue-Kitty message spread like wildfire throughout my body. Kitty would die if we couldn't locate her soon. We were her only hope.

"What with the wonky dreamwalk and discussing our engagement with Larissa, we didn't review your observations about Kitty's spirit," I said as Mayes turned onto the spur. "Did you learn anything new when Kitty was in my body?"

"A little. I wish we'd gotten more from her, but I was very concerned you weren't you," Mayes said. "She said she met her abductor online. At his insistence, she hid the dating app on her phone. She called him Joe. We're not sure if that's his real name or a screen name."

Sunlight and shadows entwined patterns on the asphalt road. Light and dark were joined at the hip, same as good and evil. The same as an innocent young women and the man who caged her. Evidence suggested Kitty's kidnapper embraced the darker side of human nature.

I shook my head to focus on finding Kitty. "Did you find the app?"

"Wayne reached out to Tamika's teenaged nephew. He's a wizard when it comes to cell phones. It didn't take him thirty minutes to check everything and reboot the phone. The dating app popped up on the Home screen and last I knew, Wayne was working on getting access to her account. Kitty's brother Shawn had no idea about the app or her password, so we need permission from the site owner to view her posts."

My teeth ground together at the mention of Kitty's brother. "If not for Shawn's lax attitude toward his sister, we could've searched for Kitty on Saturday. Every moment we struggle following the cold trail, she's starving to death in a cage. It isn't right."

Up ahead, three mixed breed dogs trotted across the road. I tapped Mayes' arm lightly. "Careful. We might need to find where they belong."

Mayes slowed and the dogs bolted into a mostly fenced yard. I let out a long exhale that they were safe for now.

"I hope access has been obtained," Mayes continued. "Once we have a sketch from your vision, we'll search online images of

Georgia's kaolin mines. We could locate her today."

I let out a long sigh. "Something's been bugging me. Kitty is the same size as the murdered women in the suitcases. Her captor is making her smaller through starvation. Does her abduction tie into the Suitcase Murders? Were the other women starved?"

"From my recollection of victims, only one was found within a few weeks of when she went missing. The grueling heat accelerated decomp, so her weight status is unknown." It was his turn to sigh. "I know you want to solve both cases, and there is an overlap in victimology, but objectivity is crucial. The cases might not be related."

My head was shaking before he finished speaking. "I don't believe in coincidences."

"Neither do I," Mayes said, "which is why we must remain open to ideas. Solid police work will solve the case. The edge we have is you. The killer doesn't know about your abilities. Even better, they can't change the past, and that's how we'll find them. People follow familiar patterns and we'll find those routines."

Talk about pressure. "My dreamwalks aren't foolproof. Often they're cryptic. You know that."

"I know what each dreamwalk costs you, and I'm here to assist you. We're a good team, a solid team, and all the crooks in Georgia better watch out."

I giggled at his notion that we had superhero like abilities. My glee faded quickly as he pulled up to the entrance in the employee parking lot and idled the engine by the door. "You're not coming in?" I asked.

He gazed at me with veiled eyes. "I have an errand to run. Tell Wayne I'll be back in an hour. If something breaks in the case, call me immediately."

He was telling the truth, but he'd been careful to say little. I didn't like being his message boy to our boss, but I supposed that came under the heading of teamwork. Still, I couldn't contain my curiosity. If I was covering for him, I wanted to know where he was.

"What kind of errand?" I asked.

"One of those wedding details. I won't be long."

I hesitated. "Should I mention the engagement to Wayne?"

"Wait, if you don't mind. I don't have your mother's permission yet."

"Is that where you're headed?"

He nodded. "I set it up last night. They're

expecting me in fifteen minutes. Wish me luck?"

Relieved, I gave him a quick kiss. "You'll be fine."

"One more thing," he said, pressing a slip of paper in my hand. "Raymondia LaFleur's number in Tampa. Call Rose's associate from the office when you are alone."

In all the to-do with our active cases and engagement, I'd forgotten my spiritual mentor transported us body and soul to Tampa to do God knows what. I needed to find out what Raymondia knew. Otherwise, our actions there might destroy our careers and lives.

"Will do."

"You break up with your boyfriend?" Wayne asked when I entered his office.

"Not hardly. He asked to speak privately with my mom. He'll return in an hour."

"I didn't authorize any leave."

My hand shot up to forestall Wayne's notorious temper. "Don't shoot the messenger. You and Mayes can square things when he arrives. What about Kitty's phone? Do we know who she was messaging?"

"We have a phone number, but her contact used a burner. Any minute now, I should hear from the judge about a warrant for her account information, then I'll shoot that to the owner of the dating site. Meanwhile, the sketch artist from Savannah is waiting for you in the conference room."

"Okay. That's where I'm headed. What happened with Roger Lavene and the Suitcase Murder suspect? Did that interview happen?"

"It did, and we had no grounds to hold Otis Clement. We had to let him go."

I couldn't mask my disappointment. I wanted to take Otis Clement's measure in person. If I touched him, there might be a glimpse of Kitty in his mind. "Sorry I missed it. Really sorry. I believe the cases are related, Wayne."

"Let's not get ahead of ourselves. These cases are separate until I say they aren't. Our priority is finding Kitty. You were too wiped out to do anything more yesterday, which is when the Clement interview occurred. Don't fret. After you finish with the sketch artist, your next task will be to view his recorded interview."

It wasn't as good as an in-person read, but it was something. I managed a wry smile. "Will do."

An African American of my mother's generation awaited me in the conference room. A statuesque woman with a near regal bearing, Eula Mae Jenkins rose and shook my hand when I entered the room. Good energy flowed from her firm and welcoming handshake, a miracle of sorts in this energy-sapping institutional setting.

After introductions, we got right down to business. "The perspective is from an elevated vantage point," I explained as I pointed to different quadrants of the page. "In the foreground is scrub vegetation, very sparse. A scraggly pine over here, a maple seedling here, and maybe sedge grass. A ridge line of clay soil snakes from left to right and then arcs back toward the center. Where it snakes back, I saw a lighter slope. Below that is a tree line and another white slope. That gives way to dirty-looking level ground that became a turquoise pond."

Eula Mae sketched until the elements were in the right proportion. I nodded and remembered another detail. "There was a building off in the distance. Here." I pointed to a spot on the drawing. "It looks old, like weathered wood, two-story, with a rusted tin roof."

"How's this?" Eula Mae asked after we'd changed a few things.

The sketch looked exactly as I remembered. "Really good. Do you exhibit your artwork anywhere?"

She mentioned a gallery in Savannah and added, "But art doesn't pay as well as police work."

I nodded. "I have the same issue with my Pets and Plants business. It's what I enjoy doing, but the income is sporadic. Being a police consultant pays the bills."

"I've heard about you," Eula Mae said, stowing her supplies in a canvas satchel.

"Oh?"

"Nothing bad. Some of the investigators in Savannah are talking about this hotshot psychic with a hundred percent case closure rate down in Marion. They'd love for you to freelance up there."

"My life and my family are here. I prefer to stay here on the coast."

She gave me a pained look. "Oh, honey, I'm so sorry."

"About what?"

"Your sheriff promised you'd help on some big, whoop-de-do case."

"He did?" Under the table, my hands coiled into fists. Wayne had no right to loan me out like a piece of tactical equipment. Clearly I needed to remind him of the rules of our association.

"Yeah. Somebody is murdering women and putting them in suitcases."

"Oh. I know about that." Relieved, I sank into the molded plastic chair. "We have an open case right now that could be the work of the suitcase killer, but we shifted our resources to focus on our missing young woman."

Eula Mae gestured toward the sketch. "And she's in this place?"

"Yes."

Her head cocked to the side. "I hope you don't mind me asking. Did you have a vision?"

Though she was friendly and I enjoyed her company, Eula Mae was a stranger with loyalty elsewhere. I chose my words with care. "It's complicated."

"But you saw this place and that's why we're making the drawing."

"That's true."

Eula Mae studied the drawing. "Looks like kaolin country to me. That'd be middle Georgia. Maybe even over Sandersville way."

"We'll be checking online for a match. My boss is determined to find this girl. We need to find her today."

Eula Mae patted my hand. "You're all right, Baxley Powell. This gal is lucky to have you on her side."

Wayne poked his head in the door. His

florid face gave me pause. "You done?" he asked.

"Yeah, we got it." I showed him the sketch. "This is exactly what I saw."

His gaze swept the landscape. "Seems fairly specific. Let's get going on an image comparison." He snagged the sketch, thanked Eula Mae, and crooked a finger at me. "In my office. Now."

My insides did a flip-flop and not in a good way. I said goodbye to the sketch artist and followed Wayne. He was not in a good mood. I thought over what I'd done the last few days, and couldn't remember any wrongdoing on my part. What was his temper about?

"Close the door," Wayne snarled.

I complied and kept my distance from him to avoid his negative energy. All the good vibes from working with Eula Mae dissipated in a heartbeat. I did my best to appear composed, though my knees trembled until I edged behind a guest chair and held onto the back.

Why was I so afraid? It made no sense. Had our part in the Tampa mayor exposé come to light? Would I spend tonight in prison and never see Larissa again?

"I just got reamed out by the Blair County Sheriff for stealing her employee, and I've done nothing of the sort," Wayne said. "What the hell is going on?"

Oh, boy. I especially didn't want to have this conversation. "I'm not sure. Shouldn't you talk to Mayes?"

"Mayes isn't my guy. You are. Spill. Now. Or you're finished here. I don't tolerate people going behind my back."

Now that I understood the reason for his anger, I felt more confident. I stepped around the chair, hoping logic would calm his fears. "I don't know exactly what's going on with Mayes and his job. I have a general idea why his boss called you, but Mayes and I haven't discussed his career."

Wayne glared at me. "Something made him call his sheriff this morning and give two weeks' notice. I don't like being blindsided. I hate secrets, especially when they affect my police consultant."

"We're engaged," I blurted out. "I accepted his proposal yesterday. I wasn't supposed to tell anyone until after Mayes asked my parents for permission to marry me."

"That's where he went this morning?"

I nodded, deeply distressed that I'd betrayed Mayes' confidence.

The sheriff's laser focus on me intensified. "Tell me the truth. Is he coming after my job?"

This showdown was about Wayne's job security? Good grief. "As I stated before, I don't know what his career plan going forward will be. He's mentioned a cold case task force but I truly am in the dark. He said he's moving here. So we'll live here. Is that what you're worried about?"

The air turned blue with Wayne's swearing. I winced at the scathing outburst, but I didn't feel a lick of sympathy for the man. He liked to be in control. Who didn't?

When he wound down, I seized the opportunity to speak. "Am I fired?"

"No. This is a complication I don't need."

The tightness in my chest eased. "Deal with it."

"Or what? You'll run off and join the task force too?"

"No one's running off anywhere. I love my police consultant job, and my dreamwalker gig is in Sinclair County. My place is here."

"See that you remember that." Wayne's cheek twitched, twice. He drew in a few deep breaths, looking everywhere but at me. Finally, he gathered himself and cleared his throat. "You scared me, Powell. Thought you were leaving town."

"Not that I know of, though I will probably accompany Mayes back to his stomping ground for tribal matters from time to time."

"You want me to give him a job?"

"What I want is for you two to work things out on your own. I feel uncomfortable having said anything about our engagement when Mayes specifically asked me to wait to tell anyone. Because you said my job was on the line, I went against the man I love and revealed our private business here at the office. Fair warning: if you two can't find a way to play nice, I won't be caught in the middle."

"You threatening me?"

"I'm asking you to be a mature adult and talk to Mayes." My voice rose with each word I spoke. I clamped down on my emotions. "Clear the air. Ask him the questions you asked me. Why is that so hard?"

A crisp knock sounded on the door. Wayne and I stood there, like boxing opponents between bouts. Wayne gave a terse nod and yelled, "Come in."

"Sorry I'm late. I had a personal matter." Mayes stepped in and closed the door, interest etched on his face. "What'd I miss?"

CHAPTER TWENTY-TWO

I snatched the sketch from Wayne's desk and headed for the door. "I am not doing this again. You two sort this out right now, or there'll be hell to pay."

Wayne's door rattled on its hinges behind me, but I didn't care. Those guys were overdue for a heart-to-heart. I handed the sketch to Tamika for scanning and stepped outside to call my parents. My father answered on the first ring. "Congratulations," he said. "I've got you on speaker phone so Lacey can hear as well. We couldn't be happier for you. Sam Mayes is a fine man. We're glad to welcome him to our family."

"He makes me happy, Dad. Larissa likes him too. I have a concern though. Will others think I'm moving too fast?"

"Waiting on other people's approval is no way to live. Lacey and I are in favor of this union. We're pleased he formally asked our permission to marry you."

"Traditions are important to Mayes."

My mom laughed. "If you're marrying him, shouldn't you call him by his given name?"

"Good suggestion, but I think of him as Mayes instead of Sam. He calls me by my first and last name interchangeably. It's a cop thing." I didn't mention the Cherokee endearment Mayes used for me. That was private. "We'll figure it out. He's willing to accept my obligations and responsibilities, and that means everything to me."

"He has them too, dear," my mother said. "I can't stop smiling. This marriage coming on top of everything else, it's wonderful."

"What else?" I asked.

Voices murmured softly on the opposite end of the line. My curiosity rose exponentially. What were my parents talking about?

"It's okay, dear," Mom continued. "Your marriage should take center stage, and our immediate priority is this wedding."

"Gotta warn you, Mayes wants the knot-tying to be soon. He said he'd take care of the details, but I'd love to have an outdoor ceremony at your place."

"We'd love that too," Mom said. "Whatever you two decide, we'll be there with you. We're so happy for all of y'all."

"Thanks." Voices sounded behind me as a

pair of deputies walked into the center. I instinctively curled into the phone. "I couldn't manage without you. I'm so grateful for all you do for me and Larissa."

"Of course," Dad said smoothly. "We wouldn't have it any other way."

After our goodbyes, I stood my ground on the office sidewalk. I wasn't ready to head inside, especially if Mayes and Wayne hadn't figured out how to share me, professionally speaking.

The air felt a little cooler today. Soon the thermometer would be dipping into seriously cold temps. Good chance I'd be married by Christmas. Heck, the way Mayes operated, I could be married by Thanksgiving.

"Powell," Wayne said.

I turned to see the sheriff waving me inside. His expression stayed deadpan, so I couldn't tell if he was over his man-fit or not. I hoped he was.

"What do you need?" I asked as if something else was more important than my marriage and career.

"Today's assignment is for you to review Lavene's interview with Otis Clement, one of the suitcase murderer suspects. Meanwhile, I'll network with other jurisdictions about the kaolin mine sketch you created."

"Coming." I took a last look around the tended lawn and framing pines. Stolen moments like this peaceful one made me grateful my job wasn't boring. "You and Mayes work things out?"

"Somewhat."

"Huh." I wanted to know more, but I'd get with Mayes later and figure out what the heck was going on. "Where do you want me?"

"Viewing area for Interview Two. Run the tape and tell me your impressions. Is Otis Clement lying? Is he the guy we're hunting?"

"Gotcha. I'll get right on it." I hoofed it down to the viewing room, settled behind the monitor, and activated the recorded interview.

Like the photo in his suspect file, Otis Clement looked to be a tad older than me, maybe mid to late 30s. He was a light-skinned African American, with closely shorn hair. Just enough length to suggest curliness. His charcoal gray business suit was conservatively cut. The only flair of color was his lavender neck tie atop his white business shirt.

A sheen of sweat adorned his forehead. Clement shed his suit coat and draped it neatly across the back of the chair. His gaze darted everywhere at once, and I could tell he hated being in this small room.

He fidgeted for the whole interview, jangling one leg then the other. He kept rubbing the back of his neck and staring at the door. Right away, he raised the issue of racial discrimination. "You didn't pull those other suspects in yet, did you? The first thing you did was haul in the black man and accuse him of wrongdoing."

How'd he know about the other suspects? I leaned forward, eager to see if Lavene would take that remark in stride or press him on the information source.

"What other suspects?" Lavene asked.

"I'm black but I'm not stupid. Last time you collared me, I heard cops talking about the other guys. They're both white. That's how I know I have a basis for a case of racial profiling when this is over."

Lavene slouched in his seat. "Why don't you sue me right now?"

"I'm keeping my options open, but I'm making notes about how you treat me. You better believe I'm watching you as much as you're watching me."

"No one's accused you of murder. No one's put you in handcuffs, and you drove your own vehicle here at my invitation. Tell me how you've been mistreated."

"You singled me out." Otis Clement spoke emphatically, underscoring his words with dramatic arm gestures. The whites of his eyes showed. "You made me take time off work to come down here. You made me feel like filth because you think I'm a murderer."

"How do you know I haven't already interviewed them?"

His eyebrows raised. "You have?"

"Let's clear the air here," Lavene said. "I'm an investigative team member on a new suitcase murder," Lavene replied, still looking the soul of relaxation as he lounged in his chair. "Because of the case similarities, we're doing due diligence by interviewing our previous suitcase murder suspects and moving out from there. If you have an alibi, I'd love to hear it."

Otis covered his face with a large hand and then flipped his wrist toward Lavene, inadvertently flicking sweat towards the other man. Neither appeared to notice the flying moisture. "For what day? You don't know when this gal died according to the paper. You can't pin this murder on me. I have rights."

Lavene's spine stiffened. His icy smile chilled me, and I wasn't even in the room. "Have you ever been in this part of Georgia?"

Otis waggled his head back and forth so fast it looked like a shudder. More sweat flew, making me glad I wasn't sitting next to Lavene. "I considered a territory down here once, but it meant a cut in pay. I'd have to drive more to sell less. Not a good business model. Besides, I rarely work south of Savannah. I've never been in Marion or Sinclair County before today."

"Interesting," Lavene said. "Sure you don't want to change your story?"

"It isn't a story. I've never visited this town."

"And yet your cell phone puts you in this area in June and July."

"That makes no sense. I wasn't here, I tell you." Otis shrunk into himself, his shoulders bent. "This population size and the medical professional demographic are sub-par — not enough doctor's offices here to make it worth my while to stop. Plus, this is another rep's territory. I'm the north Georgia rep except when we're rolling out a new product."

Lavene held his peace, doing a fairly good imitation of Wayne's gunslinger eyes. Otis snapped his fingers. "Wait a minute. I drove to the Jacksonville Airport a few times while I worked a product launch in Savannah because we ran out of samples. The company ships their product on direct flights to Jacksonville or Atlanta. Maybe that's what this is all about."

"Do you remember the dates?" Lavene asked.

"No, but I have a mileage log of those trips in my phone. That's where I keep my travel log. Return my phone, and I'll check the dates."

"We'll do that in a bit. Tell me, what's your state of mind?"

"You're kidding, right? Look at the sweat pouring off my head. I'm nervous as a skinned cat. I would rather be anywhere than here."

"Duly noted. Moving on, you drive a black SUV. The vehicle is large enough that it could easily carry large items, such as a dead body."

"Not this about the car again! You people are outrageous. How many times do I have to explain that I drive a company vehicle? My personal car is a tiny sedan with a post-age stamp sized trunk. I love my job, and you people are gonna get me fired. I nearly lost my job last time over your false accusations. Now you've got another case and first thing you do is grab me. I didn't do anything wrong. Check me off your list and grill somebody else."

Lavene sat mute. Did he believe Otis Clement?

Finally, after the silence felt prickly to me, Lavene rose. "I'll get your phone from the property clerk."

While he was gone, Otis Clement scowled at the camera. He paced the room, shaking his arms and legs as if that would relieve tension. The perspiration stain on the back of his shirt took on the shape of South America. Finally, he sat down in his chair and laid his head on the table. It sounded like he was talking but I couldn't make out the words.

A few minutes later, Lavene returned with a large paper bag, which he left by the door, and a clear evidence bag containing a phone that he handed to Otis. With Lavene looking on, Otis unlocked his phone, accessed his calendar, and paged through screens for several moments. "I drove I-95 to Jacksonville twice from Savannah this summer. There and back on June 21 and another round trip on July 10. If you have cell tower records, they should match those dates."

Lavene made a note of the dates in a little notepad from his pocket. Then he placed the paper bag on the table. "Here's the rest of your stuff. You're free to go."

Otis stilled unnaturally. "Just like that?"

"Just like that."

"You won't haul me in again?"

"Your records for those dates match the cell tower data. If new information comes to light, we may have additional questions."

"Great. Just great. I'll be looking over my shoulder the rest of my life. That isn't fair." Otis stuffed his wallet and keys in his pocket and headed for the door. Lavene followed, his face inscrutable. The tape flickered, then cycled off.

Hmm. The evidence suggested Otis Clement was innocent, but there was something about him that didn't ring true. Trouble is I wasn't sure what that something was. Otis Clement had been scared, but not so scared he couldn't answer questions. He'd said he never visited our town, but the crime scene wasn't in town. It was less than a mile off the interstate.

Was that relevant?

I didn't know.

I ran the tape again, listening for nuances in his speech. On closer inspection, I could see why he'd failed a lie detector test previously. Between his sweating, nervous mannerisms, and octave ranging vocalizations, it was hard to get a clear read on Otis Clement.

It dawned on me there was a phone in this

room, and I was alone. This was the perfect time to call Rose's alleged sister in Tampa. Maybe she could shed some light on what happened down there, and I could figure out if I was going to jail. No judge in the world would believe the defense that an undercover angel made me tie up the mayor. I withdrew the slip with Raymondia LaFleur's name on it from my pocket. A woman answered on the first ring.

"Raymondia?" I asked, my voice squeaking with pent-up tension.

"Aack! Stop talking," a woman said. "Don't call this number again."

"I need to talk to you," I said, deepening my voice again.

"Too risky. Bye."

I hung up, disappointed. Stuffing the phone number in a pocket, I wandered down the hall to reception. "Any word on the kaolin mine search?"

"Still waiting," Tamika said, admiring her long pink fingernails.

A small bowl of candy on her desk made my mouth water. "Where's Roger Lavene?"

"He's working out of his Savannah office today trying to locate Darius Bronson. Why?"

"I wanted to discuss my interview impressions of Otis Clement with him. Is he coming here today?"

"You'll have to ask the boss."

A loud voice filled the corridor. "Powell!" Wayne yelled. "In here."

CHAPTER TWENTY-THREE

I entered the bullpen. "We need to work on your communication skills, Wayne. I don't like being yelled at."

"Can't change a tiger's stripes, so you're out of luck there. But, you're gonna wanna see this," Wayne said, waving me forward.

I joined him as he stood behind Mayes. On the computer monitor was a real place that closely resembled my sketch. "We found it?" I asked.

Wayne nodded. "Sure did. Grab your gear. The three of us are headed to Sandersville. I can't spare anyone else, but the three of us have an excellent chance of finding Kitty Ballenger. She'll sleep in her own bed this evening."

"I, uh, don't have any gear," I said, wringing my hands.

"Figure of speech. I've got your bulletproof vest in my Jeep already. Mayes, your stuff handy?"

"In Baxley's truck. Should we follow you?"

"My consultant rides with me, but it would be a good idea to have a backup vehicle that's unmarked. Follow in her truck. The county will pay for her gas."

"If we're headed out of town, I need to make alternate childcare arrangements with my folks."

"Go ahead outside and make the call. I'll be there in a sec," Wayne said. "First, though, report on the Otis Clement interview."

"He spoke the truth," I said. "Though he appears very anxious, I don't think he's our guy."

"Got it. Let's rescue Kitty. She'll be able to ID the S.O.B. that snatched her."

Mayes followed me out and listened while I made the call. My parents were happy to meet Larissa's bus. No worries at all.

After I pocketed my phone, I searched Mayes' eyes. "You okay after meeting with him? Wayne can be overbearing."

"Wayne's used to being king of the hill. My presence here challenges him in ways that make him uncomfortable."

"Is that one of your Zen comments?"

"Nope, that's one of experience after listening to him ream me out for ten minutes straight. You'd think I kidnapped you or beat you or something. The guy thinks he owns you."

"But you set him straight?"

"I did. We're going to be married. My tribe is in favor of the union, and your mother gave us her blessing."

I nodded, but a wedge of unease threatened my calm. "What's this about your tribe? You asked their permission?"

"It was assumed that I would marry within our race, to strengthen intertribal bonds, but a union with you brings honor and prestige to our people. And our children will have the best of both worlds."

"Children. We haven't talked about children." Good grief. Was I ready to start over with an infant in the house? "This is happening so fast."

"I already love Larissa as if she were my own. It is my hope that our union will yield children."

I must've made a face because he reached over to stroke my hair behind my ear.

"Don't you want to make babies with me, u ge-yu-di?"

"Maybe. I mean yes, I mean, I don't know. This is so sudden. We need to discuss this."

He studied me, concern bracketing his dark eyes. "Were there medical complications during your prior pregnancy or delivery?"

"No, nothing like that. But babies change your life. There's a lot of not sleeping and plenty of colic and dirty diapers. You have no idea what you are asking for."

"I'm asking for a life with you and whatever comes with it. I'm not asking you to give up your career, or be a stay at home mom. We are a team in all things."

I searched his face, not daring to breathe. "You sure?"

"More than sure. You are my heart." He kissed me lightly on the lips, his eyes soft with emotion. "You are my life."

My arms wrapped around his neck, but my eyes brimmed with moisture. He wanted kids. How many men would admit that?

He noticed I was crying right away. "What's this?"

"I'm a sucker for a man who loves babies, that's what." I gave him a quick kiss. "I wanted more children with Roland, but the timing was never right. Truthfully, I'd given up on the idea of having more children. I'm not repelled by the idea. I'm taken by surprise. We have so much to talk about with the marriage between our jobs, tribal responsibilities, dreamwalker responsibilities, and our families. Surely, the talk of babies isn't our top priority?"

He broke into a radiant smile. "Whatever you say."

That's what he said, but suddenly I knew with every sense I possessed that he was holding out on me. "What?"

The door banged shut behind us, and we startled apart. Wayne strode toward us. I studied Mayes' smug expression and leaned over to whisper in his ear, "You will tell me later."

"New plan," Wayne said. "We're meeting Lavene in Savannah at the airport. The GBI has a helicopter we can use, which will be invaluable if Kitty is alive. We can airlift her to a hospital. Everybody in my Jeep. Mayes, grab your gear."

"One sec." He reached into the bed of the truck and removed a black duffel with his name sewn on it. "Ready."

Wayne nodded appreciably. "Your boss spring for the gear bags?"

"She did. Our deputies kept getting their gear interchanged. The monogrammed duffels eliminated the gear mix-up issue. We keep the duffels in our duty car or in our locker."

"We'll be ordering those duffels for down here. This cross-pollinating of squads couldn't have come at a better time."

Like I believed that. I barely suppressed a snicker as I headed for the Jeep's back passenger door. Wayne motioned me forward to the front seat. I did as he said, thinking he was being petty about not letting Mayes and me sit together. I didn't fuss though. If we were going to find Kitty Ballenger, I needed to conserve my energy for whatever dreamwalker challenge the afternoon brought.

To my surprise, Lavene piloted the helicopter. Wayne rode shotgun, while Mayes, and I sat in the rear. We programmed the coordinates of the location into the flight plan, and Lavene and Wayne had other agencies and the Washington County Sheriff's Office on standby.

Blue sky stretched endlessly before us and the ground passed swiftly underneath us. We were high enough that I couldn't make out the people below, but houses and forests were visible. The seat had an interesting vibration that permeated the marrow of my bones.

After the crazy tumbling I was used to in the drift, I was surprised at the queasy sensation being in the helicopter brought on. As if he sensed my distress, Mayes reached across and held my hand. My fingers closed around his thankfully.

At the same time, a lullaby sounded in my head, deeply resonant and comforting. I smiled, letting him know I was grateful for his kindness.

The flight took barely an hour, with only one hundred thirty-eight miles between Savannah and Sandersville. We'd donned our bulletproof vests before takeoff, ear muffs too. Mayes and my ear protection sets had no com links, but Wayne and Lavene had the works in their ear protection helmets.

Finally, we circled a large canyon cut-out of earth. The ridges and the water exactly matched my vision. I didn't see any kind of enclosure, pen, or cage in the area where I thought it should be. I chewed my lip as we sat down on a flat surface near the turquoise water.

The rotor blades slowly wound down. I unhooked my seat restraint, my fingers clumsy with emotion. This was the place. I knew it as well as I knew my name.

"Where is she?" the sheriff asked me.

"I don't know. I need to get my bearings."

"Make it snappy." He shuddered. "All this place needs is creepy music, and it could be the site of the next alien invasion."

Mayes helped me step down from the

chopper. It felt beyond strange to be standing in a place I'd seen in a dreamwalk. I pointed east of our position. "This was what she saw. To get the correct perspective of looking down on this vista, she had to have been up there."

"Want to try a life scan search?" Mayes asked. "That would narrow down the directionality."

My mind screamed no as I crossed my arms over my chest. I hastened to explain. "Kitty hijacked my body last time I connected with her. I won't give her the opportunity again."

"Then up we go," Mayes said.

I eagerly trailed him up the manmade ridge. Every now and again, I stopped to look back. We zigged a bit more to the north after the second turnaround-and-study-the-view moment. The tree cover, which had been sparse to nonexistent, began to fill in and the going became tougher as we slogged through briars and underbrush.

We shouted her name repeatedly, certain we were close enough Kitty could hear us. The echoes of our voices died down, but there was no answering response. "We're too late," I said. "It's too quiet."

"She's here," Mayes said. "I trust your dreamwalk."

"Something's wrong." My skin prickled. "I feel it."

"Call Oliver," Mayes said. "Have him track her."

I brightened at that idea. "Okay. Hang onto me. Don't let the sheriff interrupt the process."

Now that I'd interacted with Oliver multiple times, I could enter a lucid dream quickly. The disorientation of going from my reality to the murky one where earthbound spirits existed was minimal. I suppressed a wave of pride and called my ghost dog. He came immediately as if he'd been waiting on me. I made a fuss over him, calling him handsome and rubbing his ears. He licked my face until I laughed.

"Okay, boy. We need to find Kitty. You searched for her before. She's still missing and she was here yesterday. Can you find her?"

Oliver took off running. I followed him virtually, glad to be no longer challenged by underbrush. We moved through the objects in our path until we came to a hidden clearing. Oliver stopped and barked.

I glanced around. No Kitty. No cage. No nothing. I turned in a circle, studying the view in every direction. The kaolin mine stretched behind me, so she had to have been facing the other way. I turned in that direction, but the foliage blocked my line of sight. She had to have been higher.

Glancing up, I saw missing bark from a large branch overhead. Something had been slung over that branch, a rope or a chain. Kitty had been suspended from that tree.

I thanked Oliver, made note of the location, and vectored back to where the men clustered. No one would like the answer I had to share, but there was no help for it.

I awakened and found Lavene and Wayne standing beside us. Wayne seemed like he barely had made a climb, but Lavene's shirt was sweat-stained. Moisture dotted his florid, scowling face.

Uh-oh. He's pissed. I wonder why? I wished I had better news, but I wasn't in the fiction-writing biz. I was in the finding people biz, and we'd missed.

"I found the spot where he kept Kitty, but she's gone," I said. "He knew we were coming."

"That's ridiculous," Lavene said, stomping a foot. "Only a small number of people knew we were on our way here. This whole trip was a wild goose chase. You wasted my time and valuable taxpayer dollars."

"I wasted nothing." My fingers curled into my palms so tightly the nails bit into the soft flesh. "I can take you to the place. Bring your scent dogs or whatever you like to check my findings. Kitty was here, but she's gone now."

"This is a crock," Lavene said. "There's no physical proof. We've wasted half the day on this trek to nowhere. My boss will be livid. I should arrest you for misuse of government resources."

"Easy on my consultant, Ace." Wayne turned to me. "Take us to the spot. Perhaps the kidnapper overlooked some evidence."

Mayes took my hand and we walked to the location, some five hundred yards distant. I gestured to the raw mark on the tree branch overhead. "The view I saw was from overhead. She was suspended from that tree."

"Everyone stand still," Mayes said. "I'll check for prints and tracks."

He ranged out from the area immediately under the tree. Lavene and Wayne started arguing again, but no matter what negative thing Lavene said, Wayne never wavered in his faith in me.

Mayes returned. "A large vehicle came here from the north. If Kitty's in a cage, the guy's got a flatbed and a hoist of some kind."

"There are no tire tracks that I see,"

Lavene said. "You're making this up."

"The tire tracks begin a little further out. He wiped the tracks from this area. I found two rotting apples. I think they were used to drug Kitty."

"We'll need those apples," Wayne said. "Let's get photos of the site, castings of the tire tracks, and collect any additional evidence we find."

"What a waste of time," Lavene said. "We should be interviewing suspects instead of chasing after shadows and dreams."

"Not a waste," Wayne replied with a snarl. "This is police work 101. We're collecting evidence and generating leads. Maybe bigshot GBI agents don't do it this way, but I do."

My stomach rumbled, making my face flush with heat. "Sorry. We left so abruptly, I didn't have time to grab a lunch."

"I've got snacks in the chopper," Lavene said. "Might as well help yourself."

"You know what this means," Wayne said, ignoring Lavene's grumpy mood. "The killer has someone inside law enforcement feeding him information. I can tell you right now, it isn't my department."

Lavene planted his fists on his hips. "It sure as hell isn't mine either."

"And," Wayne continued, "by virtue of

extrapolation from the fact you didn't nab your Suitcase guy last time, Kitty's abductor stands a good chance of being our Suitcase Killer. Not much chance two serials would be working the same M.O."

"I strongly disagree," Lavene said. "No one in my shop is a rat. This is all a ruse to discredit me. Burnell Escoe warned me about you people and he was right. I've done everything by the book. No one could be more diligent about following procedures."

Burnell Escoe was a GBI agent we worked with on another case. He'd been a thorn in our side the entire time. Now it seemed Lavene was cut from the same mold. Pity that.

"Wasn't my guys," Wayne said with certainty. "I'll go to the mat on that. Someone tipped this guy off that we were coming, and the only people who knew our destination on my end rode in the chopper with us. They haven't been out of my sight. That means the problem is in your shop."

"Huh." Lavene stubbed the ground with his shoe. He seemed to be deep in thought. "I see how you may believe the leak is at my end. I'll humor you. Here's what I did. I notified the GBI and the Sandersville Sheriff's Office. I also filed a flight plan at the airport," Lavene said. "I can't believe one of our own would aid and abet a serial killer."

"The physical evidence suggests the guy drives a big rig. Somehow he can get the person-sized cage on the rig and travel without his victim being seen."

"It's easy to cover up flatbed objects with a secured tarp," I chimed in. "I see vehicles on the road all the time and wonder what's bulging under those odd-shaped tarps."

"If he drove on the interstate, he's required to enter the weigh stations," Wayne said. "I'll request the footage at the nearest ones for the last twelve hours, then we'll follow up on their load deliveries. No delivery will be a red flag."

"That's a lot of man hours. Worse, we're back to needle-in-a-haystack mode. We don't know that she's even in the state," Lavene said, his shoulders bowing. "She could be anywhere."

I thought about the rotting apples we'd found. Kitty wasn't eating. Her life clock kept ticking faster and faster. We needed a break in the case, more than the location of where she used to be.

"Time is against us," I said. "This guy is starving her to death. All along we've thought our guy was a copycat killer so I believe he stayed on his home turf. We have to move fast."

The only way to beat a leak was to back-channel everything, but even then, time was working against us. Could we flush the kidnapper in time to save Kitty's life?

CHAPTER TWENTY-FOUR

We helicoptered back to Savannah and then drove south on the interstate to Sinclair County. I opted for the backseat this time and Mayes rode shotgun. After navigating the heavy traffic around Savannah, Wayne engaged Mayes in a football conversation, and I faced my disappointment about the case.

I'd failed to rescue Kitty. Her abductor knew we were coming and moved her from the kaolin site. The only way I knew to find her was to try another dreamwalk. I dreaded it. What if she hijacked my mind again? Could I block the intrusion? Rose would know, but my Other World contact was unavailable.

I absently massaged the rose tattoo she'd placed on my wrist, but it felt like skin instead of an energized conduit. That spiritual connection I shared with Rose had ceased. Three days ago she kidnapped us

251

for that Tampa jaunt. Had she gotten in trouble with her boss? Or had she pulled another crazy stunt and not fared as well?

Rose worked from a hidden agenda. She claimed to be an angel masquerading as a demon, both powerful beings. Working undercover was dangerous, what with the threat of exposure and possible indoctrination into the adversary's mindset. Rose had a boss on the angel side, so she must have one on the demon side as well. Glad I wasn't her. Dealing with Wayne was enough for me.

I removed my sunglasses, rubbed my throbbing temples, and wished I knew another way to find Kitty. Mayes glanced over his shoulder. "Headache?"

"All we have are questions. Kitty's still a captive, the Suitcase Killer is at large, and Rose is offline. Nothing feels solid. It's like I'm standing on a wobbly platform and I can't catch my balance."

"Sounds like we should knock off early and grab a beer," Wayne said.

My stomach rebelled at the thought of alcohol. "I was thinking more of my mom's restorative broth and meditating in the woods."

Wayne groaned. "Boring."

"Sounds perfect," Mayes said. "They

invited us for dinner to celebrate our engagement."

"I won't make it to dinner," I said, donning my dark glasses again. "I'm hungry now."

"Gee, Powell," Wayne said. "You got a tapeworm or something? We just ate."

"Chips and soda aren't my idea of lunch. I need protein. Can we stop somewhere?"

"Nope. I gotta get back for damage control. Lavene is pissed about his organization's leak. We have to restrict information flow. Lavene's agreed to follow my lead, so I gotta figure out our next move. Y'all got any ideas?"

"Find Kitty," I said. "I need to do another dreamwalk, but it has to wait until tomorrow."

"Why's that?" Wayne asked. "We got plenty of afternoon left. You're still on the clock."

"I pushed my limits yesterday doing five dreamwalks. Since I get one vision per item, I can't waste an attempt." I chose my words carefully. "Connecting remotely with a living person is different with scary consequences. I'm very concerned for Kitty, but I need to safeguard myself. Essentially, each time I connect with her, I'm walking a tightrope with no net."

"We can't lose you," Mayes said. "What about Tab? Does he share this ability?"

"I don't know," I answered. "He rarely volunteers information about his dreamwalker days unless I ask. Luckily, we have an eyewitness available who can answer this question."

"Who?" Mayes asked.

"If Daddy searched for living people, it would've been at the sheriff's request. Wayne? Did y'all work any missing person's cases?"

"Lemme think for sec," Wayne said. "I remember one instance. A little gal went missing over Thomasville way. Me and Tab rode over there and checked things out on their sheriff's invite, but Tab had nothing to offer, as I recall."

I leaned forward, straining against my seatbelt to hear every word. "How'd that case turn out? Was the child dead or living?"

"Now that's the downright interesting part. The kid was hiding with her Mama, but I didn't get the word for a coupla years. Meanwhile, the dad took up with another woman, beat the tar out of her, nearly killing her, and got arrested for it. During his trial, his wife's hospital records came to light. Turned out he'd also beat his kid. The

254

judge and jury threw the book at him."

The way he drew that out, I knew there was more. "And?"

"Kid abusers are despised in prison. This guy didn't last long. Found him dead in the showers, beaten to a pulp."

Gross, but, the story offered a glimmer of hope for me. If my dad believed the Thomasville man was a bad guy, he wouldn't put a child back in danger. He might have advice for my current situation.

"Good to know," I said, settling back into the seat.

"I know what you're thinking." Wayne's eyes met mine in the rearview mirror. "You think your dad held out on me because he knew the score. I always wondered if he did. I asked him pointblank one time and he mentioned the wheels of justice revolved slowly. Never figured him for a philosopher. He always seemed more of a throwback or retro type to me."

"Whoa," Mayes said, as if he were halting a horse. "Watch what you say about my new family."

I smiled inside. Mayes had my back. Maybe the wheels of karma were turning here as well. I may have lost Rose, but I'd gained Mayes as a helpmate. An excellent trade-off, in my opinion.

"Thanks, Mayes," I said. "So we're all on the same page, I'm grabbing lunch soon as we get back. I don't care what time it is."

"Might as well get burgers for all of us while you're out," Wayne said, exiting the interstate. "I need Mayes following up with the weigh stations and reviewing their films. Join him on that when you return. I'll give a press briefing to the vultures on our lawn, then I need action items from both of you. Don't let me down. The world is watching our every move."

He seemed to be seeking reassurance, so that's what I gave him. "Sure."

Ignoring the flock of reporters at the main entrance, I kissed Mayes goodbye and drove away in my truck, glad for my ball cap and sunglasses. Maybe the vultures wouldn't recognize me. To my dismay, two vans followed me, so I hit the drive-through at the nearest burger joint and inhaled my lunch on the short ride back to the office.

Wayne had a strict policy on use of the employee parking lot. Media were not allowed. That didn't stop one woman from yelling through the fence. "Baxley Powell!"

I glanced her way. The woman behind the chain-link fence was dressed for an Atlanta boardroom, with a hint of exposed cleavage, gleaming white teeth, big hair, and flawless makeup. Her shapely legs seemed to go on forever beneath her pencil thin skirt.

I mentally dismissed her request and focused on juggling the sack of burgers and fries with the drink carrier of milkshakes. My mouth watered for more vanilla shake.

"What can you tell us about the FBI investigation of your boss?" the woman demanded.

My feet stopped, while my brain processed the question. Was the FBI here? And if they were, in what regard?

"Ms. Powell, two agents from the Jacksonville office entered the building," the woman continued, her voice sounding authoritative. "Are y'all close to making an arrest in the Suitcase Murder case?"

Summoning my best eat-dirt-or-die smile, I answered, "No comment."

CHAPTER TWENTY-FIVE

When I entered the building, everyone clustered at the opposite end of the hall from Wayne's office, trying to eavesdrop and knowing Wayne would fire them if he caught them listening. Virg and Ronnie bummed a pack of fries from me before I found Mayes looking at grainy films of trucks on a computer monitor.

"What's going on?" I asked.

"Keep your voice down," Mayes said, reaching in the bag for his late lunch. "The feds were in Wayne's office when we returned. According to Tamika, they've been systematically checking each computer."

I sat beside him. "For leaks on the case?"

"For connections to Tampa. To the disgraced mayor and the bank swindle."

No way. I scooted my seat closer and whispered, "What? How?"

He spoke softly in words meant for my ears only. "Raymondia LaFleur is right in the middle of everything."

The fluorescent bulbs seemed overly bright. The room threatened to spin. "They said that?"

"I heard Wayne deny knowing any Raymondia LaFleurs and trying to throw the feebs out. Hell, the whole office heard him yelling. I thought the roof would fly off."

My pulse sounded so loud in my ears I could barely think. Oh. My. God. The trail from the Tampa heist led straight to our city. And Wayne. That wasn't good. Wayne was blameless in the matter, but Mayes and I weren't. We'd tied the man up and who knew what else.

"What now?" I whispered, my hasty meal feeling cannonball heavy in my gut.

"We're following orders, that's what. Wayne asked for leads on the trucks. That's what I'm doing."

"What if they question us?"

He regarded me with a strange, shuttered expression. "We have an alibi for Sunday night."

"And Wayne doesn't?" I shot back.

"Let's hope he does. Otherwise, this could go badly for him."

The thought of Wayne going to prison for something we did was wrong. Out and out wrong. "I can't let him take the fall for us."

"Keep your voice down," Mayes cautioned. "Help me cross check the license plates and the bills of lading."

He was right, though I hated being in the dark like this. I kept my ears cocked toward the hall, hoping to hear Wayne's voice at any minute. Virg and Ronnie came in briefly. Virg grabbed Wayne's burger and Ronnie took his shake. I didn't care. If Wayne wanted lunch when his interrogation was over, I'd make another food run.

"Bingo," Mayes said.

"You found something?" I asked, lifting my gaze from my monitor to his.

"Yep. This guy's an indie trucker. He claimed to be headed to Orlando, but his rig didn't go through the Florida station on his route. He should've checked in there hours ago."

"But his box trailer looks like every other truck on the road. It isn't an open flatbed carrying a woman in a cage."

"Which could be how he's escaped detection so far."

The energy in his voice infected me. "How so?"

"If the cage fits inside a trailer and he's drugging his captive, all he needs besides a forklift is a rope, a pulley, and a heavy counterweight to suspend her cage over a branch. The trailer itself would be a counter-weight."

"I don't understand why anyone would do this. Who would enjoy starving another human being? And then why stuff the bodies in a suitcase for disposal? This guy is good at flying under the radar, so why not bury the bones afterward? The evidence trail makes no sense."

"It makes sense to him, that's what matters. I'm issuing a statewide BOLO for this rig, but we'll keep looking in case this lead runs dry."

The sheriff would hate Mayes being proactive. I decided to gently remind Mayes he wasn't the boss. "Shouldn't you wait for Wayne?"

He jerked his thumb toward Wayne's office. "The feds have been gnawing on Wayne for over an hour. They've got leverage on him, or he would've thrown them out."

"I don't understand."

Mayes gave a cold smile. "Wayne has a certain reputation among the sheriff's association. My boss warned me about his God complex. I've seen firsthand how he operates, and it doesn't surprise me that he plays fast and loose with the rules."

That news took the starch out of my spine. "This is terrible."

"Maybe. Maybe not."

I tugged on my ear. Mayes was always so direct, so sure. "What?"

"Let's wait and see. I hope he comes through unscathed, but if he doesn't, there's an opportunity here."

The dots connected, and I froze for a long breathless moment. "You *are* after his job!"

"I admit, I'm in a strong position right now. I've been temporarily detailed here. I have prior experience as interim sheriff. I play by the rules. If Wayne is sidelined, it could be good for me. For us."

For us. He was right. If the sheriff were out of the picture, Mayes had a better than average shot at running this place until the next election. He was a proven leader, unlike Wayne's deputy pool of non-self-starters, and Mayes was conveniently at hand.

Loyalty mattered to me. I'd been loyal to Wayne because of the job, but now my loyalty was to my fiancé. My heart knew this, but my head balked at the new truth. Mayes came first in my heart and in my loyalty. The sheriff came in a distant second. Sure, I felt sorry his current trouble was our fault. I had to try to make this right.

"I see," I managed. "Anyone else connect the fed visit with Tampa?"

"Who knows? None of them are on task right now, and I don't have the authority to order them back to work. If I'm in charge here, things will change."

Everyone around here was used to how Wayne operated. Mayes wouldn't have an easy task if he stepped into Wayne's shoes. Even so, my loyalty split. I wanted Wayne to rise or fall on his own merit, but if Mayes was sheriff, he wouldn't have to work all over the state on that cold case squad the state forensic anthropologist wanted to launch.

We found two more discrepancies among the truckers who stopped at the weigh stations in our time-frame. Mayes issued a statewide BOLO on all three rigs.

Five o'clock came and went. The feds didn't emerge from Wayne's office. Tamika packed up and switched the phone lines over to the 9-1-1 center. She mentioned that Mayes had a package on her desk and left. Virg and Ronnie rotated off shift and second shift came on. Mayes handled the informal shift change briefing, and the men accepted his authority without question.

Just when I was thinking we'd never get to go home, Wayne's office door opened. Mayes and I hurried to the conference room door where we'd been waiting for Wayne to emerge. Two dark-haired men in black suits stepped into the hallway, one of each side of Wayne. My heart leapt in my throat as they strode our way. Was Wayne free to go? Would they question us next?

They made straight for us. The suited men wore stoic expressions. Wayne looked like he'd lost his last dollar in a slot machine.

"Powell, call my wife and tell her I won't be home tonight," Wayne said. "Mayes, you're in charge until I return. I sent out an email to everyone announcing your status as interim sheriff. Take the keys to my Jeep and my office."

"What's your status, and what are my orders?" Mayes asked, accepting and pocketing the keys without a flicker of emotion.

"Business as usual for the office, and my status is confidential." Wayne followed the feds out the back door.

The door slammed, echoing down the empty corridor. "Crap!" I said.

"You didn't see this coming? Even after our conversation?" Mayes asked.

"I saw it coming, but I drew the short end of the assignment stick. You manage the deputies while I handle the wife. Dottie will be livid. She'll blame me, and this time she'll be right."

CHAPTER TWENTY-SIX

Chicken that I was, I phoned Dottie instead of telling her in person. She answered my call, but it could have been because I used the line in Wayne's office. She probably thought it was her husband calling instead.

After the hellos and how-are-yous, I got down to business. "Dottie, there's no easy way to say this. Two FBI agents out of Jacksonville came here today and spent the afternoon with Wayne in his office."

"Why?" Dottie demanded.

"All he told us was that his status was confidential."

"What?" Dottie shrieked.

Her voice blasted through the phone like an air raid siren. Grimacing, I shifted the phone away from my ear. "Please, let me finish. When they finally emerged from his office, Wayne appointed a deputy to be in charge while he was gone and then he left with the feds."

"When's he coming home?" Dottie asked.

"He said he wouldn't be home tonight. That's all I know."

"This isn't right. They got no business coming after my Wayne. I don't believe it. You're covering for him."

"I'm telling you the truth."

"Something's rotten. Y'all think I don't see what's going on. I know you're to blame. What did you do?"

I swallowed around the lump in my throat. "Wayne's my boss, and I follow his orders."

"Humph. A likely story. The whole time your Daddy worked with Wayne, the feds never came a-calling. You brought this trouble down on his head. Virg and Ronnie and the others don't have sense enough to rate a federal investigation."

I winced. "I'm sorry you feel that way. If we hear anything at the office, I'll let you know first thing."

"What about that Jeep? Can I come get it?"

"Uh, no. Wayne handed the keys to the interim sheriff."

"The boys there understand that's my car. I'll come right down and get it."

"No ma'am, that won't do. Sam Mayes is the interim sheriff. He needs the computer and radio access in Wayne's Jeep as he goes about his job."

"Humph. I don't know any Sam Mayes. Where'd he come from?"

"North Georgia. He's on a work detail down here."

"Hold the bus. This is your boyfriend we're talking about? No way am I standing for this claptrap. I'm coming down there right this minute and getting my car."

"Dottie, please calm down. Take care of your kids. Wayne will check in with you when he can."

"He's got his phone?"

"Far as I know."

"I'm calling that rat bastard right now. He can't do this to me. Darn his sorry hide."

The phone slammed in my ear. I turned to Mayes who'd overheard the last bit of the exchange. "That went well. Not."

"She needed to vent," Mayes said. "She'll be okay now."

"Betcha she blows up Wayne's phone with calls."

"I'd lose that bet." He extended his hand. "I have something for you."

I clasped his hand and felt myself tugged his way. "Is it dinner, because I swear I'm hungry enough to eat an entire horse, not that I would eat a horse. That would be gross."

267

He kissed me quiet to cease my babbling. "That's better," he said.

When he withdrew a small velvety black box from his pocket, I felt all fluttery inside. "Is that what I think it is?"

He nodded. "Your engagement ring arrived while we were working. I hope you like it."

The package on Tamika's desk. It must've been the ring. My eyes misted. "I'll love it."

"If you don't, we can choose something together. This was made by Native Americans using Black Hills gold."

He opened the box, and I sighed with delight. The design was a stunning array of natural elements on a black enamel inlay of the shiny gold. A dainty diamond glittered in the center. "It's beautiful."

He slid the ring on my finger. A perfect fit. I admired how it looked on my hand. Not too girly. Not too sparkly. It was just right. I lifted my gaze to his. "I love it."

His face relaxed into a genuine smile. "Good."

After a kiss, I stepped away. "Now if we've got half the sense we started with, we better hightail it before Dottie shows up to steal the Jeep."

"I'll follow you to your parents' place."

The engagement ring was a big hit with my family. Lots of hugs and congratulations all around. Running Bear and Gentle Dove were present and genuinely happy for us. We finished off dinner, and I had a quiet moment with my father.

We walked outside to his favorite sitting place, a bench with a woody view, his grey braid trailing down his back. Twilight had come and gone and the starry sky was blanketed by night. Just enough light to make out large objects.

"You're glowing with happiness," Dad said. "It's about time you started living your life again. About time you wanted a family."

I dashed the tears of emotion away from my cheeks. "That's what Larissa said too. I hope I wasn't a drag before."

"It's like you've awakened from a long sleep. Your mom and I are very happy for you."

I hugged his approval close to my heart, warmed by the notion of enlarging our family to include Mayes. Unfortunately, I needed to get my father's take on the finer points of my unusual gifts. "Thanks, but we should talk about dreamwalking. I'm concerned about recent events. May I pick your brain?"

"Sure. What's on your mind?"

"A lot, as it turns out." He listened, stony-faced, as I recited how Rose kidnapped Mayes and me for her purposes in Tampa. "But that's not all," I continued. "As you know, a dreamwalk with the missing girl, Kitty Ballenger, led to an out of body experience. How can I prevent it? More, I want to understand how it happened. Did my association with Rose make me vulnerable to psychic attack?"

Forest noises and rustlings filled the ensuing silence. My father retreated to his thoughts, but his peaceful energy surrounded me. He never judged my actions or criticized my fumbling with my ability. One day I hoped to do the same for Larissa, but today I needed the benefit of his experience and wisdom.

"I don't have the answers you seek," my father said. "You're more powerful than I ever was, and nothing of the sort happened to me. Within these last few months, you've breezed through what for me was a lifetime of experiences, and you've done it all with your customary grace."

"Thanks, I think." I listened to the night sounds all around us, finding solace in the wholeness of creation. "How can I fix this?"

He gave a slow smile and stroked my back. "I believe your issue will resolve naturally in due time. What will be, will be."

I leaned into his touch. "I'll try to be more accepting, but it's hard for me to comprehend the unusual experiences. I feel so vulnerable. How do I hold it together?"

Dad's arm snugged me in close. His body radiated comfort and assurance. "You know, my mother experienced something like this when she was at the same life stage. I'll lend you her journals."

My eyebrows arched. "She wrote about possession?"

"Some."

"I'd love to see those."

Mayes joined us, a sleepy Larissa in his arms. "Ready to go home?"

My family. They looked great together. I rose. "Of course. Let me say goodnight to my mom."

Mom gave me an extended, teary-eyed hug, longer than normal, and it had me wondering all the way home. Was I missing something?

CHAPTER TWENTY-SEVEN

During the night, Mayes got a phone call. I groaned at the intrusion and rolled over, but I couldn't drop back into a deep sleep. Through a sleepy haze I heard him say, "I'm on my way."

After he ended the call and rose from the bed, I stirred, sitting up. Darkness blanketed the room and my windows. "What's going on?"

I heard the rustle of clothing, the rasp of a zipper. The mattress gave a little as he sat beside me. "My BOLO paid off," Mayes said. "A patrol cop spotted one of the rigs. It's parked for the night at a truck stop halfway across the state. I'm headed there now to check it out."

With each word he spoke, I awakened more. The truck. Kitty. Adrenaline rushed through my body. "Should I come?"

"Stay here with Larissa and the pets where you're safe and warm. We have a one out of three chance this is the right vehicle. No need to wake your folks for kid sitting or drag a sleeping child with us unless this is the real deal. If something's amiss, I can confiscate the semi and have it towed to Sinclair County. For obvious reasons, I'd rather not do that unless I'm certain, and I have to be careful I don't run afoul of the sheriff up there. We don't want to tip our hand to anyone if this isn't our guy."

That was a lot to process with a muzzy head, but I got the gist. He was going to slay dragons for the cause, and I was to keep the home fires burning. As much as my practical nature agreed with his reasoning, part of me resented being left behind. "What about Lavene?"

"He's out of the loop for now. Not that I think he's dirty, but he plays by the rules. Any information sent his way feeds into the federal knowledge bank. With a leak over there, we can't risk updating him."

"Understood." And I did, which sucked. My face must have revealed my disappointment.

"Don't worry," Mayes said, kissing me goodbye. "You have a major role in this investigation. Right now I need to do my job. I'll touch base once I've vetted the rig."

"Be safe," I managed to say.

He bent down to kiss my engagement ring. "Always, u ge-yu-di."

A moment later, he was gone. He walked so softly through the house that none of the dogs or cats even stirred, as if they already knew this was the new status quo. I hit the pillow, pulled the covers up all cozy and tight, but sleep wouldn't come.

I checked the time. Three a.m. Wednesday night had become Thursday morning. I'd normally be rising at six thirty to get Larissa ready for school. If I stayed awake, I'd miss hours of sleep. I tried to find a quiet place in my mind, but my thoughts wouldn't settle. Kitty was out there somewhere. My fiancé might be heading into danger. A serial killer was stalking defenseless women in our state. Wayne was in trouble, and Tampa, how could I forget that? I might have committed several crimes while Rose hijacked my body.

Rose. Where the heck was she? I fingered my moldavite pendant, my touchstone, and tried a quick dreamwalk to find her and get some answers. I zipped through the drift, waded through the Other World inky fog, but she didn't appear. However she'd linked us previously, whether it was physically or spiritually, that connection had been severed.

I awakened in my bed, hands clenched in frustration. No Rose. I was truly on my own, navigating the realm of the dead by myself. I had the general hang of it now, but I kept encountering special circumstances. My choices led to more anomalies, more things I didn't comprehend.

Maybe that was the whole point of trial and error. Something over there had it in for me and all those moments I made a good decision in the clutch, they made it work against me.

I shuddered at that awful thought. I detested other people taking over my head or body. I had no problems encountering spirits in their realm, but they needed to leave me alone in mine. Which reminded me I had the box of my grandmother's journals that dad tucked in my truck. I'd stashed the box in the dining room when we came home last night.

Quietly, I padded that way, intending to carry the box back to bed, but my stomach rumbled. I fixed a ham sandwich, downed it with a glass of milk, and lugged the box back to bed. Closing the bedroom door, I turned on the light, propped up the pillows, and looked at the journals with interest.

The spines of the leather volumes were creased and the edges of the pages yellowed.

Spidery handwriting in thin black ink filled the pages, and a date prefaced each journal entry.

Might as well start at the beginning. I carefully placed all twelve books on the bed and arranged them in chronological order. I selected the first one and began reading. Leila Nesbitt had been an only child, same as my dad and me. Same as Larissa, come to think of it.

Her younger cousin, Emerald drove her nuts tagging around after her. I'd known Uncle Emerald vaguely, and once as a child I got trapped in a bad dreamwalk in his favorite chair. That's when I learned to shield my thoughts.

Teenaged Leila wrote of normal everyday things, of yearning for more, of wondering about boys, of despairing to fill her mother's shoes. Her mom was the Dreamwalker at that time, and her dad was a fisherman, so she was often left to her own devices. She learned to cook the bounty of food left at their door, and she befriended stray animals. I felt an immediate kinship with her.

She began the journal with entries about being her mother's caretaker in the aftermath of dreamwalks. She developed the recipe for restorative broth that my mom currently made for me. I noted the page number so that I could come back later and copy the recipe.

In the second journal, I read that tragedy struck at fourteen when her parents were both lost at sea. Leila went to live with her cousin Emerald's family. The dreamwalker talent awakened full force the night her mother perished. She struggled to learn the ropes, same as me. Her dark hair developed a telltale white widow's peak, which made her livid. I totally got where she was coming from. My hair color change had also started with a white streak. We had so much in common.

A boy came into her life, briefly, an upper classman friend of Emerald's from school, but he moved on and enlisted in the military. A training accident took his life, and just like that, Leila Nesbitt became an unwed mother. His family wanted the baby to take his father's last name, but Leila said no. The child would be a Nesbitt.

I heard a toilet flush and dog claws ticking on wooden floors. A glance at the windows showed day had dawned. Reluctantly, I set the journals aside and rose to care for my child.

"Where's Mayes?" Larissa asked while eating her scrambled eggs. The cats looked on from atop the fridge, the dogs guarded her chair.

"Off following a lead that developed overnight."

"Oh. He's coming back, right?"

"Yes. Of course. Why do you ask?"

"Mama Lacey and Pap have a good marriage, but that's not the norm for our family."

Her comment brought me up short. "Oh?"

Larissa nodded with the uncanny wisdom of a ten year old. "I read those journals last year. If your life goes the way of Great gramma Leila, you may have many sorrows."

I rushed over and hugged her. "I'm not Leila, and I make my own decisions. I'm not going anywhere, either. I'm your Mom. Don't you forget it."

"Thanks, Mom." She pushed out a little so she could gaze at me. "I wasn't questioning your commitment to our family. Just saying that if history repeats itself, Mayes might move on."

I mulled her words for a few moments before I answered. Mayes wanted to be part of our family, wanted it more than sticking close to his home and tribe. He wouldn't distance himself from us on purpose, of that I was certain.

"Here's what I know. We can't control

what anyone else does. We take them at their word and focus on our own actions and hearts. We meet each day with grace and do our best. Mayes wants to marry me. He wants to be part of me and you. I want that, and I thought you did too."

"I do. Only, I was wondering about the future, thinking about what our family might look like in five years."

"I don't understand your concern. Are you worried he won't stay or that he will stay?"

"Both." Larissa shrugged. "I want to know the future to protect myself. I don't want to jinx him or us. I don't want to go through losing someone again."

"Oh, honey. I'd love to tell you that you'll never lose anyone again. I'd love to say that loving someone doesn't hurt. Here's the thing. Humans aren't meant to last forever. All of us, even you and me will die. As dreamwalkers, we have an inkling of what comes next, but even if someone dies you go on loving that person."

I hugged Larissa, her soft body adhering tightly to mine. After a long moment, I caught her gaze. "What's this really all about?"

"There's a new girl in my class. Her family just moved here. I showed her around school yesterday, and I like her. She's different. But I'm scared. I liked June Gilroy a lot. She was my best friend and she died. What if I'm the reason everyone is dying?"

I breathed a sigh of relief at finally knowing her true distress. "You're not to blame for anyone's death, especially not June's. Set those negative thoughts aside and get to know the new girl. Tell me about her."

"She has one tooth in the front that turns a little so that the edges don't quite meet and she has a purple backpack and she doesn't believe in socks. She's never been out in a boat and one time she fell off the jungle gym and broke her arm."

"Wow. Y'all did a lot of talking yesterday if you already know so much about her. What's her name?"

"Mary Janey."

"Is Janey her last name?"

"Nope. It's part of her first name. Her last name is Braun."

"You should invite her to dinner. Or maybe do a play day?"

"Mom! I'm too old for play days. Fourth graders get together and hang out."

Chastised, I tussled her hair. "Got it." *My girl is growing up.*

Chapter Twenty-Eight

With Wayne out of pocket on Thursday morning, his cop shop felt like a classroom during a recess break. Mayes apparently phoned in shift change instructions from his semi-truck investigation. Tamika polished her nails. Virg and Ronnie joked in the breakroom over bad coffee. I spoke to everyone and then sat in the computer lab. Wayne always directed my work effort, and I had no instructions.

Tough. I couldn't sit here and do nothing. We had two active cases. I could review the files for leads that might have been overlooked.

Yesterday Wayne said he wanted me to try another dreamwalk with Kitty's phone, but I needed Mayes for that. Or did I? If Mayes was gone all morning, I could call Bubba Paxton. That would be my backup plan. First the files then the dreamwalk.

Virg and Ronnie left for patrol, and Tamika chatted happily with all her friends and relatives by phone. Other deputies, including Clark Ryan the K-9 officer, drifted through the office and went out on patrol. I was studying the photos of Kitty's home and car, remembering both from my own personal experience, when Lavene joined me.

"Where is everyone?" he asked.

"Hey, Lavene. The feds descended yesterday and left with Wayne. No one has heard from him today. The deputies are out on patrols or calls."

Lavene sat across from me in the computer lab, the chair creaking under his weight. "What's this about Wayne and the feds?"

"I don't know much." I relayed the few facts I knew and said I thought it had to do with the Tampa mayor's problems.

"Tampa. Right." Lavene nodded like an insider in the know. "Big mess down there."

"That it is."

He gestured to the dual stacks of folders by the keyboard. "Is there a new lead?"

"I'm comparing the Suitcase Murder files and Kitty's file for common ground. We have no proof this is the same guy, but it could be."

"The chances are slim," Lavene said. "No

one would believe such a coincidence."

His smugness irritated me, especially since he'd dismissed my idea. "The Suitcase Killer victims are small-boned women who are petite in stature. Kitty fits that description."

"So do a lot of women."

I worked my back teeth apart. "As far as we know, Kitty's the only woman abducted in recent days. My vision of our Jane Doe at the morgue showed an emaciated woman. Like those Suitcase Murder women, Kitty is being shrunk down until she's flesh and bones."

"Visions carry no weight in law enforcement." He flicked his wrist dismissively. "We can't withstand another boondoggle like chasing your woo-woo hotline over Sandersville way."

That did it. "I had nothing to do with the decision to fly a helicopter up there. Cops follow leads all the time. They don't all pan out. In fact, most of them go nowhere."

"On that we agree. However, my supervisor won't release the chopper again without solid evidence. We can't go tearing off on the basis of a vision. Might as well chase rainbows."

If he hadn't been such a showboat, we could have driven there without the fanfare and no one would be the wiser. Not even the killer.

"As I understand it," I said, "there's a leak in the GBI. Someone in your organization is feeding case information to a suspect. I believe the same leak occurred during your investigation of the Suitcase Killer. That's another reason I believe the same person killed all three women, and now he's got Kitty."

"I disagree, but I see how you could reach that conclusion."

I wanted to do a zany happy dance at his concession, but I had to work with this guy. Antagonizing him wouldn't be helpful.

His phone buzzed. He read the display screen, and pumped his fist in the air. "Got 'em."

"Got who?" I asked.

"My other two suspects are on their way to our Savannah office. My standing orders are to route interview suspects to this office so Wayne can participate in the interviews, but he's in the wind. Is Mayes around?"

"Nope. I'm it."

"Pack your stuff. We're headed to Savannah. You can analyze the interviews real time and funnel your questions to me."

He hadn't asked me to go. He'd told me. Difficult as that was to stomach, I wanted to go. I closed the folders and forced a smile. "Sounds great."

Lavene enjoyed classical music, and he liked it loud, which made conversation a no-go for our one-hour drive to Savannah. We were nearly to Richmond Hill when his phone buzzed. He pulled it out, recognized the number, and switched off the radio.

"My brother," he said. "I need to take this."

His car rode so quietly that I heard both sides of the conversation. I surmised from the call that Lavene's brother had arrived unexpectedly for a visit and wanted to know what happened to the spare key.

"I moved the key to the largest rock by the bird bath," Lavene said. "I don't like leaving it in the same place."

"Uh. Okay . . . Just a sec . . . Yep . . . I found it. Apologies for the intrusion. I'm off for a few days and wanted to hang out with my big brother. When I didn't see the key in the usual spot, I thought you didn't want me coming around."

"No. Not that. Never that, bro. It was a security precaution. Let yourself in and make yourself at home. I may be working late tonight."

They talked more, but I quit paying attention because my cell phone chimed with a text message. I withdrew it from my pocket and saw the message came from Mayes. He was headed to Sinclair County from middle Georgia, finally. His lead was a bust.

I replied by text that I was en route to Savannah to observe Lavene's interviews of his former Suitcase Killer suspects, Darius Bronsen and Jared Springfield.

Mayes texted he'd meet us there. I pocketed my phone about the same time Lavene concluded his call.

"Sorry about that," Lavene said. "I try not to deal with personal business during my duty hours, but some things can't be helped. My brother is starting to turn his life around, and I support his journey to wholeness. Sometimes he crashes with me between jobs."

My attitude toward Lavene softened. He may be a jerk, but he put family first. "He's lucky to have you in his corner."

"I enjoy his company. If we weren't on a case, I'd take off a few says and we'd go fishing. He understands I'm working an active case right now."

"Where does he live?"

Lavene's face flushed red. "He has no fixed address. Sometimes he stays with friends. Sometimes he camps out. He said mortgages and rental payments cramp his style."

"Being a nomad must suit him," I said. "All that drifting around would drive me nuts. I need to put roots down, to plant things and watch them grow."

"To each his own."

It was nearly noon by the time Lavene interviewed Darius Bronson. Mayes hadn't arrived yet, so I had the observation room to myself. It was nicer than ours, with upholstered chairs and swivel wheels on the bases. The monitor was a flat TV screen mounted on the wall, so I had a bird's eye view of Mr. Bronson. Not quite as riveting as an actual observation window, but it worked for me. Flipping a nearby toggle switch would put my words in Lavene's earpiece.

Bronson was older than me, but not as old as my parents. He had gray at the temples of his short black hair. He was big all over, with a corded neck like a pro football player. His button-down collar shirt had been ironed, his jeans creased. He wore slip-on loafers with no socks. His face was red. Guess he didn't like waiting for Lavene.

The door opened, and Lavene entered. After greeting Bronson, Lavene placed his manila file folder on the table between them and got right to the point. "Another Suitcase Murder victim surfaced," Lavene said.

"It wasn't me," Darius said. "I resent getting pulled in here every time I turn around. You have no right to do that. I'm innocent."

"You crossed paths with each of the former Georgia victims," Lavene countered smoothly. "You bought groceries from Deb Teal in Atlanta, you frequented the South Fulton County Library where Chaundra Mallory worked, and you rented a boat at the Tybee marina where Hannah Blake worked."

"Not this again!" Bronson bolted to his feet. "Someone must've followed me around and killed those women. It wasn't me. I feel persecuted by your continued harassment. I'll file a lawsuit if you don't stop demanding that I submit to these degrading interviews."

"Sit down, Mr. Bronson," Lavene said. "I have questions about the new case. You've already refused permission for us to search your vehicle. Do you want to look even guiltier by trying to leave?"

"This sucks." Bronson sat down in a huff. "What do you want to know? I get around. We established that last time you talked to me. So what? I've got grandkids in Atlanta and Savannah. I run the roads regularly."

"Have you ever been to Marion, Georgia?"

Bronson scowled. "Where is it?"

"About an hour south of Savannah. You ever been there?"

"Not on purpose."

"You trying to be a wiseass?"

"I'm trying to get out of here."

"Answer the question."

"I did. If it's near the interstate, I drove through the county twice taking my Savannah grandkids to the theme parks in Orlando. You questioning everyone who rides up and down I-95?"

Lavene sat a little straighter. "What about the truck stop at the Marion interchange?"

"What about it?"

"You gas up there?"

"Not that I know of."

"You might have stopped there?"

"I was traveling with a pack of hungry, peeing kids." Bronson gestured with both hands. "You don't want to know how many times I stopped."

Lavene stared at the man for a long moment. "You ever visit online dating sites?"

Bronson snorted. "Of course not. I got me several lady friends at home. I don't need a computer for that. You can't tell chemistry without an in-person meeting. I don't know why anyone would trust a computer over their own gut instinct."

"You consider yourself as a player?"

The crimson color on Bronson's face and neck deepened. "I don't like what you're implying. Let me be perfectly frank. All of us seniors chase after our grandkids. Whenever me and my lady friends are home at the same time, we go out to dinner or a show. If something else happens, that's on us. I'm no sex fiend. I don't date children."

"So you know something about the latest murder?"

"I pay attention to the news same as everybody else." Bronson shook his finger at Lavene. "I've been a good sport and answered your questions. I want that on the record, but I'm not wasting all day sitting here at your convenience. You got something on me, charge me. If not, I'm walking out that door."

"Thank you for coming in. I appreciate your cooperation," Lavene said.

"I can go? Seriously?"

"Yes," Lavene said. "You're free to go."

Mayes joined me. "What'd I miss?"

I kissed him hello and waved him into the upholstered chair beside me. "Not much. Lavene interviewed Darius Bronson." I was giving Mayes a quick rundown when Lavene

290

joined us.

"What'd you think?" Lavene asked me.

I thought back over the interview. Nothing stood out as a red flag. "He believes what he's saying."

"I knew that. I thought you could tell if he was lying."

"I didn't detect any lies." That was the truth. Darius Bronson had good cause to be angry with Lavene for pulling him in.

"Bronson is innocent?" Lavene asked.

"He believes what he's saying," I repeated. After Lavene read me the riot act on the way here about wasting police resources, no way would I overstate anything and risk getting into trouble with him or his boss.

Lavene turned to Mayes. "I cut Darius Bronson loose. My last interview is with Jared Springfield. He's being escorted into the same room right now. Changing the subject, you hear anything from Wayne?"

"He hasn't called me," Mayes said. "Why?"

A warning flag lifted in my head. Mayes wasn't lying but he knew something. I narrowed my eyes and studied him. He knew something about Wayne he didn't want me to know.

Lavene shrugged. "Just wondering what the feds are doing with him."

"Aren't we all?" I added so that Mayes wouldn't have to answer.

On the screen, a slight man matching Jared Springfield's description entered the room with a uniformed officer. He paced the small area, stopped in front of the camera, and made animal noises. I grinned at his comic antics. At first glance, he resembled my father's laidback friends. He wore leather sandals, jeans with frayed bottoms, an untucked uniform shirt with Jared embroidered on it. His shaved head gleamed from the overhead light. He had at least three visible tattoos: a snake head adorned his neck, a scorpion was inked on his left arm, and an ace of hearts covered his left forearm.

"That's my cue." Lavene exited our room with his file folders and joined the truck-driving suspect. "Mr. Springfield, you know why you're here?"

"Because you couldn't catch any flies to torture?" Springfield replied.

I snorted with laughter in the observation room, glad that we were soundproofed.

Lavene frowned. "Because we found another Suitcase Victim."

Springfield's expression mirrored Lavene's. "Whatever."

"Where've you been for the last two weeks?"

"I've been everywhere. That's my job."

"How about Marion, Georgia?"

Bronson snapped his fingers. "Truck stop, right?"

"You been there?"

"I've stopped in there from time to time. Nice bathrooms and clean showers."

"Ever visit Club Frisky a coupla blocks away?"

Springfield waved off the question. "That place is shut down."

"It is, but folks still go there."

"They have good hamburgers at those places, or so I've been told."

"You didn't answer my question. Have you ever been to that Club Frisky?"

"Not that I recall."

His answer stumped Lavene. I understood his mental paralysis. Jared Springfield was his last viable suspect. After this we had nothing. Something occurred to me. I pressed the transmitter and whispered in Lavene's ear, "We've got three guys that stop at similar places. Ask him how he decides where to stop when he's on the road. Ask him if he uses an app."

Lavene shifted in his chair. To a trained eye, his shoulders came up a bit, so did his chin. "Do you use a travel app for rest stops?"

Springfield's face twitched. "What if I do? Everybody uses apps these days."

"Why? You run the same roads day in and out."

"Yeah, but guys post what they see on the app I use most. If someplace has a really good cook on shift or a hot waitress, the word travels."

"Somebody posts about a place, then guys flock there?"

"We have gal operators too. They use the same app."

"I'm only interested in the guys," Lavene said. "What's the name of the app?"

"Truck King Three is the best one. It has the most comments about food and servers."

To my right, I heard Mayes clicking away on his phone, searching for the app, downloading it. Mayes leaned forward and flipped the transmitter again. "Ask him if there are certain people's entries he pays more attention to, like an influencer."

Lavene nodded the whole time Mayes was speaking in his ear. Then he gave Springfield the "I've got you now" glance that cops seem to be born with. "Who do you follow on the app?"

"I don't follow anyone. It's a rolling forum. Guys post things all day long. No one's in charge of anything. That's what I like. It's by us and for us. No merchants chiming in to twist your arm or anything. You need a password to get in."

"And that is?"

"Uh. . . ." Springfield looked everywhere but at Lavene.

"The password."

"It's a secret. The guys will get mad if cops are on there."

"If you don't give it to me, I'll have the app shut down."

I shook my head at his last statement and turned to Mayes. "Can he do that?"

"He can make it difficult enough for the app creator that he or she pulls the app."

"I see." Turning my attention back to the view screen, I noticed the energy in the room had shifted. It felt tingling and positive. We were on the verge of an emotional cliff.

Springfield mumbled something, and Lavene called him on it. "What's that?"

"Hot wheels. All one word and lowercase. The guys are going to kill me."

Right away, Mayes tapped furiously on his cell phone. Who was he texting? No one back in Marion could figure this out for us.

It had to be someone else. Wayne would hate Mayes outsourcing anything without checking with him first. I was about to remind him when Lavene piped in again.

"The guys will never know you shared it unless you tell them," Lavene said. "I'll be right back."

Seconds later, Lavene bounced into the room. "That was brilliant, Powell! If the other two suspects use the same app, it explains how their paths intersected with our victims. I'm trying not to get too excited about the lead, but this is awesome."

"What's your IT support look like?" Mayes said.

"We contract out for the service through our headquarters, so there's no one onsite. I can send this to the contractor though and they'll figure it out. Heck, my brother's good with tech stuff, and he's staying with me right now. I could ask him about the app."

"Hold off on your usual tech support and your brother since Wayne thinks there's a leak to the killer in your shop. I know a guy who hasn't worked this case before, a guy I trust implicitly. You okay with that?"

"I should be saying no, but I'd really like to crack this case and catch this serial killer. Go for it. How quickly can you get results?"

"Should have something for you in a few minutes," Mayes said.

No one asked my opinion on the outsourcing of sensitive data, so I declined to give it. If this worked, Wayne would overlook our initiative. If it bombed, we'd never hear the end of it. I wished I knew more about apps, especially the social ones. I used one for weather and another for directions. App was short for application, all the cool kids knew that, and I guess the truckers knew that too.

My stomach rumbled again, reminding me I was empty. "Y'all got a snack machine or something?"

"We keep soda and chips in the breakroom. Help yourself," Lavene said. "If this case starts breaking so that we can't stop for lunch, I'll order pizza in."

Ooh, pizza. Yum. "I could go for some pizza either way."

"The lady wants pizza," Mayes said.

Lavene raised a hand. "Got it. Will order a coupla pizzas right away. What about Springfield? Do we cut him loose?"

"Get him some pizza too," Mayes said. "He's not going anywhere."

CHAPTER TWENTY-NINE

Between the three of us and Springfield, we polished off two large pizzas in short order. Good thing, too, as things kept hopping all afternoon. First, we tracked the creator of the app to Atlanta and talked with him about records availability. He clammed up. We requested a warrant. The judge agreed to expedite it. We arranged for a team in Atlanta to serve the warrant.

As one thing led to the next, I realized I wouldn't leave the Savannah GBI office anytime soon. With my daughter's school day ending in an hour, I needed to arrange for her care, and my first choice was my parents.

"I apologize for calling so much lately, but are you available to meet Larissa's bus today?" I asked my mom when she answered. "We've been super busy working two cases at once, and I'm still in Savannah."

"Not a problem, dear. I was certain Larissa would be joining us today."

Her prescient ability made me smile. "How do you know these things ahead of time, Mom?"

"I don't question it, same as I don't question when to tune crystals. Seems like I get that right most of the time."

"You're amazing, and I thank you from the bottom of my heart."

After talking with Mom, I tried to reach Wayne. That call bounced straight to voice mail. I didn't leave a message. My thoughts immediately returned to the case. Kitty was still out there. She needed us to find her.

I entered Lavene's office. He was cranked back in his chair, directing Mayes to add events to the timeline on a whiteboard. I pulled up a chair and listened.

"Springfield posted in the app about each of the three victims about a week before each disappeared," Lavene said.

Mayes made additional tics on the timeline.

"They had names," I said. "Don't depersonalize Deb, Chaundra, and Hannah."

Mayes wrote their names in bold letters on the board.

I nodded my approval. "If only we had

299

the app data, we could arrest the killer right now."

"Shouldn't be much longer," Mayes said. "We're close."

Lavene's phone rang. "My brother. Since we've got a few minutes, I'll take the call. Excuse me." He stepped out to the hall, but his voice carried so I heard him giving step by step directions on how to operate his new washing machine.

Mayes came over to the window where I stood. "What happened this morning?" I asked. "We didn't have a chance to talk about that yet."

"That trucker was dirty." Mayes' scowled and shook his head. "I knew it as soon as I saw his troubled aura, and he wouldn't look me in the eye. He had pat answers for everything, and his rig was packed with heavy cartons. To be on the safe side, we weighed the rig again, and the weight matched. He said he tried to hook up with an old flame, but she turned him down. With no proof of wrongdoing, I had to turn him loose."

"You think he took Kitty?"

"I think he did something else, unrelated to the missing woman. I wished I had time to lean on him and figure out the score, but Kitty is our top priority."

We both fell silent. After a few minutes, a random thought popped in my head. "You know, Wayne expected us to try a joint dreamwalk with Kitty's phone."

"Can't do that now. We're in Savannah and the phone is in Sinclair County. Assuming we haven't erred by combining the cases, following this lead will bring Kitty home and net us a serial killer."

Kitty's life clock ticked ominously in my head. Every decision we made today potentially meant life or death for her. "But he could kill Kitty in the meanwhile."

"If he wanted her dead by a violent means, she'd already be dead. He's had her for almost a week. Unless she's ill or hurt, she stands a good chance of survival. There's momentum now. The information is meshing together. Can't you feel it?"

"Don't take this the wrong way. I want to free Kitty, and I want to help, but I'm essentially a third wheel here. You and Lavene are doing a fine job of establishing physical links from suspect to victim, but I'm extra baggage. You don't need me."

"I'll always need you." He reached over and stroked my hair. "As for the case, we're only reading cops in on a need-to-know basis. The killer won't know we're coming for him until we're in his face. Officers are

301

on the way to serve the warrant to the app guy. We've coordinated remote tech support, and they're on standby. I've got a very good feeling about this lead. Don't worry about being at loose ends. You've been doing double duty with all those dreamwalks. Why not find a place for a nap? I saw a sofa somewhere in this building. Chances are this evening will be full of excitement."

A nap. Not something I normally did on the clock, but this wasn't a normal case. I stretched, and a yawn slipped out. I covered it with my hand and laughed. "Guess I could use a nap. Call me if anything breaks. I want to be on Kitty's rescue team."

"Will do."

If we'd been working the leads in the Sinclair County cop shop, I could've gone home or tended to errands until the showdown. Instead, I was passing time in Savannah. Both Mayes and Lavene shared a similar mindset. They believed the case would resolve today. For Kitty's sake, I hoped they were right.

The office sofa looked inviting, and no sooner did I sink into its softness than I fell asleep. But instead of restful slumber, a sobering scene filled my head. I recognized the weak energy signature. Kitty. I sank into her reality and experienced the scene from her eyes.

The darkness lightened, and I saw the soft glow of morning through metal bars. I shivered and clutched my legs tighter, my teeth chattering with cold. The cage swayed.

Sobs escaped my mouth. "Why me? What did I ever do to you?"

A voice came out of the sky, startling me. "Why won't you die?"

I sat up, arms wrapped tightly around my empty belly. I searched in all directions, but I was alone. "Please. Water. I need water."

"No water. No nothing," the disembodied voice continued. "Game's over. The cops know where you are. I can't have that, so you have to die."

"I'll eat the apples. I'll do whatever you want. Please. Give me another chance. This isn't fair."

"Life's not fair, girlie."

"My name is Kitty," I whispered.

"Quiet. I can't stand sniveling. We're moving to home base. They'll never find you there."

A loud motor cranked nearby. I cringed and cried out when the platform lurched wildly. I slid across the container, jolting into the cage bars. A moment later, the floor angle changed, and I slid across the platform again. I screamed, the shrill sound echoing into nothingness.

I jolted awake and nothing looked familiar. Heart racing in my ears, I sat upright and tried to orient myself. The sterile office. The brown sofa. The muted light in the hallway. I was free. I was not in a cage.

Those experiences belonged to Kitty, not Baxley Powell. My breath came easier. My pulse slowed. I was in an office. In Savannah, with Mayes and Lavene. We were at the GBI office. I'd had a dream.

A Kitty dream. It must have taken place very early in the morning, before we flew the chopper to Sandersville. As we'd feared, her abductor knew of our pending arrival. He'd moved Kitty to someplace called home base.

Footsteps pounded down the corridor. Mayes burst through the doorway. "You all right? I heard a scream."

"I'm all right. I . . . I had a dream. From Kitty. Sorry about the scream. I thought it happened in the dream. Everything was so real. I was in her head experiencing her exact feelings."

Mayes sat beside me, his arm around my shoulder. "You want to talk about it? Is she dead?"

His warmth seeped into my body, and I felt more like myself. "She was still alive yesterday. Her captor knew we found the location so he moved her. He said it out loud."

"You see his face?"

"No. He spoke to her through a hidden speaker. It was creepy."

"Your dream confirms his connection to law enforcement. You remember anything else?"

"He wants her dead, but so far he hasn't hurried things along. Except he's refusing to give her water now. She won't have long. Maybe not even a day."

Mayes' grip tightened on my shoulder. "I want to save her, too," he said, "but with time running out, I can't promise we'll find her soon enough."

His statement brought tears to my eyes. "She's frightened and cold. Whatever equipment he used to move her, it flung her all over the cage. As thin-boned and exhausted as she is, she might have broken bones now."

"Let's hope not. I'm sorry the dream was so disturbing. I hoped you would rest."

"I wanted rest too. I haven't had a sleep visitation like this in months. The intensity surprised me, that's all."

"Look on the bright side, at least this time she didn't invade your body."

He was right. Kitty's consciousness lent

me the memory. Guess she knew my mental URL. "Nope. She only invaded my dreams, which may be worse. Her scream echoes in my ears."

"We're even because I'll never forget the sound of your scream. I thought something happened to you."

"Something did happen. The dream."

"Did she reveal anything else?"

I ran through the brief dream sequence in my head. "Not that I recall."

Mayes muttered something under his breath. It sounded like one of Wayne's litany of swear words. What was it about being in charge that made men swear more?

"What's that?" I asked.

"I hoped the killer mentioned where he was moving her."

A slow smile filled my face. "Thanks for the memory jolt. He did mention a place."

"Where?"

"Home base."

He groaned. "Not funny."

"It's true. He said we'd never think to look for her at home base."

Quick footsteps sounded in the hall. Lavene rushed in, breathless and red-faced. "I hate to end the hug-fest, but we have an ID on our latest victim. Johnna O'Neal. She's an unmarried orphan who used social media, and get this. Her name is in the Truck King Three slipstream of posts two months ago."

"We're close," Mayes said. "Very close."

"I feel it too," Lavene said. "This guy's going down."

"Who else knows about the positive ID?" Mayes rose and stood toe to toe with Lavene.

"The three of us and the DNA tech. It came through on my secure office email. I changed all the passwords on my office account this morning. No one else knows my password, guaranteed."

"Good. Keep the need-to-know circle tight. Hold off on updating the system about the positive ID. Let's flash Johnna's driver's license photo in front of Springfield and see how he reacts."

"Good idea."

The men hurried away, leaving me alone with my thoughts in the quiet office. I understood their excitement. Even I felt the pieces of this particular puzzle knitting together. The sooner the serial killer case wrapped up, the sooner Kitty could come home.

Though I had no connection with Kitty right now, I sent her a shout out through the universe anyway. *Stay strong, Kitty. We'll find you soon.*

CHAPTER THIRTY

After stretching and freshening up, I made my way back to the GBI's observation room. Mayes' eyes warmed as I joined him at the view screen. "They just started," he said. "Springfield is pissed about being held so long."

I scooted my chair close to his. "He has a point if he's innocent."

"Trust me, he's not completely innocent. Something's off with this guy."

"Like what?"

"Can't put my finger on it yet, but he's slimy. I stake my reputation on that claim."

"No need to stake anything. I believe you." As I listened to Lavene calm Springfield down inside the interview room, another thought occurred to me. "We know this guy uses the app Truck King Three. Is it possible for app users to have multiple accounts?"

"Ah, I like the sneaky direction of your

thoughts. He could have one identity he posts under routinely and a second identity for posts where he wants to be anonymous. Let's see how he reacts to the photo, then we'll cue Lavene with the question."

I turned my attention back to the screen. Lavene had the suspect seated once again. The GBI man placed his thin folder on the table in front of him and waited. Cops did that a lot. Waited. Most people couldn't stand the conversational void.

"What do you want from me?" Springfield asked. "Ask me your questions so I can get out of this hellhole."

Lavene's gaze shifted down to the folder and then back to the suspect. "We have a photo for you to view."

"Not another set of bones. I have nightmares from the last set you showed me."

"Someone's targeting these women."

"I don't kill women. I admire them. Big difference."

Lavene waited again, and Springfield twitched silently in his seat. With a sigh, Lavene opened the folder and slid Johnna's photo across the table.

His start of recognition alerted me to the truth. We were on the right track. Springfield knew her!

Springfield slid the photo across the table.

"I don't know her."

I flicked the toggle to speak in Lavene's earpiece. "That's a lie."

"We know that isn't true," Lavene said smoothly. "Your path crossed hers at least once."

"Look, I didn't kill this girl. I don't know her. You can't pin these murders on me."

"We combed through your phone records and the GPS unit in your rig. You stopped at her place of employment several times in recent months."

"Don't. Know. Her."

"The post on Truck King Three said she was a hottie with a warm smile."

"I remember that post. The Welcome Center chick." Springfield brightened. "She was sweet, only she isn't there anymore. I thought she quit."

"Nope. Suitcase Murder victim. You're our prime suspect."

The trucker paled. "I don't kill women. How many times do I have to say that?"

"You're repeating yourself, and you're in trouble."

Mayes flipped the switch and told Lavene about our two user name theory.

"You don't have any evidence," Springfield said.

"I know you withheld information. Something you wanted to remain hidden."

A defiant gleam in his eye, the man shook his head. "I'm a regular guy doing his regular job. I'm no criminal mastermind."

"You've got two accounts on Truck King Three," Lavene lied smoothly. I was certain Springfield believed the bluff, but the lie registered with me.

In answer, Springfield put his head down on the table and wept, his hands atop his gleaming, bald head.

Mayes elbowed me gently. "We got him. He's guilty as sin, even if he isn't the killer. He teed up these women for a stone-cold killer."

Lavene put two and two together in the same way as Mayes. "You commented about these nice girls on Truck King Three on your secret account. Then you posted about seeing them later. You're the killer's spotter, aren't you?"

He straightened, dashed away the tears on his face. "I didn't kill anyone. I don't know who killed those girls."

"You aided and abetted a serial killer. That makes you guilty."

Springfield recoiled in his seat. "I didn't know anything would happen to them."

"And yet it did. This isn't the first time I've questioned you. You must've recognized the young women from our prior interviews. Not even their murders kept you from posting about other women. You targeted them for this killer."

"You don't understand." Springfield pounded a fist on the table. "Girls looked through me all during school. Once I became a trucker, I became part of a community, a brotherhood. We hang together."

He paused for a ragged breath. "I can't help it if some sicko gets the wrong idea from my posts. I thought every one of those girls, and a whole bunch more, were drop dead beautiful. They treated me so nice when I came to their jobs. I wanted to share that with others. Women saw me. Deb, Chaundra, Hannah, and Johnna saw me."

"I see you," Lavene said. "I'm not registering any prize. I'm seeing a spoiled millennial who played Russian roulette with innocent women's lives."

"It wasn't like that." Springfield shook his head too fast. "I didn't kill them."

"You were an accomplice," Lavene insisted.

"You can't prove that."

"Yes, I can. And the judge and jury will see it the same way. You're guilty, and I'm charging you with murder."

"No! You can't hold me."

"Yes, I can. You'll be remanded to the Chatham County Correctional Facility by day's end until you come before a judge for a bond hearing."

He glared at the GBI man. "I want a lawyer."

"Suit yourself. Here's my opinion. You need a miracle instead of a lawyer. The only way for you to walk free is to tell us what you know about the killer."

"You'll drop the murder charge?" Springfield asked.

"Things will go a lot better for you if you cooperate with our investigation. Are you revoking your request for counsel?"

"Yes. I didn't murder anyone. Make sure that goes on my permanent record."

Mayes and I exchanged a hopeful glance. We hadn't expected insider information.

"You know who the killer is?" Lavene asked.

"I got suspicious after a while. I went back and checked who read my posts, who pinged in the same locations I reported. One user turned up at all three employment places of the victims."

"Name."

"I don't know his real name. Only his screen name."

"For someone in need of a miracle, you're

dragging your feet all of a sudden. Don't you want to be a free man? Maybe you like living with gang members and criminals who'd just a soon drive a shank into your heart as not."

Springfield's Adam's apple wobbled. "Hammer. His name is Hammer."

CHAPTER THIRTY-ONE

Hammer. I connected the dots in my head. If we learned Hammer's real name and pinged his cell phone, chances were that Kitty might be at that location also. I turned to Mayes, my heart racing. "Can we get the guy's identity from the app guy?"

Mayes swiveled his chair to face me. "We had to move heaven and earth to get his cooperation for the previous information. But now that we can show the link between Jared Springfield, Truck King Three, and the murder victims, maybe a judge will give us a nod."

Lavene hurried into the observation room, leaving Jared Springfield with his head resting on his arms in the adjacent room. "This is it. I know it."

"Roger that," Mayes said. "We have to be smart about this. Only the three of us can know we're closing in on this guy. If he spooks, he may go underground, assume a new identity, and become another state's serial killer."

"I want to nail this guy," Lavene said.

"You got that judge on speed dial?" Mayes said.

"Yes. I'll call his office as I type the warrant." A buzzing sound emitted from Lavene's pocket. He withdrew the phone and silenced it. "My brother. He can wait a few hours. Probably lost the TV remote. I'll be glad when he moves out again."

After Lavene left, I smiled at Mayes. "This is happening."

"It is. We're on track to catch a serial killer today. And if our luck holds, the serial killer is also Kitty's abductor."

"There's a chance someone else took her."

"A very slim chance. She fits the victimology of the serial killer women."

Kitty needed to be rescued today. Her time was quite literally running out. I wanted to believe Mayes, but his theory needed testing. "Her name wasn't in any of the Truck King Three threads. I would've noticed."

"It's the same guy. Like I said, he's been in our pockets the whole time. He knew enough to change how he acquired victims or risk getting caught. Someone in this office or in Lavene's circle of law enforcement

317

acquaintances knows this man."

The facts of the case glimmered in my mind, sliding around each other like whirling teacups. I fingered my moldavite pendant to center myself. Unable to string thoughts together in my head, I began voicing my thoughts aloud in hopes of sparking a discussion.

"Jared Springfield made the connection that his friendly female posts inspired our killer to select them as victims," I said. "Springfield liked his finder role, a lot. What if our killer contacted Springfield anonymously with a burner phone? He might've asked for a new lead and convinced Springfield not to post the name on the app."

"That's a pretty big leap, but if that's true, we should focus on Springfield's phone records again —"

"Especially in the few weeks before Kitty Ballenger went missing," I finished for him.

Mayes got a faraway look in his eyes that I called his thinking mode. "Lavene's got the case files secured in his briefcase," he said.

I popped out of my seat, unable to contain the wave of hope that swept through me. "Let's review the phone history listing right now. Until today, we didn't know Springfield was linked to the killer through an app. With that connection established, Springfield's activities bear closer scrutiny. He could still be lying to us by omission." I gestured to the man on our monitor. "Look at his defeated posture. He looks guilty."

Mayes gave a cursory glance at Springfield who hadn't lifted his head from the table since Lavene left. "Agreed. Let's go."

We hurried to Lavene's office. He handed us the list of phone numbers. "I didn't check out the numbers all the way to Kitty's abduction. This guy made lots of calls. One of the numbers near the end of the list looked familiar, but I don't remember where I saw it before."

"Hmm," Mayes said. "Which number?"

Lavene huffed a breath of air up his face as if he were annoyed to be interrupted, but he reached for the file, started about two-thirds of the way down. His finger dragged across the list. I held my breath watching and waiting and hoping. He was nearly to the end of a page, then he backed up and pointed out a number. It had double threes in the center of the last four-number sequence.

He grabbed a pen and circled the number. "This one."

"Should we dial it?" Mayes asked.

"Not yet. If that's the number, we don't want to tip our hand. Run a trace on it first.

Let's see who owns this number. We can ping it afterward, if need be."

Mayes sat at a nearby workstation, logged in with his credentials and ran the trace. "Burner."

Meanwhile, I grabbed the list and highlighted all instances of the number. It first showed up five weeks before Kitty's abduction. There were exactly seven calls, all two minutes or less in duration. Since we had Springfield's phone, I checked his list of contacts. The number wasn't identified in his phone as belonging to anyone.

Lavene's phone chimed again. He silenced it again.

"Your brother?" I asked.

Lavene finished typing a mile a minute, theatrically tapped a key and said, "Done. We'll be in business soon as I collect the warrant. And yes, that was my brother again. He must've locked himself out of the house again to be calling me so much. He can be such a pain in the ass. I should call him."

"Maybe." Mayes leaned back in his chair, crossed his arms, and contemplated the ceiling tiles.

The speculative tone of his voice caught my attention. "What's up?"

"We know there's a leak in this office or

320

the GBI communications array," Mayes said, his gaze locked on Lavene.

Lavene put a hand up as if he could ward off whatever was coming next. "I've devoted the last five years of my life to catching this killer. No way am I the leak. Three other agents work out of this office. They're in the field right now."

"Exactly," Mayes said. "All the information is contained now. What if we purposefully leak something, say to your brother?"

"My screw-up little brother isn't a serial killer," Lavene asserted, red-faced. "I'm outraged you'd suggest such a thing."

"Humor me. Your brother knows your passion for this case, and I'm guessing he knows the names of our three suspects."

"Of course he does, but he's discrete. Besides, I didn't mention anything that wasn't already in the newspapers. I never shared confidential information with him."

"Tell me about your brother again," I said, hoping to distract Lavene long enough for him to gather himself. "I remember you saying he was tech savvy."

Lavene gave a bittersweet smile as if he recognized the interview technique I'd used. "Comes from a youth spent on video games. That kid is a whiz on computers. He was always quick to pick up anything that interested him, but he never cared for most book knowledge."

"Smart enough to hack the passwords on your devices?" Mayes asked, turning Lavene's protests against him. "Smart enough to obtain your work logins?"

"This is preposterous. My little brother wouldn't do that. He knows this job means the world to me."

"Put it to the test," Mayes said. "Text him that you're about to interview a suspect in the case and that you can't be disturbed. If I'm right, he'll blow up your phone with multiple texts until you answer him, or he'll attempt to contact Springfield. If he's innocent, he'll respect your request for radio silence and not bother you or Springfield."

"Wait a minute," I said slowly as another realization dawned. I drifted close to Lavene's desk. "Didn't you say something once about your brother working from time to time as a short hauler?"

"I did, but that doesn't make him a bad guy, just one who can't keep a job. I tell you, he's a screw-up."

"Send the text," Mayes said, moving up to stand beside me.

"All right, I will. To prove you wrong." Lavene tap-tapped away on his phone and placed it on his desk. Less than a minute later, his phone lit up. "Who?" Joey wrote.

"That doesn't prove anything," Lavene said.

"Don't respond," Mayes said.

"The trucker?" was the next message.

Three more texts followed asking about the interview. Lavene shook his head, rose, and backed away from the incriminating messages. "No. It can't be."

"It can be. And it probably is," Mayes said. "We won't know for certain until we question him, but we certainly have grounds to pull him in for an interview."

"I've looked after Joey for years," Lavene said. "He's my step-brother because his dad married my mom. Our parents died in a car wreck a dozen years ago, and he's been struggling ever since."

His voice held all the angst of a parent whose teen has done something wrong and the law got involved. It must be awful feeling that gut betrayal, wondering if he was to blame for how he mentored his brother. I'd worked cases before where brother had gone against brother. Festering family wounds didn't heal. Worse, and this hadn't occurred to Lavene yet, if Joey was our guy, Lavene's credibility would suffer and his career would tank.

"The first documented Georgia Suitcase

Murder was six years ago," Mayes said. "I wonder what his trigger point was."

Mayes assumed Joey began killing six years ago. I wasn't so generous. "Or there may be more suitcases with bodies out there, waiting to be found," I said.

Lavene took a considering moment where he constantly shifted his weight from foot to foot. He shook his head. "This can't be. I don't accept it. Not my brother."

"Ping his phone right now. Let's pick him up," Mayes said.

"He should be at my place over in Rincon." Lavene wrung his hands. "Accusing him will shatter his trust in me. I don't want to do this. He's too fragile."

"Ping the phone and let's roll. The three of us will move in lock step until he's detained to make sure no information flows outside this circle of trust. We'll collect the warrant on the way to picking up Joey."

"No, please," Lavene begged. "There has to be another way to approach him."

Springfield's phone chimed. An incoming text message lay on the screen like a fat ugly toad. I leaned over and read it out loud. "Don't breathe a word, man, or you're next."

I glanced up at the men. "It's from the burner."

Lavene wept openly and sagged against the wall.

"Proof positive," Mayes said. "Let's bring Joey in. What's his full name?"

Lavene's voice broke as he spoke the name. "Joseph Furnell."

CHAPTER THIRTY-TWO

Lavene's place was a modest one-story home that looked to be fifty plus years old. There were no trees or landscaping, only patchy lawn. For someone who had a prestigious job, this state cop didn't live very high on the hog.

Once we parked a few houses down, we gathered outside the vehicle. Mayes carried his service weapon in his holster. My Beretta was tucked in my waistband. I'd been at this long enough to know that things can and did go sideways. Though I didn't plan to shoot anyone, I didn't want to be caught in a firefight unaware.

"Hands behind your back," Mayes said to Lavene.

"I already gave you my gun, my phone, and my word. What's wrong with you?"

"You can't be involved in Furnell's capture. It's against every reg in the book. You know that. I'm bending the rules by even allowing you onsite. Your brother can't be trusted, and you are too close to the situation."

"You don't understand. Joey is fragile. You can't storm into my house, guns blazing."

"No guns will be blazing, if I have anything to say about it. You're here as a professional courtesy, but that's as far as I'm willing to go."

"I outrank you, and you're out of your jurisdiction."

"Think again." Mayes went nose to nose with Lavene. "I have the approvals and authority I need. I made sure of that before I agreed to come out here."

"You didn't go through my chain of command for that approval."

"My boss did. My sheriff who expects to be the next governor of Georgia. If being the brother of a serial killer doesn't wreck your bureau career, pissing off the next governor will seal the deal."

Lavene flinched. "You don't know he's a serial killer. You have no hard evidence."

"I'll have the proof I need, as long as you don't foul up this arrest. Hands behind your back. Now."

Grumbling, Lavene complied, and Mayes cuffed him. "Too tight. Show some mercy."

"This will ensure you stay put. Once Furnell's in custody, you'll be questioned on the record." Mayes opened the Jeep's back door. "Inside. You make so much as a peep, and I'll add abetting to your charge. Think of what that'll do to your career."

Lavene slid into the backseat, glaring but silent.

All through the conversation, I'd held my peace. Mayes' treatment of Lavene seemed harsh, but if Joey Furnell was the serial killer, we may only have one chance to collar him.

"Should we call for backup?" I asked.

"Nope. This guy is smart. He's been keeping tabs on the investigation all along, probably through tracers in Lavene's phone and computer. Since we've been off the grid all morning, and since Lavene's phone is in his office, Joey won't suspect he's living on borrowed time."

"How do you want to play this?" I asked Mayes.

"I'm counting on him running when he sees you at the front door. But, if he answers the door, tell him you're looking for Lavene. That'll give me time to open the rear entrance with Lavene's key."

Mayes left, and I stood beside the car, thinking of how far I'd come. A few months ago, I didn't know the first thing about police work. *Look at me now. About to go knock on the door of a serial killer's house.* I glanced down at my hand. Steady-eddy. Amazing what experience did to calm the nerves.

On the way over, I'd studied Joey's driver's license photo. It showed a clean cut young man, but he wasn't smiling. At first glance the photo didn't set off any alarms, but I wondered about the blank expression in his eyes. The photograph was mandatory for all licensed drivers, but he'd done it on his terms. The button-down Oxford shirt, so like the ones his brother wore, the choir boy haircut, the clean-shaven face — they contributed to his disguise.

He was a chameleon hiding in plain sight. That made him very dangerous. Add in the loss of his parents, the parenting of a doting older brother, tech skills, and part-time employment in the trucking industry, and, oh, let's not forget the homicidal tendencies, and you had the makings of a serial killer. He'd been snowing his older brother since day one.

Now that the blinders were off, we saw Joe Furnell for who he really was. A cold-blooded killer. The fact that he starved women to death and threw them away in suitcases really pissed me off.

But I would do my job and arrest this guy. I would survive and so would other women because we'd figured this out. I zoned back in on the modest home and the pricey motorcycle parked in front.

Furnell didn't bother to maintain his choir boy image when it came to his ride. The Harley parked outside Lavene's house was all muscle and shiny chrome, definitely bad-ass.

"Nice bike," I said grudgingly to Lavene through the closed window.

"He's keeping it for a friend who was deployed," Lavene said, his voice tired and sad.

"Interesting," I said, not believing him for a moment. Furnell had been lying to his brother for so long that Lavene didn't call him on his crap. Furnell was a piece of work, probably always had been. I wouldn't be surprised if Lavene's head was chock full of lies his brother told.

"You don't believe me?"

"I believe family is important to you and that you spent your life bending over backward to help your brother."

He grimaced. "Got me there. I did everything I could to help him."

I thought of Furnell's clean police record and connected a few more puzzle pieces.

"Including making sure a few charges against him here and there got dropped?"

"Every cop does that. Besides, if Joey had a criminal record, he'd lose his job. Every man needs to work, to pull his own weight."

"You said he had a job. With a trucking company."

"He does, but he's not one of their regulars. Some long term drivers have to retire before they'll hire him on full time."

"That doesn't sound right to me." Lavene looked confused, so I continued, "Why would a grown man settle for temporary employment when he needs a fulltime job to pay his bills?"

"He kept his expenses low. He had a place once with a roommate, but that didn't end well. The roommate ran off with Joey's girlfriend."

"How long ago was that?" I spoke softly. After I asked, I realized how important the answer could be.

"About six years ago." Lavene paused. Then he swore and slumped against the back door. "Six years. That's when first Georgia Suitcase victim was found. Because of the intense heat, the body decomposed rapidly. I never made a connection to Joey's personal life. Never once thought about how he dealt with that betrayal. He told me so

331

matter-of-factly, and I was so busy trying to make something of my career. I didn't see it. Oh, my God."

More puzzle pieces came together. Furnell wasn't wired like everyone else, from everything Lavene said. When he lost the woman he loved, he retaliated. "What was the girlfriend's name?"

"Emily Holt."

I'd never heard that name before. "Did you run her name through the system?"

"Why would I? Joey never brought her around to meet me. Once they broke up, she wasn't on my radar."

"So, either she's still out there, she's dead, or he lied about her name. What if the first victim, Deb Teal of Atlanta, was his straying girlfriend?"

Lavene blanched. "These are questions I need to ask my brother."

"Mayes and I will question him. You can't be part of this. You know that."

"I need to protect him."

"He's a grown man. He has to be held accountable for his actions."

A wild look came into his eyes. "I need to hear what he says, to see how he looks as he says it."

"If your story checks out, you can watch the interview video after the fact because

332

we'll question you on the record," I said, "so we will discontinue this conversation now."

My phone buzzed. Mayes was in place. "Time for me to go. Sit tight."

CHAPTER THIRTY-THREE

As I marched up the gravel drive, my calm evaporated and my heart beat double time. The last serial killer I'd encountered tried to suck every ounce of energy from my body. I'd beat him, but it wasn't a good memory. All I knew about Joe Furnell would fit in a cereal bowl, but his reign of horror had to stop right now. With that mindset, I purposefully clomped my feet as I mounted the front steps and stood on the postage stamp sized porch.

I knocked on the plain white door. The crisp sound vibrated through my hand and up my left arm. My right hand hovered near my waistband so I could grab my Beretta if needed.

Footsteps approached the door. Was he looking through the peephole right this second? I stood tall, hoping I was doing a good job of looking harmless.

"What?" a man said from inside.

Furnell was still home. Good. When we left the office, his burner was here, but he could've left in the eighteen minutes it took us to drive over. Had he seen me approach, or was he hanging back to hedge his bets?

"I'm looking for Roger Lavene," I said, pleased at the ring of confidence in my voice. "This is his place, right?"

"Who wants to know?"

"Baxley. My name's Baxley Powell. I work with your brother."

Something shattered inside, and I heard footsteps running away from me. I kicked at the locked door, near the knob, but it didn't budge. In frustration, I rammed my shoulder into the barrier, but the hardware held fast. Time for a change of plan.

I retreated into the yard a few paces between the Harley and the door. If the panicked man saw Mayes in back, he might rabbit toward me. I pulled my Beretta, unlocked the safety, and gripped it with both hands. I aimed the barrel at the doorway. More crashes sounded inside. Did Mayes have him?

The front door flung open, and a man charged out, going one stride on the porch before halting. His hands rose automatically. "Don't shoot."

Joey Furnell looked exactly like his photo,

even down to the closely cropped hair light brown hair, Oxford shirt, and khakis. His whip-thin body vibrated with a dangerous urgency, and I had no idea if he'd charge me or stay put. I summoned a fierce look and held my gun steady.

"Stay where you are," I commanded.

Mayes appeared in the doorway, holstered his weapon, and cuffed Furnell. In moments, he patted the man down and led him down the steps. He pointed to the second stair. "Sit."

He came over and gently eased the barrel of my pistol to aim at the ground. "Good work, Bax."

"Thanks." The surge of adrenaline sluicing through my bloodstream was surely two hundred proof. I engaged the safety on my gun and stashed it as Mayes called for backup.

Our captive hung his head and cried. Bawled and sobbed like there was no tomorrow.

"Knock it off, Furnell," Mayes said. "We're not as gullible as your brother."

Joe raised his face, his eyes both sorrowful and defiant. "I haven't done anything, but my brother will make you pay. Nobody touches me ever."

"Think again. We've got Lavene in cuffs

too. For helping you kill all those women. Where's Kitty?"

If looks could kill, Furnell's gaze was an automatic weapon spraying bullets. "Lawyer."

"Fine by me. Meanwhile, we have your brother's written permission to search his house and its contents. We'll analyze the soil type on your motorcycle tires. We'll find the evidence we need to find Kitty since you refuse to cooperate."

A few hours later, I wasn't sure of anything except I was still stuck at the Savannah GBI office. Neither Lavene nor Furnell were talking and all we had were questions. There'd been no sign of Kitty in the house or on the property. The agents who searched the property after we came up empty found nothing related to serial killing, trophies, or murdered women.

The hum of the fluorescent ceiling light in the Savannah GBI office reminded me of an annoying mosquito. I wanted to swat at it or turn it off, but there were no windows in Lavene's interior office.

"We should return to Lavene's place," Mayes said from behind Lavene's desk. "A touch test on items Furnell used would be very helpful at this point. A spontaneous dreamwalk, even better."

I'd known this was coming, and I had an excuse ready. "But if the victims weren't there, that won't help us find Kitty Ballenger. She doesn't have much time left."

"I want to find Kitty, but even more than saving her life, I have to stop Furnell from killing again."

My stomach rumbled. Again. I flushed. "Sorry. I can't seem to fill up these days."

"It's okay. We'll run through a fast food place on our way to Rincon. The clock is ticking on how long we can hold Lavene and Furnell. If this doesn't pan out, both of our law enforcement careers are over."

"You're kidding."

"Charging a fellow law officer is a serious matter. We've found no evidence of collusion between Lavene with his brother, and we haven't firmly established Furnell's guilt yet. A clever attorney might get the text messages thrown out or dismiss them as coincidence. I can't take our gut instincts to court. We need hard evidence. Fast."

Voices and footfalls sounded in the hall. The door to Lavene's office burst open and Sheriff Wayne Thompson strode in, flanked by his deputies, Virg and Ronnie.

"I leave town for a few days, and y'all take on the entire GBI," Wayne said, shaking hands around the room like a politician. He stood with his feet braced apart, his hands fisted on his hips. "I had to hightail it up here to get my car back. Now somebody tell me what the hell is going on."

"Good to see you, boss," I said. "We found the GBI leak. Lavene's phone and computer were infected with some kind of tech. The GBI tech support guys found the problems and neutralized them. But the bigger problem is we can't trace the leak to his brother. We can't trace anything to his brother, but he's the guy."

Wayne listened to the rest of what I said about the app, Springfield, and Furnell, but his steely eyes were locked on Mayes. After I finished my report, Mayes didn't rush to add anything. Mayes and Wayne stared fiercely at each other.

What was it with guys and their silent communication? I thought these two had worked through their issues. Seems I was wrong.

"Keys," Wayne said.

Mayes fished the set of keys out of his pocket. He laid them on the desk before him. Wayne nodded to Virg, who reached over and picked them up.

"How are we going to nail this bastard?" Wayne asked.

"Baxley and I were headed out to Lavene's place to do a touch test now that the crime scene techs are finished," Mayes said.

"Kitty's in trouble. She needs food and water," I added. "We have to find her tonight."

"Understood."

Silence surged through the office like a rogue wave, crashing into walls and rebounding with force. I instinctively skirted the desk to be near Mayes.

"What are you waiting for?" Wayne asked. "Get me some evidence. Now!"

"What vehicle would you like us to use?" Mayes asked, his face cop tight.

"You may borrow mine, but bring it back in one piece."

In one motion, Mayes palmed the keys from Virg and gestured for me to go first.

"A word, Powell, alone," Wayne said.

Mayes bristled. The tension in the room escalated to volcanic levels. "I'll be right behind you," I told Mayes.

Virg and Ronnie shut the door behind them, and I was alone with a hundred and eighty pounds of angry man. "You all right, boss?" I asked.

He marched over to me. "No thanks to you."

The fierce energy waves coming off him

worried me. He was upset, of course, but something else rode under the wings of that anger, something that mattered. My brain went haywire, knowing this was about Tampa, knowing I couldn't explain my involvement to his satisfaction. What did he tell the feds? Would he arrest me?

Ice formed in my gut. It quickly encased my heart. "What?"

Wayne leaned close to my ear and whispered, "I denied it, of course, and the feds cleared my name, but something fishy went down in Tampa. Clothing and hair aside, the couple who kidnapped the mayor and left him for media fodder looked exactly like you and Mayes."

I tried a breath, but my lungs didn't cooperate. "Everyone has lookalikes."

"Not you. And not Mayes either. Both of you are quite distinctive." He grabbed my arm and held my tattooed hand close to his face. "This is the only thing that saved you from a life behind bars."

With the touch connection, the mixed energy came though clearer. Anger ruled, but fear and disappointment were strong seconds. What did he have to be afraid of? The answer surfaced on the next thought. Me. He was afraid of me? I could understand his disappointment, but fear floored me. Dear Gussie. I was going to jail.

I tried to speak but my voice came out strangled and breathy. "What do you mean?"

He dropped my hand and stared right through me, his shoulders squared for battle. "Neither kidnapper bore tattoos. The woman's hand was visible as she held the gun and ordered the man around. I have photos of your hand and rose tattoo on my phone but I didn't need to use them. The feds don't know it was you and Mayes."

"We have an airtight alibi," I insisted, sticking to my story. "No way could we have been in Tampa and answered that early morning homicide rollout."

"I get it," he said, "and I covered for you."

His loyalty unnerved me. Worse, I felt hollow inside at the steel-sharp edge to his words. I'd broken his trust, and we both knew it. There was no going back to our previous professional relationship. Metaphysically, I stood on a great cliff, jagged rocks and treacherous seas below.

The room wavered a bit, and my legs felt wobbly. "I have to sit down for a moment."

Wayne pulled out a chair for me, as if he weren't just reaming me out. "Put your head between your knees," he said gruffly.

I started to fuss at him, but putting my

head between my knees was exactly what I wanted to do. It didn't take long and the lightheaded moment passed. I sat up straight again and regarded my boss. I couldn't tell him about Rose kidnapping our bodies. I just couldn't.

"You got anything to say for yourself?" he asked.

I shook my head.

"Take it easy out there, then," he said. "And one of these days you can tell me how the hell you managed to be in two places at once."

CHAPTER THIRTY-FOUR

Once we pulled onto the night-drenched highway, Mayes asked, "What was that about?"

My empty stomach growled, distracting me. The pizza I'd eaten for lunch seemed a lifetime ago. "Don't forget to stop for dinner," I said.

"Noted," he said. "You didn't answer my question."

"He knows."

"You lost me."

"Tampa. Wayne knows we were there."

Mayes jerked the wheel hard to the right, pulled into a nearby empty parking lot, and stopped the Jeep. "How does he know?"

"He knows what we look like, that's how."

"I don't get it. If he knows, and the FBI knows, why aren't we in custody and heading to Tampa?"

I gave him a long look before I answered. "You don't know Wayne very well."

"No," Mayes said. "I don't. Tell me what's going on."

"Wayne has one priority — self-promotion. He wants the world to notice who he is and how great he is. Like when he was the high school football quarterback. As long as everyone acknowledges that he's the big man on campus, Wayne is happy."

Mayes scowled. "And?"

"Ratting us out would make him look bad because he'd be harboring criminals. Losing us from his team would cost him two valuable crime-solving assets."

Mayes stared at the abandoned building before us, his thoughts fully occupying him. After a long moment, he turned back to me. "He values his honor over truth."

Wow. I'd never thought about Wayne in that particular light, but it made sense. "You got it."

"Honor is very important in my culture as well."

I sensed a "but" coming on. Taking a lesson from the guys, I didn't say anything. This time the silence didn't feel uneasy, it felt right. I nestled into my seat and waited.

"This career and my heritage have taught me another lesson," Mayes said. "There are many colors of truth."

Maybe it was the empty belly, maybe it

was the long day, but my snarkiness surfaced. "So it's okay to rationalize if we make poor decisions?"

"That's not okay. Honor is about being true to your beliefs. Wayne believes in you. He wants to keep you around. He made the call to protect you. I understand his reasoning."

"He protected you, too."

"Because of your involvement. He hasn't accepted me into his tribe. I'm an outsider."

"Do you?" I studied his angular profile, so clearly stamped with his heritage, so noble. "Wayne is threatened by your competence more than anything."

He closed his eyes and massaged his temples. "I couldn't close this case while he was away. That's the opposite of competence."

I tugged on his sleeve until he opened his eyes again. "Now he gets to swoop in and take credit for catching a serial killer. If you'd solved the case, he'd feel unnecessary. This way is much better. We do our thing and catch this killer. Wayne takes the glory."

"Only if we figure out how to nail this guy."

"We'll get him."

■ ■ ■ ■

A fried chicken dinner later, I felt more like myself. I was also thinking about loosening the button closure on my slacks, but I couldn't risk my pants falling off in public. The fancy undies I wore were for Mayes' eyes only.

One vehicle remained in Lavene's gravel driveway, a squad car from Effingham County Sheriff's Office. Mayes and I showed our IDs, the guy checked the access list, and we were good to go. Furnell's motorcycle was gone, taken into evidence by the forensics team. I hoped the lab worked fast to analyze any trace evidence that might be on the bike.

"You ready?" Mayes asked.

I nodded, trickling my pocket crystals through my fingers to steady my nerves. I'd touched items before that killers had touched in a rage, and the resulting visions had been horrific. Those images couldn't be unseen. I shook off a shudder. Kitty needed my help. I didn't have time to be squeamish. I could do this.

I strode into the house and glanced into the living room from the threshold. Except for fingerprint dust everywhere, the room looked normal. A lumpy brown sofa, a deluxe chestnut recliner tricked out in leather, a wingback chair stacked with linens, a blanket, and a pillow. Two ugly lamps squatted on boxy end tables flanking the sofa. A braided rug covered most of the floor. Sunlight slanted in through the closed blinds, illuminating dust motes in the air.

"Where do you want to start?" Mayes asked.

Instinctively, I crossed my arms, keeping my sensitive fingertips close to my body. Most of the time I needed to physically touch items to read them, but on another case I'd had a spontaneous dreamwalk. I didn't want to get caught off guard. "Let's walk through the whole house first. Looks like someone slept in here."

"That's my take too."

We strolled through the rooms. No drapes, no afghans on the sofas, no dainty anything to soften the strong lines. Everything served a function. Dishes were stacked in perfect alignment in the cupboards, silverware aligned soldier straight. Matching shiny salt and pepper shakers topped the small table for two. Someone had a penchant for order and positioning. I hadn't noticed that about Lavene. He'd always been presentable, but not spit-shined. Did Joe Furnell organize

348

his brother's belongings when he stayed over?

Plain white towels hung in the utilitarian bathroom. Not a glob of toothpaste anywhere, not even on the small mirror over the sink. Toothbrushes were missing, but the techs probably took them into evidence. The shower gleamed. Bet the forensic team hated that.

We entered Lavene's bedroom last. I recognized his clothes hanging in the closet, his shoes lined up in rows underneath. Maybe Lavene was the neatnik after all. "Feels like we're intruding in his life," I said.

"We are. Lavene lost his right to privacy the moment a serial killer lived under his roof."

Mayes went through the dresser drawers with a methodical efficiency, lifting stacks of stowed clothes, checking the folds or pockets for concealed items. He found nothing.

I glanced around the room. "This is Lavene's bedroom, so his brother slept on the couch. I'll read Furnell's bedding first. If I get nothing, I'll scan Lavene's items."

"Sounds good," Mayes said.

Gathering my nerve, I returned to the living room and plunged my hand into Furnell's folded bedding. A shock wave jolted through my body, followed by a backwash of nastiness and degradation I'd never believed possible. Nausea, dizziness, and revulsion shuddered through me as a thicket of dark spider webs appeared in my thoughts.

This guy was a creep all right, but was he our killer? His essence laid down in the clothing indicated an aberrant and dangerous personality, but I didn't sense any direct information about him taking captives or killing women. He was off his rocker, but how far off?

I had to go deeper into the memory he'd laid down, to experience more of the awful things in his thoughts. I vectored through the chaos of his thoughts. A dark object appeared on my mental TV screen, which meant he'd viewed this lumpy, angular, object. I needed a zoom feature to see more clearly. What was he studying?

I kept blinking and looking, hearing his sighs of contentment. As my eyes adjusted to the low light, the image sharpened. It appeared to be nearly circular, like a deflated ball. Some of the lumpy parts came into focus. Shadowed depressions pockmarked a mostly pale surface. After a few moments, I searched the shadows for a recognizable pattern.

Two dark circles. A lighter, angular protrusion. A dark circle, larger than the others. The chill of dread made me mentally clumsy as I identified the features of a human face, the jaw gaping in a silent scream of death. The greater ball shape came from the fetal curl of the body. This was a corpse. Most likely one of his victims.

Ohmigod. It was gruesome. My eyelids closed, and I forced them open. For Kitty. I had to do this to save Kitty.

The image flickered, replaced by another similar one, but the hair around the face looked different. Not the same woman. Must be another victim. The image shifted to a third ravaged face. I mentally reeled. This man was terrible. Awful. Rotten. Vile. Evil.

I couldn't take anymore. I shut down the probe and jolted back to reality. It seemed surreal that the overhead lights still shone, that the room remained neat as a pin. My stomach didn't transition so smoothly to reality. I raced outside and emptied the contents of my belly over and over again.

Mayes handed me a damp paper towel. "You saw something?"

I nodded, not trusting myself to speak yet, but I crawled away from the stinking pile of vomit. A slight breeze helped me feel a semblance of normality.

"Can we convict him on what you saw?" Mayes asked, his hand warm on my shoulder, his energy giving me strength.

I waffled my hand from side to side to indicate I didn't know.

"Damn. I'd hoped for more than that," Mayes said.

"Me too," I croaked through my dry throat. What I wouldn't give for some ginger ale right now, but we couldn't leave here without answers. Kitty's welfare came first.

We sat in silence for a few minutes. "What else you got, Powell?" Mayes asked.

The energy he'd been transferring boosted my flagging spirits. Bottom line, I felt strong enough to talk about it. I lifted my chin and caught his worried gaze. "He took pictures."

CHAPTER THIRTY-FIVE

"Pictures? Where are they?" Mayes demanded as he knelt beside me on Lavene's lawn. Shadows drenched the area beyond the pool of illumination from the porch lights.

I tried to focus on the night sky, but those terrible visions kept intruding. I wrung my hands and tried to rein in my circular thoughts. For my own good, I needed to think about something besides the case, except this was my job. I couldn't shy away from my responsibility because it was difficult.

"I don't know where they are, but this guy is messed up," I said slowly. "If he isn't the killer, we have another problem on our hands. From the things I saw, the sick thrill I felt as he viewed the images, Joe Furnell is more than a bad egg. He's an entire hen house full of bad."

"Did you see Kitty this time?"

"Not that I know of. I saw poorly lit images of three dead women. Furnell studies the photos, and he derives pleasure from viewing them. He treasures these pictures."

"Trophies."

I'd heard of trophy wives, but trophy photos of dead people creeped me out. I couldn't imagine wanting to remember those horrific images. Revulsion swept through me. "That's gross."

"Not all serial killers take trophies, but this guy's trophies will put him behind bars. Given his lack of a permanent residence, those pictures will be in this house or on his bike. Trophies must be accessible so the serial killer can relive his moments of triumph. They have to be portable." He fell silent for a minute. "No snapshots were found in his personal possessions. He must have a secret hiding place."

"Like in his shoes or in his jacket lining?"

"We'll check those. I want to go over this house again, looking for where he might have stashed photos."

I thought back to the images. They looked flat, and I didn't remember seeing any kind of white border. "I'm not certain about the format. They might be digital."

"Hmm. I'd rather find a snapshot than hunt for a flash drive. Those tiny storage devices come in many shapes and sizes. The salt and pepper shakers on the kitchen table, for instance, would make great hiding places for a flash drive."

"The jump drives at the office are rectangular, narrow, and about an inch long. We can find something that size."

He held his silence again, so I did too. He was the first to speak again. "You feeling better?"

I ran a quick self-check. "Yeah. You're the best. How come it doesn't drain you to recharge me?"

"It's a mystery to me as well, but I want to spend the rest of my life figuring it out."

My thumb sought the engagement ring he'd placed on my finger. "Me too."

"Meanwhile, I'll curry favor with Wayne by giving him the tip to search Furnell's personal items and the evidence collected here for flash drives and victim photos."

"He'll like that."

Mayes smiled. "I figured as much."

We were still searching Lavene's house when Wayne summoned us back to the Savannah GBI office. He'd found the thumb drive and the photos.

Mayes and I made it in record time. Truly, it was the fastest I'd ever seen Mayes drive.

He must be feeling the same urgency I felt to save Kitty.

"You saw these already?" Wayne asked me, pointing to a dark image on a computer. Both Virg and Ronnie's eyes bulged, and they left the room.

Knowing exactly how they felt, I averted my eyes from the screen. "I did. I rather not see them again. I may never stop seeing them in my head as it is."

"I'm sorry about that, but I'm not sorry your vision helped us find this tangible lead," Wayne said, his expression gleeful. "We'll have no problem holding Furnell for the murders. The jury's still out on Lavene, but we should know soon if he's more than an unwitting accomplice."

"Where'd you find the flash drive?" I asked.

Wayne held up a necklace on a silver chain. One blunted point of a black star-shaped pendant was missing. "No one tried to pull this apart. I found the hidden flash drive right away. Great lead, by the way."

"Glad to be of service," I said, recognizing the necklace Kitty's abductor wore in a vision I'd had in her car back at the beginning of the case.

"What's the plan?" Mayes asked. "How will you get the girl's location?"

"He'll want a deal," Wayne said. "They all do, but I won't let a serial killer walk."

We ordered and ate Chinese food while we waited for the lawyers. Virg and Ronnie were assigned guard duty in the hall, to make sure neither prisoner escaped during their private conversations with their lawyers. Virg held his Taser at the ready, while Ronnie practiced his quick-draw moves.

When the prosecutor arrived, Mayes and I settled behind a monitor in the observation room. Wayne and Tommy Lott, a forty-something prosecutor with graying temples, looked positively stone-faced as they entered the room where Furnell sat with his attorney, Evelyn Lancaster, an older woman who looked like she ate cops for breakfast.

"They say confession is good for the soul," Wayne began.

"My client has nothing to confess." Ms. Lancaster's voice frosted the air. "I demand you release him immediately."

"Of course you do," Wayne said, "but your client isn't going anywhere anytime soon. We know, Furnell. We know what you've been doing and who you've been doing it with. We know you have Kitty Ballenger."

Lancaster returned Wayne's death glare full force. "Is a question in there somewhere?"

Mayes whispered to me, "She's tough."

"Shh," I said. "I don't want to miss a single word."

Wayne selected a page from his folder, rotated it, and slid it across to where Furnell sat. I started with recognition at the victim photo, my fingers digging into my palms.

"We found the photos, dipwad," Wayne said.

All the color drained from Evelyn Lancaster's face. She shifted her body away from her client.

Furnell, on the other hand, turned florid and fought the restraint cuffing him to the table. "You can't have that," Furnell said. "That's my private property."

"Think again." Wayne retrieved the photo and shoved it in a folder. "The image is one of the Georgia Suitcase Murder victims. Mr. Lott will be indicting you for all three murders, four if we don't locate Kitty Ballenger in time to save her."

"You can't prove a thing," Furnell said. "You don't know how I came by those beautiful pictures. I coulda stole them from my brother."

Wayne exchanged a glance with Lott. Guess they realized, as I did, that Furnell incriminated himself by calling the photo beautiful. This guy thought he'd walk. No way. We'd shake him yet.

As if he read my mind, Wayne kept his reaction internalized. "We'll interview him next. You're welcome to tell us your side of the story right now."

"Got nothing to say."

"Georgia has the death penalty," Wayne added.

Furnell shook his head defiantly. "Nothing."

Wayne and Tommy Lott strolled out and joined us. "He's cocky, but the picture rattled him," Wayne said. "Let's shake Lavene's tree and see what falls out."

"I want to convict this guy," Lott said. "Give me something to work with."

Lavene and his attorney waited in another interview room, a few doors down from where we held Furnell. I noted that Furnell's lawyer had stepped out of the office, probably deciding whether she wanted to represent a murderer.

Jordan Berry, Lavene's attorney, looked to be my age. His navy suitcoat's sleeves were too short for his long arms, as if he'd worn this jacket in high school. If I guessed correctly, Lavene had arranged for the more experienced attorney to represent his brother and he'd taken whatever he could get on the cheap. For his sake, I hoped Berry knew his stuff.

"My client had a change of heart and wants to speak to you on the record," Berry said.

Wayne and Lott exchanged a glance. Lott gave a nod.

"Go ahead," Wayne said. "We're listening."

"You've got this all wrong," Lavene said. "Even if my brother somehow hacked into my tech, he doesn't have the constitution to be a killer. He's a screw-up. Always has been. He can't hold down a fulltime job. Accusing him of anything is a mistake."

"Sure you want to clear his name? Because that leaves us with you and these pictures."

Lavene reared back in his chair, whimpering as Wayne laid out each photo of the victims. Lavene heaved three times, the third time spewing the contents of his stomach all over the floor.

"You've seen these photos before?" Wayne asked, ignoring the vomit and most assuredly the pungent odor.

"No. I've never seen these before. Take them away. They're awful," Lavene said.

I tore my gaze from the monitor and glanced at Mayes. "I believe him."

"Me too."

Jordan Berry found a handkerchief in his suit pocket and covered his nose and mouth, muffling his words. "Agent Lavene has cooperated with you. You have no evidence against him, and he has the right to press charges against you for harassment."

"He can press whatever the hell he wants," Wayne threatened, "but he jolly well better tell me where his brother got these pictures."

Lavene's chin quivered. "They're Joey's pics?"

"They are. He wore the trophies everywhere in that necklace of his."

"What?" Lavene asked. "How?"

"Hidden flash drive," Wayne said, his tone harsh and unyielding.

Lavene broke. He cradled his head in his hands and sobbed unabashedly. "Joey, oh, Joey. Where'd I go wrong?"

"Save the recriminations for later, Lavene," Wayne said. "Pull yourself together, or there'll be another murder charge. Kitty Ballenger's life is at stake. My consultant says she doesn't have much time left. Furnell has been starving her to death ever since he kidnapped her a week ago. Do you know where he took her?"

Lavene's sobs subsided. He sat up, tears wet on his cheeks. "Joey doesn't own any property."

"What about you? Do you own any property other than your home place?"

The way Wayne worded his question rang a bell with me. Home place. No, home base. I'd heard that phrase before. In a dreamwalk. Yes, it was coming back to me. The killer said he was moving Kitty to home base. I flipped the toggle to speak directly into Wayne's ear.

"Wayne, something just clicked," I said. "Ask him about home base. Kitty is at home base. I'm certain of it."

"Home base. You know where that is?" Wayne asked without a moment's hesitation.

Mayes rose and stood behind me, his hands on my shoulders. His touch filled me with love and comfort, two things I sorely needed on this long and difficult day.

"Home base," Lavene repeated woodenly. "It's the last base on a baseball field."

"Not that home base. Something from your life. A place you might have once called home base."

Lavene jolted upright, realization dawning on his stricken face. As one, Mayes, Wayne, and I leaned forward. My heart raced. Adrenaline spiked in my blood. As soon as he gave us a location, we could rescue Kitty. I prayed it wasn't too late.

"Lavene! Snap out of it, man," Wayne said. "Home base. Where is it?"

His eyes rounded. "Can't be."

"Tell us where it is."

"My grandparents had a farm in the woods, a couple of miles from my house. Pop always called it home base, but when my grandparents passed away, they owed so much money we had to sell the place. Last I heard, the guy who got the property went bankrupt. No one's lived there in a very long time."

"The address, Lavene," Wayne said.

"That was before house numbers. Lake Forest Drive. I can get you there quicker than GPS or an app."

"How far is it?"

"Twenty minutes, tops."

We made it in twelve, lights flashing, no sirens. Wayne drove Lavene in his Jeep. Mayes and I followed in Virg's cruiser, while Virg and Ronnie stood watch over Furnell at the GBI office. Our high beams illuminated the crumbling farmhouse. The old homestead was a tear-down waiting to happen, with a huge hole in the rusted tin roof, busted stairs, and a missing front door. The grass was knee high around the home, and scrub trees grew randomly where once

363

must've been lawn.

From appearances, no one had visited that dwelling for years. However, a well-traveled route circled the left edge of the lot. I pointed it out to Mayes, and we turned onto it, Wayne hard on our bumper. The trek took us down a winding lane, branches scratching the undercarriage and the sides of our vehicles.

"This better be the place," I said.

"Can you sense Kitty?" Mayes asked.

"I can't do a life scan check while we're moving, but she has to be here. I'm glad we keep extra water bottles in all Sinclair County vehicles. Kitty will need every one of them."

Mayes focused on driving and I held on as we hit a rough patch in the rutted grass. My head bonked the roof of the cruiser, even though I'd securely fastened my seat-belt. Mayes immediately eased off on the gas pedal. "It's okay," I said. "I won't break, but Kitty might. Every minute counts."

"Look."

I gazed ahead where he'd gestured. An old eighteen wheeler lumbered ahead of us like a sleeping elephant. Mayes parked, ordered me to stay put, and joined Wayne. The two of them approached the semi with guns drawn, flashlights atop their weapons illuminating their way. I sensed their battle-ready tension from here.

Kitty wouldn't be returning fire. I closed my eyes and did a life scan of the area. Five people in the immediate area. There were no additional gunmen lurking about. Just the four of us and Kitty, and right this second Kitty was alive.

I grabbed a water bottle and raced toward the truck.

CHAPTER THIRTY-SIX

When we opened the back of the semi-trailer truck, the smell of human waste gagged me. My flashlight beam highlighted a yellow forklift and behind it, a metal cage. I lowered my beam to the floor, angled myself so that I could see beyond the machine, and saw a huddled mass.

"Kitty!" I tried to clamber inside when she didn't move, but Mayes held me back.

"Wait until we can get to her. We'll be quick."

Moments later, they'd pulled a ramp from underneath the truck and attached it to slots on the trailer bed. Mayes cranked the forklift and backed down the ramp. Wayne and I rushed onto the vehicle, but a stout padlock secured the cage.

"Kitty!" I called again, tugging against the bars. Kitty didn't move. Were we too late? I turned to Wayne. "Get her out of there."

Wayne withdrew his gun and shot the lock

off. I didn't realize his intentions until too late. My ears rang like church bells on Sunday morning, but the cage opened.

I raced to Kitty's side. "Kitty! We're here. You're safe now."

No response.

Breath stuck in my throat, I searched for a pulse and couldn't find one. Tears flowed down my cheeks. We were too late.

Mayes lifted Kitty, carried her outside into the fresh air, and stopped in the pool of light made by our vehicle headlights.

Her head moved.

"She's alive!" I said. "Let me get some water in her."

"I need a tarp to lay her on and a blanket to wrap around her," Mayes said to me. "Wayne, call for a medevac."

"Got it," Wayne said.

I unfolded a tarp from the gear bag in the trunk and grabbed a blanket from an adjacent satchel. Mayes carefully lay her down on the blanket-covered tarp and wrapped her in the blanket. He kept his hands on her shoulders. "Are you giving her energy?" I asked.

"Figured it won't hurt," he said.

"I'll help too once I get some water in her." I switched to dribbling water into her mouth. So far, I'd managed to spill most of the liquid down her chin.

"Not worried about her hijacking your mind again?"

"After all she's been through, she's overdue for a little R&R."

"Not at your expense," Mayes said. "I urge you to reconsider."

"Her mind has to be troubled, I could help calm her," I said.

"No need to put yourself at risk today. I will help by singing to her."

Much as I wanted to help Kitty, jealousy wormed its way into my thoughts. "I see."

Mayes caught my gaze. "The healing is similar with other recipients, but the intimacy isn't. What you and I have is special. Never doubt that. You are my heart. Forever."

My cheeks flamed, and I felt awful. "I'm sorry for misunderstanding. Please, do everything in your power to help her."

Wayne talked the chopper pilot in, while Mayes sang a healing melody and shared energy with Kitty. I placed my hands on Mayes' shoulder so that my energy flowed through him to her. Each time she stirred under her blanket, I shifted to give her more water, succeeding in getting her to swallow little drips and drabs. So far, so good.

The chopper arrived in a flurry of whirling blades and flashing lights, and the crew of medics scrambled to get her airlifted and hydrated. Once Kitty was airborne, we processed the scene. We dusted for finger-prints inside the truck and on the fork lift. After we finished evidence collection, we escorted Lavene over to hear what he knew about the vehicle.

Behind us, a tow truck idled and waited to take custody of the rig.

"First, before you say anything," Wayne gestured to a handheld device, "this conver-sation is being taped for official use. Do you acknowledge that you've been read your rights?"

"I do," Lavene said.

"Tell me what you know about this vehi-cle," Wayne said.

"I've never seen this truck before," Lavene said.

"Your brother was an independent hauler," Wayne said. "You told us his oc-cupation. Didn't you wonder how he hauled loads on his motorcycle?"

"Joey had an answer for everything." Lavene's head hung low. "He said he checked a truck out of the motor pool whenever he got the chance to make a run."

"You're a trained investigator," Wayne continued. "Didn't his situation arouse your suspicions? Didn't you encourage him to find full-time employment?"

That was exactly what I wanted to know. Sometimes it seemed like Wayne read my mind. Of course, that was baloney. Mayes could read my thoughts, if I let him, but right now I was staying tightly shielded.

"Joey knew which buttons to push when it came to my sympathy. He was always short on cash, and he had ready excuses why he couldn't change careers. His health for one wouldn't allow him to sit at a desk all day, and he said he didn't have the stamina for physical labor. Even in school he said his grades suffered because he was bullied. I believed his excuses. I can't tell you how much money I've given him over the years, especially in the last six years. Things got tough for him once he lost that shared apartment."

"I'll bet." Wayne snorted. "He probably quit working all together to stalk and kill women. Since he was homeless, your financial contribution was all he needed to survive. You supported a serial killer."

"You don't know that. He's innocent until proven guilty," Lavene insisted. "My brother doesn't have the wherewithal to be a brilliant strategist. He's a manipulator. I acknowledge that, and I realize he used me.

But I clung to those times when he visited because I didn't see or hear from him otherwise. I was supposed to take care of him."

"He is guilty, or Kitty Ballenger wouldn't have been here at your family's property."

"We don't own this land anymore."

"Think about it, Lavene. Who else would think to use your family homestead as a body stash? Especially a real estate holding that wasn't listed on any property record as belonging to you or a family member. Your brother is a serial killer. He played you from day one, unless you're the mastermind. Did you kidnap Kitty Ballenger for him?"

"Hell no. I enforce the law. I don't break it."

"Just the right amount of outrage and hubris. How can we believe anything you say? A case could be made for you, a brilliant crime investigator on an upward trend at the GBI, as the serial killer mastermind. It could be a family package deal. The two of you pulling the wool over everyone's eyes. Are Furnell and Lavene the next big deadly duo?"

"Stop trying to trip me up. I'm innocent, and you know it. That's not what happened. I had no idea Joey was involved in anything like this."

Lavene's words rang true. I believed him. "He's telling the truth."

Wayne scowled at me, but I didn't care. It needed to be said. If Lavene was guilty of anything, it was poor judgement about his brother. He'd tried to be brother and parent to Furnell. He'd loved wholeheartedly and blindly. His psychopath of a brother took advantage of him and screwed him in every way possible. That betrayal must cut to the quick.

Lavene deserved love, respect, and security, same as everyone else. How he was holding it together was beyond me. I couldn't have been so strong in the face of this new evidence.

I studied the interplay of emotions on Wayne's face. He appeared to be unimpressed and unwilling to cut Lavene any slack. "Wayne —"

"Can it, Powell," Wayne said. "I'm not done with Lavene yet."

Wayne waved the tow truck forward, and we stepped closer to our vehicles. I hoped questioning for tonight would be tabled until tomorrow and that we were finally headed home, but Wayne had other ideas.

He placed the recorder he'd held on the hood of his Jeep and turned to face Lavene. I had a moment of alarm as I watched him tense and flex his fists like he planned to clobber Lavene. If he tried that, I'd stop him.

Instead, Wayne crossed his arms and glared at Lavene. "Where were you when Deb Teal was killed?

Lavene blinked repeatedly at the question. A wary look dominated his face. "I don't know. Her time of death is a several month spread six years ago from when she went missing to when she was found. I was still posted to the Atlanta GBI office."

"So you could've been in on her murder?"

"No. Ask Mayes. We've worked cases together before. I'm a cop dammit."

Wayne gave Mayes the stink eye. "You still vouch for this guy?"

Mayes took his time answering. "I do."

I silently cheered. Mayes didn't trust easily but he didn't abandon his friends either. He stuck with them. A good man to have at your back. Lucky for me, he was my fiancé. I liked knowing I had someone solid on my team, much less scary than being alone. Which is how Lavene must have felt with his homicidal brother. Very alone.

The brothers possessed such different values. It was a wonder Furnell hadn't murdered Lavene in his sleep. How much did Joe resent his successful brother?

Wayne silently studied the GBI agent. "You were stupid, Lavene. You didn't think things through. You didn't make the connections you should've made."

Lavene rubbed his wrists, shook his arms. "How was I to know my brother owned a semi-truck or that the flashy motorcycle was his? I trusted him. He's my kid brother. I failed him because I didn't teach him the difference between right and wrong. This is a nightmare for me."

I patted his hand in reassurance. "It's okay. We all have blind spots when it comes to family."

He glared at my hand resting on his. "You're checking me with your spidey senses? Why does no one believe my innocence?"

His sincere words and the physical connection showed me how genuinely upset he was over his brother's heinous acts. I gave him a gentle squeeze and released his hand. "No one put me up to touching you. It's basic human nature to comfort those in distress. I wanted to reassure you that you weren't alone. People make mistakes with their trust. It happens."

"Not to me it doesn't," Lavene said. "I should resign before the bureau fires me."

The tow truck lumbered by with the big

374

rig snugged behind it. Was it just me or did the air feel less troubled with the truck out of sensory range? Maybe it was because Wayne was clearing the air. Lavene wasn't part of a conspiracy. Joe Furnell had acted alone, or at least without his brother's knowledge.

"No one's resigning just yet," Wayne said. "You help us debrief your brother, remotely, of course, and that redemption should put your career back on track."

"To hell with my career. I'll help you because it's the right thing to do. Obviously, the person who killed those women deserves to rot in prison and to be sentenced to death, but I intend to lobby for my brother to get life in prison instead of the death penalty. Let's be honest about my future. We both know my law enforcement career is over."

"So noted. The official interview with Roger Lavene is completed." Wayne nodded to our vehicles. "Saddle up. We've got a case to close and a family reunion to attend. I'll call Kitty's brother as soon as we get underway. Shawn will be delighted to hear she's alive."

Kitty was alive, but how much had our energy boost and spiritual retuning helped her? Would she spend the rest of her life cowering in her room, afraid of every shadow?

CHAPTER THIRTY-SEVEN

"Aw, I get the psychic this time. Will I find riches or true love soon?" Joe Furnell asked, the chains on his wrist cuffs jangling as he tried to move his hands. "You must be grasping at straws to use her."

Fueled again with milk and chicken nuggets, I ignored his jab at my extra gears and sat beside Wayne. Anyone in this small interview room could've predicted a much different future for him. He wouldn't see freedom ever again, much less the woman of his dreams. But more than half the people of Georgia, the women, would sleep easier knowing they wouldn't be his next victims. Lost in my thoughts, I missed what Wayne asked.

"Mr. Furnell, remember to speak through me," Evelyn Lancaster stated in a firm tone. "My client has no comment."

"We're certain of your guilt, Furnell," Wayne said. "Ms. Powell is here to assist me with information."

Good old Wayne. He may be a jerk, but he knew how to look out for his staff.

Furnell's eyes glittered as they swept my torso. "I'll bet. She's cute, but a little too heavy for my taste. I prefer smaller women."

Starved ones. I bit my tongue. Somehow I hung onto my composure. The case wrap-up would play out like others before it. Furnell was guilty, and the trick was to wring information out of him without giving anything away. Wayne excelled at this.

"Please refrain from speaking, Mr. Furnell," Ms. Lancaster said. "The officers are fishing for information. Anything you say can and will be used against you."

Furnell jerked his hands like he wanted to throttle her for talking down to him, but he followed her advice and hushed.

"First off, we have you dead to rights on the kidnapping charge," Wayne said. "Kitty Ballenger is alive and well, no thanks to you."

Furnell's foot tapped noisily on the tiled floor. "Kitty Ballenger. Now why do you think I know that name?"

His lawyer made a "shh" sound to Furnell before facing the sheriff. "What's the point of this line of questioning? It's late. You've detained us for hours. My client doesn't have to answer your questions."

The lawyer was in for a surprise if she thought legal bluster and intimidation would work on Wayne. If anything, her legal posturing made him more determined.

"He doesn't have to answer," Wayne said, "but he won't be considered for bail if he doesn't cooperate."

The lawyer must've had a cup of the same strong coffee. "Given the nature of the charges against Joseph Furnell, he wouldn't be considered for bail anyway. We won't help you build your case."

"We don't need to build a case. We have three murders and an attempted murder in his case file. This criminal investigation will make national headlines. FBI investigators will arrive shortly to determine if Furnell committed distant but related crimes. He might find himself in a federal lockup soon, maybe Jessup or Dodge, but far from home."

"You can't scare me," Furnell said. "And I'll be rich. Everyone will want my story."

"Criminals can't profit from their misdeeds," Wayne said. "You won't get a dime from your story."

Evelyn Lancaster deflated and gave a heartfelt sigh. I understood she wanted her client to clam up, but Furnell had no intention of quieting. Killing the women wasn't enough for him. He craved fame and fortune now. Too bad my newspaper reporter friend Charlotte wasn't available. She'd love to write his story.

"Further," Wayne continued, "access to you could be restricted to immediate family only. Roger Lavene could be your only visitor until the day you get the needle."

"Cut me some slack," Furnell said. "Rog is okay for a place to stay and a wad of cash. Seriously, man, have you ever tried to talk to him? He's about as riveting as wet paint."

"Mr. Furnell," Lancaster warned, "don't engage the police. They're clever at extracting confessions out of people. Let me do my job." She glared at Wayne. "Unless you have something to offer my client, this interview is over."

"I say when the interview is concluded," Wayne said. "You're welcome to stay or leave, your choice." Wayne squared his shoulders toward his real target, pinning Furnell with a hostile gaze. "Was Deb Teal your girlfriend?"

Furnell said nothing. The lawyer threw in a "No comment" for the record.

"Did you know Chaundra Mallory?" Wayne asked.

"No comment," the lawyer said.

"Hannah Blake," Wayne continued evenly. "Were you friends with her?"

"No comment," the lawyer repeated, looking annoyed.

Wayne clamped a hand over his ear, as if straining to hear something coming across his com. Mayes must be sending him a message through the ear com.

"We found your phone and computer in the truck's hidden compartment," Wayne said. "Investigators noted your Truck King Three app. That software links the women and the previous suspects. Now it links you to them also. You're going down for three murders and a kidnapping."

Joey Furnell didn't react. He looked repeat-offender tough, as if threats held no meaning in his world.

Wayne stood, so I followed suit. "We no longer require your cooperation because we have you dead to rights."

Furnell's mouth twitched. "Aw, and I was just beginning to get to know you guys."

That statement struck me as a boldfaced lie. I laid a hand on Wayne's arm. "What is it?" he asked.

"He's lying," I whispered in Wayne's ear. "There's something else involved. Something he doesn't want us to know."

"Can't you be specific?" he grumbled in return.

"I got nothing solid."

"Time to go fishing." Wayne nailed the young man with a look so full of hate I'm surprised he didn't catch on fire. "We have your GPS as well, Furnell, from your real phone. We'll know where you were and when. We can already tie you to the location of Hannah Blake's body."

"All right," Furnell yelled. "I killed Hannah, but she had it coming."

Evelyn Lancaster lost it and shouted, "Shut up!"

No one so much as batted an eye her way. The real story was Joe Furnell, and now he was confessing.

"Why's that?" Wayne asked.

"She refused to go out with me. She thought she was better than me because she worked at that fancy marina. I showed her who was boss. I erased her from the planet."

"We have records of your visits to her in Tybee, as well as the trips you made to the Fulton County Library when Chaundra Mallory was at work."

Furnell cackled with glee. "Sounds like you can't place me at Deb's grocery store."

"I'll place you there or die trying," Wayne said. "If we can match calls to her with calls to Lavene at that time, it will establish that phone number as yours."

While I winced inwardly at his poor choice of words because we didn't need any more deaths in this case, I silently cheered him on. For a redneck from the swamps, Wayne did all right in the figuring-stuff-out category. Scrambling to make plays as a quarterback stood him in good stead for being an investigator.

"Leave my brother out of this," Furnell said, tugging at his restraints.

"Your brother should've known the score. You dragged him into your mess. He'll die in prison, you know that, right? Cops are targeted by inmates and killed. They might get him in the shower or maybe in the mess line. One quick stab to the heart or lungs and he'll be done. Because of you."

"You can't accuse Rog of something he didn't do. My brother is innocent."

"Earlier today, you sat in that chair and made those same claims about yourself. Why should I believe you now?"

"You gotta believe me. Rog is my only safety net. You can't take him away from me."

"Shoulda thought of that before you started starving women to death."

CHAPTER THIRTY-EIGHT

The rest of the night passed in a blur of evidence confirmation. The weekend came and went, same as the reporters and the state's top brass. Wayne got credit for solving three homicides and a kidnapping, so he was happy. The GBI got to do the legwork connecting Joseph Furnell to Johnna O'Neal's murder, so they were happy. Kitty was recovering, though she'd been moved to a rehab center. As he'd predicted, Lavene was done in the GBI.

A few days later, I turned in my final case report on the Georgia Suitcase Killer and headed to the bathroom before I took off for lunch with Mayes.

To my surprise, Wayne followed me into the Ladies Room. "Let's hear it about Tampa, Powell," Wayne said, standing much too close.

I should've seen this confrontation coming. Wayne was like a dog worrying at a

bone when it came to gathering information. "Mayes should be part of this conversation," I said. "This involves him too."

"I don't give a flying fig about Sam Mayes.
I want to know what you were doing in
Tampa and how you managed to get there
and back so quickly."

"Uh. You're not going to like the answer."

"Try me."

"I don't know."

"You don't know how it happened? Or
you don't know the why of it?"

"Both." At his baffled expression, I hastened to explain. "Mayes and I woke up in
clothes that weren't our own. We had no
memory of how we got to the post office
near my home, where the clothes came
from, or what happened."

"That's impossible." Wayne's loud voice
echoed through the bathroom.

"Is it? If you'd asked me a year ago about
the possibility of any of the dreamwalker
things I do now, I would've said they were
all impossible."

"The LaFleur woman. How's she connected to all this?"

"I don't know."

"But you spoke to her before, to give her
a message from the Other Side."

"She freaked out and told me never to call

her again. I don't know her, and I certainly can't recall seeing her. Do you have any idea what it's like having a gap in your memory? It's terrible."

Wayne's eyebrows rose in tandem. "What happened?"

"Something, and I say something because there's no rational explanation, grabbed us while we were sleeping, physically relocated us hundreds of miles away, forced us to do something, wiped our memories, and returned us a few hours later to a deserted location."

"You think this entity on the Other Side that helps you, this Rose, is responsible?"

"I don't know." When he bristled again, I hurried to explain. "I can't find her. I've looked for her every time I dreamwalked on this case and she's not there. I don't understand what that means. You think I'm an expert because I can cross over to the realm of the dead, but visiting a place where all the rules are unwritten, unknown, and variable is a daunting task at best. Sometimes it's my worst nightmare."

Wayne looked like he wanted to keep reaming me out, but he chewed on his thoughts instead. "The Feds don't know it was you. They didn't recognize you or Mayes, and I certainly didn't tell them. No one was killed, and they're thankful to have the mayor's thievery exposed. Most of the stolen money has been recovered, which is another plus. Their investigation into calls to LaFleur, the mayor's side piece, led to our office, but it's officially a dead end, same as other calls to LaFleur. She vanished, by the way, just like your friend from the Other Side. Whatever con they were running, they aren't reaping any reward, but the mayor's goose is deep fried."

"Bottom line it for me," I said, leaning into the wall. The welcome coolness from the painted concrete wall seeped into my bones.

"No one suspects you or Mayes of anything. The feds are satisfied, and our office is in the clear. You sure you can't tell me anything else about this?"

I raised my hands in surrender. "I'd tell you if I knew, but I don't. Something used me as a pawn, and I despise that level of powerlessness."

"What about evidence? You didn't leave any prints down there. What about the clothes?"

"Gone. Mayes took care of them."

"Sounds like damage control is in place. That's the best we can do."

Nothing positive I could add so I kept my

thoughts of confronting my abductor to myself.

He squinted through narrowed eyelids at me. "Your folks invited me and my family for Thanksgiving dinner. You know about that?"

"First I've heard of it, but I've been busy documenting everything for our case files. Tracking a serial killer is exhausting."

"You did good work. You and Mayes."

"You've made your peace with each other?"

"We will. I'm offering him a permanent slot as my second in command."

Good thing I was hugging the wall or I might have fallen, so great was my surprise. "Really?"

Wayne nodded. "Figured this was the best way to keep you close."

Brutal honesty, that was Wayne. "He may not take the job."

"He'll take it. He did a good job while I was gone and he knows it. Having a secure income will appeal to him now that he's gaining a wife and a family."

I wasn't so sure. "And if he doesn't accept?"

"You don't get it, Powell. My offer won't be refusable."

Now I was worried. "Are you talking

blackmail?"

"I'll throw everything I can at him to make the job his dream position. He'll be begging me for the job."

"I love him. Don't screw this up for me."

"Wouldn't hear of it. I need a happy consultant."

CHAPTER THIRTY-NINE

What with one thing and another, Mayes only returned to north Georgia to clear out his desk. We'd agreed he'd keep his place there for when he needed to return for tribal business. As days passed, more evidence from Joey Furnell's truck and phone confirmed what we believed about how he stalked and killed all three, nearly four, women.

Mayes and I visited Kitty Ballenger at the rehab center. Her brother met us outside the door of her room with bear hugs for both of us. "I owe you, big time," Shawn said.

"We did our job," I said, stepping back and taking Mayes' hand again. The hubbub of people coming and going, the two nurses conversing at a nursing station, and two residents talking with guests faded into the background.

Shawn clenched and reclenched his fists.

"The doctors warned me not to get my hopes up, saying she couldn't fully come back from an ordeal like that. Somehow, she managed to walk and talk again. She has her wits about her, and I don't think any of it was luck. Whatever you did, even if you deny it, I thank you from the bottom of my heart."

"She's lucky to have you for a brother," I said.

"I nearly lost the only family I have in the world. I won't make that mistake again. Family comes first. Kitty is getting counseling here, but I'm also seeing a shrink. I never realized how much my choices matter until now. I won't let Kitty down again."

After another round of hugs, we entered the room. Kitty sat in a chair beside her bed. Her face was still much too thin, but she appeared radiant. Shawn introduced us, and another round of hugging ensued.

"Thank you," Kitty said after we'd been seated in the extra chairs the nursing staff brought in. "I feel like I've been granted a second chance. I nearly squandered the first one by making bad choices. I want to make the most of this second chance. I've decided to take courses at the community college in criminal justice."

"Good for you," I said.

"I'd rather become a psychic like you," Kitty said, "But that's not something a person can study and become. What's it like?"

"It feels good when I can get answers for people, and I wish I had that outcome every time I do a dreamwalk."

Kitty stared at her hands in her lap for a long moment. "I remember."

"What do you remember?" her brother asked.

"Being in her head. Seeing him." She pointed to Mayes. "It didn't freak me out then or now. It felt safe, and I hadn't felt safe in a long time, no offense, Shawn."

"That was a first for me," I admitted. "You were brave."

"I hung on because I knew you were trying to find me. No way could the cops find me. That jerk wad kept moving me around, starving me, and I was so thirsty . . ." Kitty shuddered. "I don't want to think about that right now, but I can't tell you how much it meant to me, those few moments in your head. I will never again take life for granted."

The Wednesday before thanksgiving, my back bothered me so much I begged off on doing the dinner dishes and went upstairs to lie down. I'd spent hours helping my mom cook and clean their place. Mayes and my dad set up outdoor tables and chairs, borrowed from Bubba Paxton's church, for the big crowd they'd invited to Thanksgiving dinner. For the meal, Mayes and my father had bagged a deer, so we had venison and corn along with all the traditional turkey fare for our feast.

I wore my overalls every evening and on the weekends because my waist wasn't cooperating with my wardrobe. Living with Mayes and being happy had wrought changes to my metabolism. He hadn't noticed my rounding figure, but it was of concern to me. I needed new work clothes. Not only were my slacks too snug, but the blouses looked like they'd been painted on.

"Baxley?" Mayes called from downstairs. "You done down here?"

"Yeah, I'm done." I was so done I could barely keep my eyes open as I unlaced my work boots. Tomorrow would be a big day of doings to feed the nearly one hundred people my parents had invited. When I questioned my dad about their intention, he'd said they had much to be thankful for this year. I'm guessing he was glad not to be the Dreamwalker any longer, seeing as how the job had been literally killing him.

I fell into bed, fully clothed, but Mayes undressed me. He whispered soft words of Cherokee in my ears as I drifted off to sleep, his hand splayed over my belly. My dreams were peaceful, and I awakened fully refreshed.

When I reached for my overalls, Mayes shook his head and called for Larissa to join us. I immediately hiked the covers to my neck to hide my naked body. Larissa and the entire pack of dogs and cats bounded onto the mattress.

Mayes knelt beside the bed and withdrew a large box from underneath. "For you."

I opened the package carefully. My breath caught in my throat as I recognized the unique "tear" styling of the dress. I'd seen examples online when I'd researched Cherokee wedding traditions, then I'd gotten busy and not given our pending wedding another thought.

A white organza dress overlay on rose taffeta met my gaze. My eyes misted as I ran my fingers over the fabric. "It's beautiful."

"It's a Cherokee wedding dress," Larissa said, beaming from ear to ear.

"Will you marry me today?" Mayes said, capturing my hand in his.

"Today?" My gut reaction was to say no, that we needed time to plan, when it dawned on me that the wedding was the reason for the big community dinner. "Ah. The Thanksgiving feast. All the people. I'm not a very good investigator to have that co-incidence slip past me."

"That's not all," Larissa said. "Charlotte and Duncan are coming, and Mayes' people are here, camped in the woods. Running Bear and Bubba Paxton will do the honors beside the ceremonial fire. I'm so excited I can hardly wait."

So a traditional Cherokee service but also a Christian one as well. Someone had cleverly covered all the bases. Little Elvis crowded close. I collected him in my arms, grateful that he also found this surprise overwhelming. "I seem to have been woe-fully unobservant."

"It was all part of our devious plan," Larissa said. "Mayes, Mama Lacey, and Pap said if you stayed busy with other stuff, we could take care of all the details and surprise you."

"Everyone knows?" I searched their smil-ing faces. "Is the wedding what Wayne was hinting at when he said his family was invited to Thanksgiving dinner?"

"Yep."

Mayes grinned. "I promised to arrange everything, and I have. Today is our wedding day, if you agree."

As if I had any choice. All those people knew about it. But I couldn't feign anger because laughter bubbled inside me like an artesian well. "Yes. I will marry you today."

Hours later, I sat wrapped in a lightweight blue blanket, along with Mayes as per Cherokee tradition, full of good wishes and good food. My family and friends surrounded me, and their love overjoyed me. Life could not get any better.

"I need to prepare you for the second part of the feast," Mayes whispered. "The shower."

"Gifts? I love gifts," I said, admiring the matching wedding bands.

"Baby shower gifts," he added.

"Baby?" I laughed out loud, then sobered. "Oh, for Charlotte and her husband."

"For us. For our baby. The one in your womb."

Mirth died in my throat. A baby? My world shifted on its axis. "I need to sit down."

"You are sitting down, lovely." His smile vanished. "Aren't you happy about the news?"

"I . . . hadn't considered the possibility. I believed I was barren, that I couldn't get pregnant. Roland and I tried to give Larissa a brother or sister, but it never happened. When you and I began seeing each other, I assumed I couldn't conceive."

"Rose," he said.

Realization dawned. The day I'd jumped Mayes at the office, courtesy of Rose. The day she'd turned me into a sex machine who couldn't get enough of Mayes.

"You knew that long ago?"

"I hoped it was true that long ago, wife."

I made two more mental connections. "Mom knew after she helped bring me back from the most recent rogue dreamwalk. That's why Dad gave me his mother's journals about when she was carrying him. I can't wait to dive into them again."

"Yes, Lacey knew about the baby," Mayes said. "She pointed out the physical signs to me and made sure I knew I had a responsibility to get you wed as soon as possible."

My hand covered my tummy bulge. Joy and hope radiated from my heart. "A baby. It's a miracle. If it's a girl, can we call her Miracle?"

"Our son will be strong," Mayes teased. "He will have a warrior's name."

"Okay, we'll agree on names later. No wonder my clothes don't fit. No wonder I run out of energy so easily. No wonder I feel so good when you recharge me. It all makes sense now."

"Are you disappointed I took the job as Wayne's second? I wasn't sure if you had your heart set on the Cold Case Task Force."

"How could I be disappointed? We both have good jobs, great friends, and it seems, large families."

He drew me in for a kiss, and everyone cheered. We broke apart, and I turned to face the smiling revelers. "Mayes promised gifts. Bring 'em on."

ABOUT THE AUTHOR

Formerly a contract scientist for the U.S. Army and a freelance reporter, mystery and suspense author, **Maggie Toussaint** has twenty published books. Her previous mysteries include *Confound It, Dadgummit, Gone and Done it, Bubba Done It, Doggone It, Death, Island Style* and three titles in her Cleopatra Jones series: *In For A Penny, On the Nickel,* and *Dime If I Know.* Her latest mystery, *Dreamed It,* is Book Six in her Dreamwalker series about a psychic sleuth. Maggie won the Silver Falchion Awards in 2014 and 2018 for Best Cozy/Traditional Mystery and Best Attending Author, respectively. Additionally, she won a National Readers Choice Award and an EPIC award for Best Romantic Suspense. She lives in coastal Georgia, where secrets, heritage, and ancient oaks cast long shadows.

Visit her at www.maggietoussaint.com.

The employees of Thorndike Press hope you have enjoyed this Large Print book. All our Thorndike, Wheeler, and Kennebec Large Print titles are designed for easy reading, and all our books are made to last. Other Thorndike Press Large Print books are available at your library, through selected bookstores, or directly from us.

For information about titles, please call:
  (800) 223-1244

or visit our website at:
  gale.com/thorndike

To share your comments, please write:
  Publisher
  Thorndike Press
  10 Water St., Suite 310
  Waterville, ME 04901